# CONFRONTING THE BOUNDARIES

# confronting the boundaries

### short stories, real and unreal

L. WADE POWERS

LUMINARE PRESS
WWW.LUMINAREPRESS.COM

Confronting the Boundaries
Copyright © 2020 by L. Wade Powers

All rights reserved. This book or any portion thereof may not be reproduced or used in any manner whatsoever without the express written permission of the publisher, except for the use of brief quotations in a book review.

This is a work of fiction, and the characters are derived from the imagination of the author. With the exception of recognized historical figures and events, any resemblance to actual persons, living or dead, is purely coincidental. In other words, please don't sue me if you think you are depicted in this story. You aren't.

Printed in the United States of America

Cover Design by Claire Flint Last

Luminare Press
442 Charnelton St.
Eugene, OR 97401
www.luminarepress.com

LCCN: 2020914031
ISBN: 978-1-64388-403-5

*For Richard Pystor,*
*friend and partner in life's trove,*
*and to all the many others*
*not afraid to meet the challenge*

# Contents

*Confronting the Boundaries* . . . . . . . . . . . . . . . . . . . . . . . . . . . 1

### PART ONE
## Family Limits

An Awkward Silence . . . . . . . . . . . . . . . . . . . . . . . . . . . . . . . . . 5
A Song for Sister . . . . . . . . . . . . . . . . . . . . . . . . . . . . . . . . . . . 11
The Hallway . . . . . . . . . . . . . . . . . . . . . . . . . . . . . . . . . . . . . . 22
Identical, Not Quite . . . . . . . . . . . . . . . . . . . . . . . . . . . . . . . . 29
Photo Essay I. How Not to Grow Old . . . . . . . . . . . . . . . . . . . 43
The Color of Remembrance . . . . . . . . . . . . . . . . . . . . . . . . . . 45
Starlight Bernie . . . . . . . . . . . . . . . . . . . . . . . . . . . . . . . . . . . 60
Butterfly Memories . . . . . . . . . . . . . . . . . . . . . . . . . . . . . . . . 67
With Open Arms . . . . . . . . . . . . . . . . . . . . . . . . . . . . . . . . . 69

### PART TWO
## Everyday Challenges

The Game . . . . . . . . . . . . . . . . . . . . . . . . . . . . . . . . . . . . . . 73
The Duck Pond . . . . . . . . . . . . . . . . . . . . . . . . . . . . . . . . . . 77
Take Out . . . . . . . . . . . . . . . . . . . . . . . . . . . . . . . . . . . . . . . 80
Photo Essay II. What People Know . . . . . . . . . . . . . . . . . . . . 82
The Dance . . . . . . . . . . . . . . . . . . . . . . . . . . . . . . . . . . . . . 84
Relay . . . . . . . . . . . . . . . . . . . . . . . . . . . . . . . . . . . . . . . . . 97
Fig Newton . . . . . . . . . . . . . . . . . . . . . . . . . . . . . . . . . . . . . 99
The Trove . . . . . . . . . . . . . . . . . . . . . . . . . . . . . . . . . . . . . 108
Renewal . . . . . . . . . . . . . . . . . . . . . . . . . . . . . . . . . . . . . . 116
Lingering Leaves . . . . . . . . . . . . . . . . . . . . . . . . . . . . . . . . 117
The Parade . . . . . . . . . . . . . . . . . . . . . . . . . . . . . . . . . . . . 118

PART THREE
# Ultimate Boundaries

| | |
|---|---|
| Incommunicado | 123 |
| Threshold | 134 |
| Shroud | 150 |
| Photo Essay III. Alien Places | 156 |
| Expectations | 158 |
| The Love Shop | 168 |
| The Miracle Workers | 188 |
| | |
| *Acknowledgments* | 220 |
| *About the Author* | 221 |

# *Confronting the Boundaries*

PHYSICALLY AND PSYCHOLOGICALLY, we all have limits. For some, the demands of life are tight, confining, and unforgiving. The world is a gray existence at best, offering only an occasional light in the omnipresent dark. Release, temporarily or permanently, is the sole reward for those without hope. Others experience varying degrees of freedom and independence that enhance and give meaning to the natural limits of our mortality, the boundary that binds us all.

A few exceptional individuals seem to have few constraints on their abilities to succeed and overcome life's obstacles. We marvel at their inherent or acquired abilities and wonder why we weren't so blessed. Sorry, we were never promised an easy road through life—were we?

Who needs a promise to exercise imagination? We fantasize about superheroes and heroines. We envy their invulnerability and their unique attributes. In the real world, some of us admire athletes, film stars, the rich and famous, and the gifted whose talents amaze and delight us. And what about the rest of us mortals...those who aren't listed in *Who's Who*, are not on the A list, not pictured on gum trading cards? Not to despair, pilgrim.

Wherever you lie on the scale—whatever your limitations—the ability to confront and survive the challenges, big and small, define who you are and whether or not you will survive. The struggle is as old as life itself—the evolutionary theme of adapt or die, live to reproduce and carry on as best as one can. But the endless variations on the theme continue to amaze and amuse us, to offer surprises as we learn to recognize the boundaries and the limitations that, at any given time, prevent us from succeeding. Perhaps we don't make the sale, win the love, or get there on time. Occasionally, the failure has greater consequences.

These are stories about the boundaries, big and small, and how we meet them, or not. As with stories about love, adventurous quests, and good and evil, tales of confrontation are—dare I say it?—boundless.

—L. Wade Powers
Klamath Falls, Oregon
April 2020

PART ONE

# Family Limits

A FAMILY IS the first social group most of us encounter. Whether it is one we are born into, one adopted by, or institutionally raised by, we come to know the individual members and their behavioral patterns. We learn that relationships between individuals and between people and ourselves can change, sometimes dramatically, as we mature. We are different people of different ages and treated accordingly.

Some changes are easy to accept, perhaps even welcome. Growing older and bigger confers advantages and privileges denied our younger selves. *Now I have a bike, now I have a car, now I am somebody.* It also means more responsibilities, more complexity, and more problems. *I need money; I need a date for the dance; I'm on my own; and I need a job.* The patterns of birth, life, and death appear to be universal on one scale, seen from a distance. Yet each pattern, in detail, is unique to each culture, to each individual, and to each time and place, with an infinite variety of families, an infinite variety of stories to be told.

# An Awkward Silence

*When is family only a designation and not the center of familiarity and protection? What are the limits of loyalty and when does allegiance end? Not easy answers for anyone, much less a teen-age boy with few attractive options for pushing on, but sometimes that is the choice—the only choice.*

He was never worth a damn, not from the beginning, not during the entire time I knew him, but especially not now. Now he's dead, and dead people only invoke responses if they stir a memory, good or bad. If they leave something for us to admire or learn from, if they stimulate an emotional reaction when named, perhaps, then the magic of redemption occurs.

He won't.

He was gray, a person devoid of any color or sharp edge—a cloud in a mist as ill-defined as any individual who ever lived. I hated him then and don't like him any better now. Long ago I sent his image into the darkness with bitter resignation for why he had earned my contempt.

Ralph wasn't evil, at least not in that gothic sense of creepy castles and nightmare manifestations. Not even in the modern sense of crime bosses, hitmen, drug pushers, or child porn barons. But he was my guardian, my mentor, my patron and he wasn't there when I needed him. Bottles and broads were Ralph's manifesto. Stay high and keep the bed warm—words to live by and, in his case, to die by.

Did it occur to him there was an obligation, a responsibility to raise me, to make sure I made it into adulthood with some modicum of success? I knew the answer to that one by the time I was eleven, when Stephen, our designated neighborhood bully, beat the crap out of me after school one dark November day. Yeah, it was one week before Thanksgiving and I said grace and "thanks" for the split lip, swollen cheek, and half-closed eye. Ralph smirked when he passed me a chicken drumstick.

"Better learn to duck—huh, Shorty?"

"I couldn't duck; he had me backed against a wall." I probed at the half-cooked chicken, our miserable excuse for a pre-holiday dinner.

"Black eyes build character; maybe you'll give out the next one."

I put my fork down and shoved the plate away. I stared at Ralph, trying to bore through his forehead, but he ignored me, as always.

"Maybe if you taught me how to fight, I wouldn't get beat up so often."

It wasn't the first time I had challenged him, but he laughed it off as he usually did, telling me the school of hard, really hard, knocks would teach me all I needed to know. Even if he had offered, I probably would have backed out. Ralph was a fat slug, lethargic, and as far from being a self-defense instructor as one could imagine.

The other thing I couldn't imagine was how he managed to attract anyone of the female persuasion to sleep with him. That's all I could imagine him doing—sleeping. He didn't have enough energy for anything else, not that I could see.

"If you ain't gonna eat your chicken, pass it over. Not wastin' good food here."

He looked at me, waiting for a denial, sass, some response. I didn't say anything.

"Your mom would be ashamed, all right, Shorty. Refusing to eat, sitting there whining about your bloody face. What the hell do ya think she'd say about that?" He pulled my plate across the table and grabbed the drumstick. "Your loss, my gain."

"Yeah, you really need a gain—don't you, Ralph?"

I was sitting on the edge of my seat, ready to bolt for the door if he twitched or made a move to reach out. It was always hard to know with Ralph. Sometimes he let my words pass as if he didn't hear them or I hadn't insulted him, but at other times he grabbed and twisted my arm or slapped me. This time he ignored me and kept on chewing, interrupted only by a swig of beer every minute or so. He was working on a six-pack, five down and one to go.

That's the way it was with Ralph and me, for eight years. Dad left when I was three, or so they told me, and Mom died when I was eight. "Uncle" Ralphie took me in and pretended to raise me until I was sixteen. For most of that time, I couldn't understand why he bothered. I wasn't even sure he was a relative, but apparently, some of the family knew him and decided it was better than an orphanage or foster home. It was several years later when I discovered Ralph had been paid by the state's social services to provide me with room and board. They didn't pay him to provide me with anything else and he didn't.

When I was sixteen, I left. I collected a few dollars from an after-school job, jumped on a Greyhound bus, and went as far as the one-way ticket would take me, about six hundred miles. I had to drop out of school, but no big loss there. I wasn't doing so well and graduation was over a year away—it wasn't going to happen. I could fix cars and work at a gas station, enough to get me out the door and on my way. No note, no forwarding address. What a joke. I didn't even know what city I would land in. One battered suitcase with a few clothes and a few dollars to eat on for a couple of days.

It wasn't easy the first month. I found some work but ended up at a Gospel Mission for food and a bed for two weeks before finding a small boarding house. No one asked me how old I was or anything else. Then I heard that Ralph was looking for me. The state doesn't like to support nonexistent dependents. Someone must have told him where I was and Ralph was trying to recover his meal ticket. There had been an article in the paper about the runaway (how did they know I hadn't been kidnapped or killed?), and the woman who ran the boarding house recognized me. My stupid fault for keeping the name "Shorty." It stands for "short on smarts," because she called a friend who told Ralph and the next thing I know, he's waiting for me at the boarding house when I get off work.

---

"Well, if it ain't Shorty," he bellows as I walk in the front door. There he is, sitting on the living room couch with his arm around his latest honey. They are sharing a beer and Mrs. Mitchell, the landlady, is hovering in the center of the room, wringing her hands. She keeps looking at Ralph and his friend as if she's regretting the decision to rat me out.

"I'm not going back with you if that's what you think." I stand there, feet apart, hands on my hips, trying to look more defiant than I feel.

"Hell, you ain't. Soon as I finish this beer, we're heading out, so get your shit together and get back down here." He smiles at the honey and she presses herself against his chest. Go figure. Mrs. Mitchell looks at me and turns to Ralph.

"He can stay here, Mr. Hudson. He's a good boy and I don't mind…uh, Mr. Hudson?"

Ralph doesn't know she's there, his eye focused only on me and his mouth twisted in a half-grin, half-scowl. For once, he looks almost dangerous, as if the slug might actually do something. Maybe he can, but I stand straight and clench my fists. Honey notices and she moves slightly away from Ralph. Whether it is to avoid a pending brawl or to free him to leap into action, I'm not sure. Instead, he takes another chug and smiles at me as if we were father and son or reunited compadres. Mrs. Mitchell clears her throat but Ralph doesn't give her a chance to intervene.

"It's okay, Mrs. Mitchell. Shorty belongs at home with us, with Susie and me." He looks at his girlfriend and she smiles back at him but doesn't look my way. "Shorty doesn't know this yet, but Susie just moved into our house. Pretty good cook too, aren't ya?"

"Ah, the bimbo has a name. Great, that makes us one happy family. Shall I call her Mom?" I turn on my heels and walk toward the front door.

That brings the action. Ralph is on his feet, hands the beer bottle to Susie, and closes the distance fast. I turn to meet him, fists raised as I put my back to the door. He freezes, about an arm's length away.

"No need for this." He begins, his voice almost inaudible. He shrugs and steps back a pace, looking back at the honey and Mrs. Mitchell. "He's just a bit upset, the surprise and all. I probably should have called and let him know I was coming."

His hesitation is all I need. I quickly open the door and am gone before he knows it. I'm down the sidewalk before I hear him yell something about my things and that he'll be waiting for me. I never look back.

---

I LEFT TOWN THAT NIGHT WITH WHAT I WAS WEARING. I HADN'T accumulated much—nothing I couldn't leave with Ralph and "Mom." Ten months later, I saw the story in the paper. I hardly ever noticed community news, but the title and picture of a smiling, younger Ralph Hudson caught my eye while I was flipping through to the sports section.

Ralph Hudson, age fifty-five, passed away at his home. He was alone at the time, discovered by a neighbor who had come to repair his sink. He had been dead for about two days and a heart attack was listed as the cause. The article mentioned a minor ward, a Neil Parsons, missing for about a year and the only known living family member. I guess Susie didn't count.

Then, I caught the next sentence: preceded in death by his sister Rachel. My mother! So, he was an uncle. She had never mentioned he was her brother, although he had visited the house from time to time.

The notice was a curiosity, a random comment on life, or the lack thereof. I had almost forgotten he existed and only numbness greeted the discovery. I had nothing to say and no one to say it to. Silence enveloped the room as I stared at the paper, not sure of how I felt. I was alone. I had never worried that he might try to follow me or get me back. He must have realized it was futile, that I would only take off again. I didn't need him and he knew it.

As I turned the page to see how the playoffs were going, one last thought about Ralph slipped along the edges of my mind, a fading teaser without an answer, but a reminder that even Ralph might have left a footprint. Had Susie needed him? Had they broken up—had she cried when she found out? Did Ralph count for something or to someone? There was no way to know.

The Golden State Warriors are playing tonight for the NBA Championship—ahead three games to one. That's something to care about.

# A Song for Sister

*It's not the size of a family that matters most, but the strength of the love shared and the bonds that unite. Sing it loud and sing it often—joyful voices will be heard.*

Her eyes were moist and one drop had crossed her cheek. "It's never gonna happen, is it, Jimmy?"

"No, I guess it won't. He isn't coming back."

I looked at her hands. They were sliding over each other with short rapid motions, as if they were dirty and she was trying to wash them, to remove an imaginary sin, the cause of Dad's departure.

"Not your fault, Sis. It's between Mom and Dad. Right?"

I tried to reassure her. She was only ten, not old enough to comprehend the machinations of a marriage gone sour. I barely understood it and I was thirteen. However, I had experience. Several of my friends were either from broken homes or watching them dissolve. We talked about it often after school. There were nine guys in our gang and only two of them had both parents at home. For how long, we wondered.

It was usually the dads who left. Some of them were still in town, visiting on occasions, but others completely disappeared. Freddie told us he was sure aliens had abducted his father. He thought it was cool because he didn't like his old man anyway. In Stevie's case, his mom had walked out one night in a drunken rage. It wasn't the first time, but she never came back. He saw her once, in a courtroom, when she tried to get custody, but Stevie told the judge how she drank and swore and had hit him in the head. He never saw her again.

Our dad had been gone for three weeks. Last week, my sister Rhonda and I received a postcard from him. He hoped we were doing well and told us to keep up our grades in school. The only sign-off was "Dad"—no cheers, love, or other words of endearment. He was that way. Not mean, but just not inclined to express feelings. Mom told us he had never been romantic and that she needed something more. I guess we all did but didn't know it until he left. The postcard was from Florida, the other side of the country. I showed Rhonda on a map where he mailed the card.

"Is that a long way from here?" she asked.

"About three thousand miles—several days by car."

She didn't look happy. Sis had always liked Dad. He worked in a factory and she would meet him at the door when he came home—tired, dirty, with a lunch pail in his hand. She would take the lunch pail into the kitchen and run through the house, announcing to anyone she found that Daddy was home. Sometimes he would collapse in his big daddy chair in front of the television. Sis would bring him his slippers and the evening newspaper, but he often fell asleep, with the newspaper on the floor and the television running with no one watching. Sis thought it was funny when he snored, but Mom was not amused.

Mom and Dad didn't fight a lot in front of us. That is, there weren't tirades of harsh words or flying fists like some of my friends witnessed. Billy had the worst stories. He came to school one day with a black eye. He told the teacher that he got into a fight with his cousin, but he later told us his dad accidentally hit him when he got in the way.

"In the way of what?" I asked at recess.

Billy took a deep breath.

"Mom and Dad were slugging it out in the kitchen. She was scratching and pulling hair and he slapped her hard in the face a couple of times. I tried to get between them when I saw him cock his fist."

"Then what?" I kept looking at his right eye. It was a beaut—red, black, blue, and swollen.

"He caught me on the side of my face. It made my nose bleed and bruised my cheek, under my eye." He pointed to it as if I couldn't see the damage from a mile away. "That stopped the physical fighting but not the angry shouts and threats. Mom took me to the bathroom and gave me an ice pack. That stopped the bleeding."

"Let's go with the story of your cousin—much cooler," exclaimed Bobby. That was Bobby, always looking for the best take on any story. He was one of the two in our group who still had both parents, along with several brothers and sisters.

I told Rhonda what the gang shared after school about their families and the problems they had. She didn't understand. Poor kid, she was too young. She kept asking why Mom and Dad couldn't love each other. I didn't have an answer, or at least, not a good one.

---

One Sunday afternoon, four weeks after Dad left, Mom sat down at the dining room table with me. She had made me a bean-and-cheese sandwich, one of my favorites, poured me a glass of milk, and placed a carton of chocolate mint cookies beside the plate. She sat across the table from me and I could tell a grown-up talk was coming. Rhonda was off playing somewhere, another clue that it was just Mom and me, and something important was going to happen or be said.

"Jimmie, you haven't talked much about your father leaving. Are you okay?"

I nodded and reached for my sandwich. She waited until I swallowed and had taken a sip of milk.

"Do you miss him?"

I looked down at my lap, then into her face. Her expression was no-nonsense serious and I knew she wouldn't be satisfied with a toss-off answer. I couldn't tell what she wanted me to say. Should I be sorry? Should I care? I didn't know what I thought, but I knew how Sis felt.

"Rhonda misses him. Sometimes she cries at night."

"I know. I've heard her. Does she talk to you about it?"

"She misses him coming home, greeting him at the door. She seems lost. After we eat dinner, she wanders around the house. She looks at Dad's big chair in the living room, then goes to her bedroom and closes the door."

I didn't fully understand why Sis missed him so much. It wasn't like he played with her anymore. He used to play with both of us and laugh and tell corny jokes. I asked him about it a week before he left, during dinner.

"Dad, how come we don't kid around like we used to do?"

Mom looked at me as if I had asked *the* forbidden question, inviting dark forces to enter the house.

Dad didn't say anything at first. He continued eating slowly, without looking at any of us. Mom froze and was staring at him, like she was going to intervene, but didn't know how. Sis was waiting anxiously for his answer, looking up with a hopeful expression. Finally, he put his fork down and turned in his chair to face me.

"I'm sorry, Jimmy." He looked over his shoulder at Sis. "And Rhonda, you too. When I get off work, I'm very tired. I don't have any energy left. Guess I'm getting old, like your grandpa."

He smiled as if it was a joke, but no one laughed.

"Maybe we can go somewhere on Saturday. Okay? Think about something you want to do, not too far away and not too expensive." He looked at Mom, but she didn't say anything and just started eating again.

Rhonda was the first to respond. "Daddy, that'd be so great. Can we go to the zoo? We haven't been there for a while and they have some new animals there and the kids at school…"

"Slow down, slow down. We can consider the zoo. Right, kids?" He was smiling at Rhonda and her eyes were bright, her grin wide enough to eat the world.

Mom glared at him as if he had violated a sacred agreement. "Ray, we can't do that; you know better." She said it with a voice brought in from the cold, harsh and bitter, an accusation that doomed any further discussion of the proposal.

Smiles disappeared and Sis lowered her head, trying unsuccessfully to stifle a sniffle. Dad returned Mom's stare, his rare enthusiasm snuffed and gone. I watched the three of them, a dysfunctional tableau of hope, despair, and frustration. I didn't think of it in those terms then; I would only use words like that after I went to college. At the time, I felt the disappointment of Dad's aborted reconciliation, his attempt to return us to happier times. I didn't understand why we couldn't go to the zoo, a trip I would have also welcomed. But Mom was insistent and wouldn't hear any more about it. We weren't going—end of discussion.

I mentioned the incident to Mom as I finished my sandwich and started on the cookies. "When Dad wanted to take us to the zoo, why couldn't we go? You never told us." I stared at her, challenging her to say something that would make it all right, to justify her refusal.

"Your dad and I had already agreed to separate, for him to leave. I wanted it to end and I thought that this was just his way of delaying it, of trying to buy you and Rhonda at the last minute. Do you understand?" Her voice had a sharp edge, cutting me for daring to side with dad and questioning her decision.

I understood more than she thought I did, but I didn't tell her. So, it was her idea, not Dad's, to leave. I didn't know the details (I wouldn't until many years later), but Mom had pulled the trigger, firing the shot that killed our family. She made no further attempts to convince me she had done the right thing. Her only comment to me, and later to Sis, was, "We'll all be better without him."

I wasn't so sure.

———

MOM TRIED TO FIND A NEW PARTNER DURING THE NEXT FOUR years. I graduated from high school and Sis went through some troubled preteen years. Although I held my temper and largely ignored Mom, Sis rebelled dramatically and often. The two of them screamed and yelled at each other and both went to bed crying on several occasions. Mom started blaming Sis for her inability to find a new man, a father for us.

"I don't want a new dad," Sis would say. "I want my old one, my real one."

Dad wrote to me from time to time, asking about Sis and me and sometimes asking how our mother was doing. He had remarried after two years and was settled down on the East Coast. He was paying alimony and child support to Mom, but she never talked about him or indicated she cared. When I received my first letter, she wanted to know what he had written, but I told her it only included inquiries about our health and how we were doing in school. I wrote him back and told him I was fine, but that Rhonda was facing a difficult, emotional road ahead.

The big difference in our otherwise unhappy little family was the relationship between Sis and me. Sometimes I was able to mediate between her and Mom, distracting one or both of them when they began quarreling. We had a Shetland collie named Shep, unimaginative as the name may sound, and I had taught him to do a variety of tricks. At my hand signal, Shep would interrupt a brewing squabble by turning quickly in circles or sitting on his hind legs, as if begging. Mom never caught on that I was directing the dog's behavior. She must have thought Shep was acting on his own accord. In any case, it made both of them laugh and forget what they were starting to fight about.

Sis loved our dog and the animal became a significant bond between us. We walked Shep together before and after school, fed him, groomed him, and played with him whenever we could. I was busier with school and playing guitar with some of my buddies, forming a makeshift garage band. We weren't good, but we were loud, and that was enough for Sis. She wanted to be our lead singer.

"Rhonda," said Stevie, who had grown up to be six foot three and rather good-looking, "you'll have to be our only singer. None of the rest of us can carry a note."

It was true. Not only could we barely play our instruments (two guitars, a cheap keyboard, and an even cheaper drum set), none of us could sing worth a lick. So, she was in. We would rehearse on Saturdays and sometimes on Sunday afternoons, and Rhonda would sing the simple folk and rock songs that we tried to play. Her voice wasn't bad and it helped drown out some of our mucked notes and chords. She started wearing sexy, tight-fitting clothes and trying to flirt with our nonexistent audience.

"Just practicing," she would say, "waiting for when we really go on stage."

Bobby summarized it for the band. "Your sister is something else again. She's gonna be a knockout by the time she's fourteen."

Despite our age difference and my growing restlessness to move on, get out of the house, and follow my dreams, Rhonda became an almost constant companion. The summer after high school, I had been accepted into the local state college to major in psychology. I received a one-year scholarship to start school, with the prospect of additional funds if my grades were adequate. I had taken a part-time job to earn some additional money but also had some free time to hang out with my buds and Rhonda. The band had improved and we were playing a few gigs here and there, sometimes for money.

Mom was still single, still harassing Sis, this time about her dress and behavior. Although I think she was proud that I was going to college, we never communicated about it or much of anything else. We never mentioned Dad, even though he and I still wrote from time to time. At one point, Dad asked me if I thought it would be okay for him to write Sis directly, especially after I left home. I told him I didn't think it would be a good idea, that it would only provoke additional trouble between her and Mom. I also knew I wouldn't be there to help defend her.

By then, Sis and I were able to discuss our parents, the divorce, and Mom's behavior in a more mature way, expressing our feelings about how complex life was and what might be in the future for us. I promised her I wouldn't forget her, that she could come and visit me anytime, and I would come home to see her as often as studies permitted. This was in early August and I had just turned eighteen.

Mom's suicide two weeks later was a shock to us. Rhonda found her after school, at home on the sofa. There was a bottle of red wine, mostly finished, and two empty bottles of a prescription tranquilizer on the coffee table. At first, Sis thought Mom was simply asleep, but when she didn't respond to Shep's raucous entry into the house, Sis investigated. Mom was barely breathing and had a weak pulse—she couldn't be aroused. Rhonda called 911 and the ambulance arrived a few minutes later. Rhonda called me at work where I was putting in some overtime. I hurried home to find my sister hugging our dog and sobbing. The wine and one of the pill bottles were still on the table.

I drove Sis to the hospital—Mom had been declared dead on arrival in the emergency room. We provided information to the ER nurse and answered additional questions from the police. They came out to the house, looked around, and removed the other pill bottle. Rhonda and I spent a very emotional night at home, hugging each other, trying to understand how she could leave us like that. Before going to sleep, I called Dad and told him what happened. He agreed to fly out the next day.

Sis and I had our most important talk the next morning as we waited for Dad to arrive. I had offered to pick him up at the airport but he told me to stay with Rhonda and he would take a taxi. I fixed us some breakfast and asked her if she wanted to live with Dad. Details were still to come, but he and his new wife didn't have children. He made it clear that Sis would be welcome in their home.

There didn't seem to be a lot of other choices available, but I told her to think about it. Dad would stay until after the funeral, about three days, and she could make her decision before he left. I still had two weeks before I moved across the state to school, and

I could help her pack and oversee the house. I wasn't sure what to do with Mom's belongings, with the furniture, or, for that matter, anything else. Dad called his sister, our aunt, and she agreed to come and help.

Shep, Sis, and I waited in the living room for Dad's taxi. We talked quietly and I reminded her of the good times we had, even though it seemed that there weren't a lot of them. We laughed about her early efforts with the band and how much progress she and we had made over the last year. I told her to join a new group when she got to Dad's place.

Her puzzled look reminded me that the decision was far from final.

"Do you want to go?" I asked. "It's up to you and if you need more time, Aunt Bess will be here."

"I'd like to stay close to you, Jimmy. I want to live with you."

She said it slowly as if she thought about and agonized over each word. She knew it was impossible, but sometimes things need to be spoken, to let another person know how you feel.

I looked at her but not clearly. There was something in my eyes.

"You'll still be with the family—a bit different from what we had before—but you'll be with people who love you."

"Do you think Dad really loves me? He never wrote me like he did you."

I told her why Dad didn't write to her. She understood and accepted it. We agreed that everything would depend on how Dad acted when he arrived. There had been no hesitation in his response to come or to invite Rhonda, but I would ask him more about his new wife and how she felt.

I didn't realize that Carrie, Dad's second wife, was accompanying him. They came in with their suitcases, we quickly introduced each other, and they settled in.

Dad seemed like a different person. He was working at a white-collar job and seemed younger, definitely more energetic than he had been four years earlier. He marveled at the changes in us and reminisced about the house. He didn't say much about Mom, other than his regrets that Rhonda had found her and the tragedy we had been forced to share. Carrie was mostly silent, but she was friendly and quickly seconded Dad's offer to Rhonda. We went out to dinner and, afterward, Dad and I talked while Carrie and Rhonda visited. It went well.

The next discussion, two mornings later, was a private dialogue between Sis and me on the back porch. We talked about our family, before and now. We tried to imagine the consequences of the decisions to come, the directions our lives, separately and together, might take. She was still unhappy that we would be three thousand miles apart.

I told her the time would pass faster than she could imagine. I reminded her that her best years of school were just ahead, that she would be a "knockout" by her next birthday, and that her singing would win her new friends and experiences.

"Keep playing guitar, big brother. Maybe we can become a bro-and-sis act, like Donnie and Marie." She laughed because neither of us was a big fan of the Osmonds. "I have something else to tell you," she said, in a meek voice. "I want to write a song, about Mom."

"Really? What will you say?"

"I'm not sure yet, but I want her to know I love her, that I forgive her, you know, for leaving us the way she did. She must have been very unhappy and I'm sorry that I couldn't tell her that before."

I smiled and told her I thought that it was a great idea and I couldn't wait to hear her sing it. It was time to get dressed for the funeral and I changed the subject.

"Do you like Carrie? Do you think you can accept her as your stepmom?"

Rhonda laughed. "She's young and pretty. Pretty young," she added. "She's what? About twenty-five or -six?"

"Dad told me she was thirty when they married, so she must be thirty-two now. That seems old enough to me." I gave her a reassuring pat on the hand.

She suddenly grabbed me around the neck and shoulders, burying her head in my chest. "Oh, Jimmy, I'll be okay, I know I will. I have Dad, and Carrie seems nice, and I'll always have you—won't I?" She pulled back and looked at me, eager for reassurance.

"You betcha, Sis. We will always have each other and that's what matters."

Shep came over to us, wagging his tail. Rhonda looked at him, then at me. "What about Shep? Can I take him with me?"

I looked at our dog, appearing to wait for an affirmative response.

"Yeah, we'll make it part of the negotiations. He's also a member of the family and that counts."

We walked into the house, hand in hand, to announce her decision.

# The Hallway

*Families don't consist of just parents and their children. Extended families are not just aunts, uncles and cousins, grandparents, in-laws, and other relatives. What about others, such as designated pets, that occupy the places we live? And what about the house itself? It may know more than you think.*

The small furry rodent quietly hugs the wall, stopping every few feet, head up, ears alert for the slightest sound. Hearing nothing but the soft hum of air conditioning, the mouse moves forward, passing the open doorway of the second bathroom. She moves cautiously, not wanting to enter the tiled room and wary of prolonged exposure in the open doorway. Being afraid is normal—it is survival. The kitchen and garage are more suitable for food and sanctuary, but The Hallway is warm, inviting—a passageway to anticipated delights.

She sniffs the air frequently but can detect only the antiseptic sweetness of a house spray. It disguises everything else, the individual smells of the people, of their food, even the residues of tobacco from Mother's secret daytime cigarettes. She is the only mouse in the house, recently arrived from a nearby field. But the house has children, three of them, and they are careless with snacks, which they generously provide for her early morning grocery shopping. Counters in the kitchen offer residues of more substantial meals, but the sugary treats in the bedroom shared by the two youngest children are the best, worth the risk of a midnight venture.

What will it be tonight? She approaches their door. As usual, it is ajar so their parents can hear them if they cry out. A bad dream, a glass of water—the twins are not shy about making their needs known. Father wants to train the six-year-old boys, to curtail the almost nightly requests, but Mother believes they are too young to ignore. Let them be our babies for a while longer. Father asks about the new kitten. He says he thought that would be the baby now. Mother shakes her head and reminds him they've only had her for a few days.

Kitty sleeps with Julie, their ten-year-old daughter. She has her own bedroom, next to the twins, but she usually keeps her door closed. Tonight, the door is also ajar. Nighttime is not the time for cats to sleep. A paw reaches playfully around the edge and the door opens wider. The hinges are well oiled and they are silent. The paw reaches again, the opening widens, and a small orange head peeks out. It is Kitty's first solo exploration since arrival.

Darkness issues an irresistible summons and he answers it without fear or hesitation, moving quietly onto The Hallway carpet. Kitty's eyes are sensitive and quickly detect the small gray shape moving away from him along the wall. The gray shape enters the twin's bedroom and Kitty follows, creeping along the same wall. His tail twitches in anticipation of the excitement ahead.

The high-pitched scream from the second bedroom is quickly joined by another, creating a piercing chorus that brings Mother, followed closely by Father, up The Hallway and into the bedroom. Lights go on in the twin's room as well as in Julie's. She follows her parents into her brother's bedroom. Sounds of reassurance from Mother are drowned out by a scream from big sister.

"Oh, Kitty, what have you got?"

"Helen, he's got a mouse. I wonder how that got into their room?"

"Mom, make him drop it. I don't want him to kill it." Julie is on the edge of hysteria.

The boys stop yelling, distracted by their sister's distress and Mother's futile attempts to calm them. Julie is yelling at the kitten to drop his prey.

A few moments later, Father reappears in The Hallway with a paper towel wrapped around the broken remains of a mouse. He carries it toward the kitchen and garage. Julie walks out of the twin's room crying, moving slowly back to her room, and closes the door. The boys are finally quiet and Mother appears a minute later, carrying the kitten.

She stops at big sister's door. "Julie, don't you want Kitty with you?"

Her muffled answer, probably from a head buried in her pillow, is angry and definitive. "No, don't bring him in here. He's a killer—he killed that cute little mouse. I don't want to see him again."

Mother's shoulders sag as she holds and pets the small cat. He responds by trying to paw at her hands, returning the strokes with a playful swipe, claws extended. A sharp cry from Mother and Kitty is on the carpet again. He looks around as if trying to decide where the next adventure is likely to be found.

Mother holds her hand and retreats to her bedroom and Father returns from the kitchen. He doesn't notice the small cat against the wall. Once again, the lights are off and the house is quiet, except for a few barely heard words between Mother and Father. Kitty leaves The Hallway and enters the living room, continuing his nocturnal quest for entertainment.

---

THE HALLWAY IS THE CONNECTOR, THE MOST IMPORTANT AREA of the house. Six doors line this residential thoroughfare—two for bathrooms and four for bedrooms. One of the bedrooms is a study, but it has a foldout couch and can be used for guests. It has been a week since the mouse massacre and Kitty now sleeps on the couch in the study. Father likes the idea of a predatory housecat, but Mother and the children are decidedly negative on the matter. Sounds of debate and disagreement lead to a bitter argument.

Mother emerges from the master bedroom, with a pillow and blanket in hand, and enters the study. Kitty, looking ruffled and a bit distraught, steps into the hallway. He licks himself carefully, reestablishing his dignity, before moving down the corridor to Julie's bedroom. The door is closed but the twin's door is still partly open, so Kitty enters the room and finds a place to continue his interrupted nap.

Father comes out of the bedroom, knocks on the closed door of the study, and calls to his wife. There is no answer. After a minute, he sighs and returns to his room. He leaves the door open, just in case the twins need him. He concedes to Mother a delay in the proposed training for the boys' independence and they call for him twice that night. Mother and Father sleep in separate rooms for two more nights before reuniting.

Julie wants her kitten back. Asked if she wants to give him a name, she tells her parents and the boys that "Kitty" is just fine with her and with her feline friend. She knows because she asked him. There was no protest from Kitty but she has warned him that there will be no more killing of small furry animals in her presence.

"At least he didn't have the chance to eat the poor thing," she tells Jimmy as they stand in front of the bathroom door.

The twins are not identical and Jimmy already has a noticeable surplus of freckles compared to his brother Joey. "Kitty didn't have a chance; Daddy took it away from him before he even got a taste." He sticks out his tongue and runs it across his lips.

"You make me sick, Jimmy face spots. You'd probably eat it yourself if you had the chance."

His response is not audible in The Hallway as he closes the door behind him. Julie walks away, satisfied she has won that exchange.

---

THE HALLWAY SENSES THE CHANGES IN THE HOUSE. JULIE IS NOW fifteen and she has friends, many friends, coming and going to her room and throughout the one-story suburban residence. The boys are older but still kids. The eleven-year-olds continue to share a room but not as peacefully as before. They have stuff—model airplanes, football and baseball gear, more schoolbooks, and more clothes. Stuff gets in their way and they acquire bigger beds as they age. Mother and Father debate the fate of the study and finally decide to convert it into a fourth bedroom so everyone has their own space. Regardless, all of them share The Hallway—they have no choice.

Cat, with its name changed from Kitty, leaves a few dark spots here and there, plus ragged edges from claw exercises. Spraying results in neutering, but Cat still leaves occasional territorial marks. The carpet is thinner, worn in a few spots, and there is talk of replacing it.

"Wait until Julie starts college," Father answers. Mother is embarrassed by it—a blemish on her house and an indictment of her as an efficient housekeeper.

"No one notices The Hallway," says Father.

"Not true," retorts Mother. Our visitors use the guest bathroom. They notice. The boys are oblivious and spend most of their time outdoors and away. The Hallway is aware of them only in the morning when they wake and at night on their way to bed. The carpet is replaced during the fall, after another summer's wear, tear, and dirt.

---

Uncle Randolph comes for an extended visit. He is old and alone, a widower with little remaining time of his own. There is no money for institutionalized health care and he isn't suffering from a dreaded disease, other than the fatal condition of getting too old to live. Mother and Father agree to take care of him and make him as comfortable as possible. The boys are reunited in their bedroom so Uncle can have a private place.

Julie is seventeen and will graduate from high school that year. Father promises Joey he can have Julie's room when she leaves the following summer. The word in The Hallway is that Julie can't wait to leave and the presence of Uncle Randolph is an additional incentive.

Trips to the bathroom are more frequent because Uncle has a weak bladder, but his steps become feebler until, by Christmas, he is using a bedpan and other people make the trip for him. He is also coughing, a deep wracking rumble that can be heard at all hours of the night through the house. What once passed for peace and quiet in the house has disappeared and Cat does likewise. One day he is there, the next day gone. No one knows where or why, but The Hallway knows the reason. Julie has outgrown him, the boys continue to ignore him, and the level of domestic stress is no longer bearable.

Mother places a portable heater in Uncle's room, hoping to compensate for small drafts. She puts it near his window, by a long red curtain. The thermostat is set for near-continuous operation during the cold January night. He calls out, as he frequently does, for his bedpan. It is just out of reach on the bedside table, next to the window.

It is Father's turn and he rises slowly, groggy, and makes his way across The Hallway. He hands the pan to Uncle and waits, half asleep, for Uncle to finish his business. Father walks down The Hallway, empties the pan in the bathroom, and brings it back to Uncle's room. Father is almost asleep and is barely aware of stubbing his foot on a hard object near the window. He drags himself back to bed and is asleep in a few minutes.

The Hallway can feel the heat and sense the smoke before the fire alarm disturbs the silence with its urgent message. It is loud and a red light flashes. Mother and Father emerge from their bedroom together and are horrified to see flames erupting from Uncle's bedroom. Julie peeks her head out of her room and the boys tumble into The Hallway, still somewhat sleepy but realizing that hell has erupted a few feet away.

Mother grabs Julie and the boys, ushering them through the living room and out the front door. Father makes a valiant attempt to enter Uncle's room, but the heat is intense. The fire spreads rapidly in the wooden structure and the smoke is blinding, choking, driving him back toward the living room opening. After one last attempt to approach Uncle's bedroom, he yields to the flames and retreats from the house.

The Hallway knows, as only it can, this is the end. There will be no tomorrow, no chance of salvation. The family is safe, except for Uncle, but the house will be a total loss. The Hallway uses the last few moments of sentience to say farewell: to walls, ceilings, the mostly new carpet, the doors to other rooms only partly perceived, and finally, to the family who used and depended on The Hallway's space, reach, and utility. The Hallway watches in silence as the structure around it collapses in a fiery roar of crashing timbers and breaking glass.

From a field two blocks away, a pumpkin-colored cat looks up at the horizon, at the red glare lighting up a moonless night. He is hunting for mice, like the small one he spied in a long hallway so many years before. He watches the flames shooting above nearby houses and hears the screaming sirens as the large red trucks speed down the street behind him. He flicks his tail once and returns to the pursuit, unperturbed by the affairs of the two-legged ones.

# Identical, Not Quite

*Some family members can be close, right from the beginning. When? It doesn't start any sooner than the single fertilized egg that becomes two. After that, anything can happen.*

Marvin and Melvin Knowland were born on August 14, 1946, four minutes and twenty-eight seconds apart. Marvin arrived in his new world first. He would always be the senior member of the identical twins, the only children that Frank and Susannah Knowland would ever have. Fortunately, to reward them for their patience through a barren marriage of six years, Melvin took his turn, squirting out of his dark place a few minutes later. Their parents were expecting twins, announced by an enormous maternal belly, a double heartbeat, and that intuitive feeling expressed often by Mrs. Knowland that her first children would arrive together. What wasn't known was whether it would be two boys, two girls, or what they hoped for the most, one of each.

When Melvin was being cleaned of the messy stuff, a prepared delivery room nurse fastened a small wristband on Marvin, identifying him as "Knowland Newborn A" because names had not yet been finalized. Melvin was relegated to "Newborn B." When he saw his new boys for the first time, Frank joked that maybe they would keep those as names, but Susannah, a trifle disappointed about not having a girl and suffering from a bit of post-partum downer, would have none of it.

"Are they really identical?" she asked her husband. She was already anticipating some of the problems that might arise with mirror image clones.

"Too early to tell," he replied. "All kids look alike for the first week or two. What difference does it make?"

He was glowing with pride, the man who produces boys who will be men. No birthing blues for him. He was ready to join his buddies at the neighborhood lounge, lift a few cool ones, and proclaim his superiority to the assembled multitude. Tonight, the drinks would be on him.

She looked at him, realizing that he might not care about which was which. *Trouble ahead*, she thought. *I need to make sure we know who is A and who is B, before they lose their wristbands.*

Two weeks later they were at home in their one-story, two-bedroom cottage in a modest suburban tract hastily erected as a response to the end of World War II and the sudden onset of family formation and baby booming. It was after dinner; the twins were tucked away, and Susannah proposed her idea.

"You still know the guy who runs the tattoo parlor downtown, right? Your Navy buddy?"

Frank looked up from the newspaper. "Yeah, he's still there." He paused and looked at her. "And?"

"And, well, he put that anchor on your left arm and I thought… Well, I thought maybe we could have him put a blue dot on one of the twins. It would be permanent and we could always tell them…"

"What! What the hell are you thinking, Susie? Tattoo the kids? They're babies. You don't just tattoo babies." He had dropped the paper and was leaning forward in the easy chair, feeling uneasy.

"It wouldn't be a big tattoo. Not a picture or writing, just a very small blue dot. Maybe on the heel or someplace where no one would see it. Just a tiny dot." She was also leaning forward, making it clear she had put some thought to it and wasn't prepared to give in without a fight. She was that way, a product of good Scottish-Irish parents.

Frank was almost thirty-five, ten years older than his red-headed, green-eyed wife. He was a mild man, a grocer who owned and managed his store in a time when local mom-and-pop-shops were common in small towns, well before the domination of chain franchises and big-box retailers.

Protest he might, but Frank knew his wife. She would eventually get what she wanted. They had just decided on the boys' names. At first, Frank wanted to name them after his father and grandfather, Paul and Alexander, keeping a good family tradition intact. But she wanted something cuter, names that reflected their identity. It was becoming clearer each day that they were indeed identical. Marvin and Melvin were a compromise, of sorts. He had a first cousin named Marvin and she liked the sound of Melvin.

*Maybe her idea isn't so crazy after all.* He retrieved the paper from the floor and held it in his lap, sat back in the chair, and smiled. "Okay, Susie. I'll talk to Big Al this week and see if he'll do it. Shouldn't cost much for a dot."

Finances were still tight. The new house and the hospital bills were not leaving much for entertainment or other frivolous expenses. No doubt that his determined wife didn't consider this to be optional. Besides, Al owed him a few favors for sending several post-discharge kids his way. The ex-GIs all wanted tattoos, of war exploits and symbols, exotic places, and the inevitable mementos to past, present, and future lovers.

---

Two weeks later, Marvin A received a small blue dot on the bottom of his left heel. Al did it at their house because he didn't want anyone to know he had marked a newborn for life. The wrist bands came off of both the boys, now one-month-old. Al had assured him that the blue dot would be even less conspicuous as the foot grew, but it would be there forever, amen.

Susannah was pleased, of course. She waited in the bedroom, holding Melvin B while Al applied the magic mark. The hospital bands were overdue for removal and now she could relax, assured that their properly-named children could now proceed through life as separate entities.

"Our boys may look alike, but they will be different," she announced when Frank held up Marvin's foot and showed her the blue dot.

---

Susannah researched the topic of identical and nonidentical twins. Her doctor had explained the difference, but she had been mesmerized by her pending motherhood, that she had finally achieved pregnancy, and long-awaited parenthood was finally in sight. The details of twinning had not been a priority until now. She learned that her boys were the products of a single fertilized egg that splits in early development to form two identical embryos. Nonidentical or fraternal twins result from two separate eggs, each fertilized about the same time. She also learned that identical twins are relatively rare, compared to fraternal twins.

She considered it a blessing before she knew that it would be the last time she would carry a baby to term. After two subsequent miscarriages, the Knowlands gave up. What she also learned, after the tattoo application, is that identical twins have similar but unique fingerprints. However, she reasoned, that is neither a rapid nor a practical method for determining their identity.

---

Frank's occupation as a neighborhood grocer provided enough income for the Knowlands to survive, but they needed furniture, better household appliances, and the culmination of the American dream—an automobile. When the twins were three, Susannah apprenticed with a local real estate office and became a part-time saleswoman. She liked showing houses, had an aggressively friendly manner with clients, and achieved noteworthy success at selling homes during the continuing boom of the late 1940s and early 1950s. The additional revenue provided an additional benefit. Before the boys started school, a parade of enthusiastic young babysitters were captivated by the identical curly-haired redheads.

Until kindergarten, the boys had been dressed in identical play clothes during the day and pajamas at night. It was Susannah's idea.

"What else should you do with twins? Oh, Frank, they're so cute this way."

Frank had the increasingly complex grocery business to worry about. It was growing as the small suburb expanded—supply chains, employment regulations, and tax laws required more of his attention. Also, there was the neighborhood lounge. He found additional reasons to stop in after work, sometimes sacrificing dinner at home, to lift a glass of suds, to complain about the headaches of modern business, to agree with his drinking friends that home life could be a challenge.

It was one of the babysitters who discovered their secret language. When Susannah and Frank were at work, Marvin and Melvin conversed quietly in what Rachel called "twin talk." She only heard it when they thought she wasn't listening and what she heard didn't make any sense, not to her, but the boys apparently understood each other.

Susannah had also noticed it before she started working but had shrugged it off as baby babble, something all young children engage in. She assured Frank it was natural and they would grow out of it, so she was surprised that, at age five-and-a-half, they were not only still using it, but that it provided an important way for them to communicate.

Frank didn't care either way. He loved the boys, but the details of their upbringing weren't his primary concern. He was the breadwinner as well as the bread-seller, and that occupied most of his energy and effort.

Susannah continued to buy identical sets of clothes for the boys when they entered the first grade. They were almost impossible to distinguish based on appearance, but their friends began to recognize differences in their behavior. Marvin was quieter, more thoughtful, less prone to dramatic episodes of temper or impatience. Melvin was more physical, faster, energetic, incautious—the daredevil of the pair.

This was especially noticeable on the playground. Melvin swung higher, scrambled more on the jungle bars, yelled louder, and was a dominating presence. Most of the time, the differences were subtle, but at other times, they were two different boys.

On a quiet May afternoon in 1954, Melvin fell off the swing during one of his patented high maneuvers, hanging upside down. It was a simple fracture, requiring a cast on his left arm for four weeks. It was no problem telling the boys apart during the rest of the school year as Melvin enjoyed the attention, the scribbled signatures on his cast, and the extra desserts prepared by his mother.

The behavioral differences were also evident to Frank and Susannah, leading Frank to tease Susannah about the still evident blue dot. "Probably didn't need that after all, did we?"

"Yes, we did. How would we know which of them became the rowdy one?"

"Just a name. One of them did; one of them didn't. From now on, we know which is which." He said it confidently as if that settled the matter once and for all and he had won.

Neither of the boys was great at school. They both passed their classes, but Marvin's grades were only a bit better than Melvin's. Melvin did better at sports and readily joined teams. Marvin spent more time with books and enjoyed reading about science, nature, and history. It was no surprise to anyone that Melvin discovered girls and the feminine mystique earlier, at the age of fourteen. He learned to flirt, to dance, to engage in the coy conversations that made him popular with the opposite sex. Marvin wasn't interested until he was sixteen, but even then he was shy and reserved. The girls teased him about being "safe" whereas his brother was considered a challenge, the desirable one.

By this time, there was no secret language or conversations and the boys were picking and wearing their own identifiable clothing. Melvin was into the latest fashion trends, rock music, and the teenage revolution occupying the early 1960s. Marvin dressed more conservatively, preferred quieter pop music, and seemed aloof from many of his peer's obsessions and inclinations.

By the time they were seventeen and in their senior year of high school, Melvin had experienced intimate relationships with three of his classmates: Beth, Diana, and his current steady, Linda. Marvin had kissed a couple of girls on dates and was showing considerable anxiety about the upcoming senior prom. He hadn't asked anyone yet and knew time was running out. He turned to his brother for advice.

"Mel, I need your help, man. I haven't found anyone for the big dance, the finale. What am I gonna do?"

They were sitting in Jerry's Hamburgers, a frequent after-school hangout. The music was loud and the place was busy, with cars moving in and out of the lot and kids mingling inside, excited about the pending year-end and the start of vacation. For many, it was the start of their adult lives.

Melvin looked at his brother, noting his sincere plea for help, his obvious distress.

"Ah, Marvy, what to do? I can't figure it out. I've always had a lotta luck with the ladies, never a problem. Just be friendly, come on to them like they want, and it's a clear freeway. We look the same. Used to dress the same. But I grew up and went with the flow. And you? You stayed Mom and Dad's little boy, head stuck in books, ever so polite. Did you ever make time with the few dates you had?"

Without waiting for an answer, Melvin pressed on.

"Look, next weekend is the Spring Fling. There's a big private party at Lucinda's place, the one up on the hill. She has a huge pool, there'll be a ton of food—and guess what? Her parents will be away and the bar will be open. Lucinda has the coolest dad and she says the fridge will be full of beer and there will be hard stuff for the taking."

Marvin looked across the table, doubt and hesitation still present. "How does that help me for the prom?"

"You ninny. There will be girls there, lots of them. I can introduce you to several and you take your pick. Some of them are juniors or younger and some of them probably haven't been asked to the prom. A couple of drinks and, who knows, maybe you can try one or more of them on for size at the party. You don't wanna pick a dud for the last big dance, right?"

Just for amusement, Melvin suggested they dress alike, just for this last occasion. "To cast a few spells, create some confusion, and have a few laughs at our classmates' expense." Marvin nodded and it was settled.

---

Lucinda's house was packed with young bodies, inside and out. Several splashed about in the pool, some in bathing suits, some in their clothes, some without anything. Beer bottles and glasses were everywhere and only a few people were drinking sodas. Some of the guys were well on their way to oblivion and more than a few of the girls were pleasantly intoxicated. Marvin and Melvin circulated through the crowd, beers in hand, greeting friends. Marvin knew most of the guys reasonably well and many of the girls by name, although not as well as his brother. The two girls Marvin dated were chatting with guys, so he merely nodded or smiled at them.

At one point, while Marvin was talking to one of his science classmates, Melvin slipped away and approached Beth, his earliest sexual partner. Adopting a different stance and subdued speech, he stood in front of Beth. It was for his brother, his poor shy brother. It was the least he could do.

"Hi, Beth. I'm Marvin. I know you dated my brother and you… well, you know, you and he were pretty serious for a while…but I was wondering if…well, I have always had a crush on you, but I couldn't do or say anything because of Mel, but now…would you like to go to the prom with me?"

Beth looked at him, studied him, saying nothing. She took a sip of the clear drink she was holding. It smelled like vodka. Melvin waited, maintaining the lost puppy look, the helpless and hopeless expression that might awake her maternal instinct. It didn't.

## confronting the boundaries 37

"You're full of shit, aren't you? If you *are* Marvin, you are too late for this girl. I have a date, so go find some other poor maiden. If you're Melvin, which I suspect you are, then go play with your new lover, if she'll have you." She turned and walked away, leaving Melvin stunned and speechless for one of the few times in his life.

His next target was the ever-lovely Diana. She was often the toast of a party. Her broad smile and well-endowed chest made her an instant attraction to the swarming drones, and Melvin had almost gone all the way with her. They had enjoyed several passionate moments in back seats, on picnic blankets, and once in her bedroom, but without committing the ultimate plunge. Maybe he could fix her up with Marvin. Mindful of his last failure, he decided on a different approach.

"Hey there, Di, you do look lovely tonight." He raised his bottle to her and took a brief sip.

"Thank you, Melvin. We've had some good times together. Hope we might still during the summer and, who knows, the years ahead."

"Yeah, that's kinda what I wanted to talk to you about. Here, let's move away from the crowd." He took her by the elbow and they found a semi-isolated spot near the back porch.

"Well, now you have me really curious," she cooed. "I hope Linda won't be jealous. Well, what I really mean is, I hope she will be."

"Yes. maybe she will. What I have to tell you, confess to you, is about our times together last year."

He sat down and she sat across from him, a small crease in her forehead about the announcement of a confession.

"I need to tell you that, well, not all of our times together was… That is, it wasn't always me that was with you when we were playing around."

"Melvin, what are you saying?" She gasped and put her hand to her mouth, as the truth suddenly flashed its revealing light. "Ohh… you mean Marvin? Marvin and you switched places."

"Yes, yes we did. Only twice. He told me what happened and I prepped him about you and what we had done and said, so you wouldn't realize it was him. It was my idea and I take full responsibility for it. I did it to help him. He was so shy and I knew you were great and might be able to give him some confidence, teach him something useful for a change."

He looked at her with a hopeful expression, waiting for acceptance and forgiveness for the lie he was presenting to her.

She sat there and took another drink. "I didn't know…didn't suspect it wasn't you. You look so much alike. Did you wear his clothes?"

"Yep. We are the same size, naturally, so everything fits."

"But he acted the same. The way he kissed, the way he stroked me, what he said. It was a perfect imitation of you. He must have practiced. Wait…." Her eyes narrowed. She took another swallow, leaving only ice cubes. "How do I know it wasn't him all along? Maybe I've never been with you, never almost had sex with you. How do I know who it was?"

She said it calmly, with no hint of anger or betrayal in her voice.

"You don't, do you?" There was an evil but friendly gleam in his eye, teasing her without punishment, challenging her to accept what he told her so he could finish the proposal. "Actually, Marvin has a very small blue dot tattooed on his heel. I don't."

"Interesting, either way. I guess I enjoyed you both and I have to be flattered that you both wanted me. I have to admit it is somewhat disturbing to find out that the man you were lip-locked with isn't who you thought it was, but I guess two for the price of one isn't such a bad deal. But why are you telling me all of this now—here?"

She looked around them, at the swirling bodies dancing a few feet away. The Beach Boys were blaring from the floor speakers and the background din had become a riot of voices and clinking glass.

"Maybe my brother and I are more alike than even we realized. Do you have someone to take you to the prom yet?"

"A couple of guys asked, but I haven't given them an answer yet. I guess I was kinda hoping that…maybe you would ask. I know you and Linda are hot items, but a girl can always wish, right?"

"Right. Well, I've already committed to dear Linda, but you can have the next best thing. Not the best thing—that would be me, of course." He laughed and took a drink. "I will ask my brother to come over and ask you to the dance. Don't tell him I talked to you about all of this; just accept his invitation. He is still shy and needs some help."

"Couldn't prove it by me. He didn't seem to need any help when we were fooling around. But okay, I'll tell him I'll be happy to go with him."

"Great, Di. You are the greatest." He gave her a kiss that was more than brotherly, but safely in the upper range of platonic, and walked back to his brother, still engaged in a nerdy discussion on nuclear physics.

Interrupting, he led Marvin aside. "Okay brother, I asked Diana if she had a date for the prom yet and she indicated she was available. If you go over right now and ask her, before someone else gets to her, she just might accept."

Marvin didn't look at all certain. Like many red-blooded fellows his age, he had admired Diana's attributes, confining further action to the unrequited fantasies of lonely nights and solo daydreams. To approach the divine goddess and make such an outrageous request didn't seem within the realm of reason, not in his universe. Only Melvin's stern scowl and the effects of two beers encouraged action.

He handed the near-empty bottle to Melvin, hitched his shoulders, and walked decisively over to Diana. While Melvin watched, his brother spoke a few words. Diana nodded her head, put her hand on Marvin's shoulder, and kissed him on the forehead. Melvin didn't see his brother during the rest of the party, which continued late into the night.

Melvin found his girlfriend with a group of other girls, boisterous and near drunk. He led her to one of the rare quiet places at the side of the house.

"Linda, we haven't talked that much about what happens after we graduate. This probably isn't the time and place, but I wanted to ask you this." She looked up at his face, six inches over her head. For the first time in an hour, she wasn't laughing.

"Marvin and I will be going to college this fall. Not sure what I am going to study or major in, but I'll do something. Linda, will you marry me? After college, when I have a job and provide for you. Will you wait for me?"

"Melvin, yes, Melvin, yes, yes, yes. I didn't think you would ever ask. I mean, I know you have had sex with dozens of women and you have your choice of them and probably many more to come, but yes, I'll wait for you."

She wrapped her arms around his neck, body stretched and pressed close. He bent down so their lips met.

*Dozens? Many more to come? Don't know about that, but she is beautiful, smart, ambitious, and great in bed. What have I got to lose?*

---

MARVIN AND MELVIN WENT TO DIFFERENT COLLEGES AND BOTH received a baccalaureate about the same time. Despite Marvin's interest in science, he struggled with the chemistry courses and scored only fair in math. He realized he could never get a decent job in science without going to graduate school, so he majored in marketing and business management. Marvin returned to his hometown after graduation, married a local girl named Jeanette, and began working for the chain grocery store that bought out his dad. Frank also worked for them as a manager and Marvin became an assistant manager, specializing in fresh produce.

Melvin joined a fraternity, spent much of his time on his back, had only a few intimate encounters, and obtained a degree in recreation. He returned to his hometown, worked part-time in the grocery store as a butcher and part-time as a recreation director at the local YMCA. He married Linda and they immediately started a family, consisting of three boys and two girls over the next ten years.

Marvin and Jeanette had twin identical girls after two years of marriage, their only children. Despite suggestions from Susannah and Melvin, Marvin and Jeanette refused to dress the children in the same clothes. and gave them distinct names,

Charlotte and Rita. Their hairstyles were different and they grew up with different personalities. Marvin never detected any twin talk between them.

Melvin died of prostate cancer at the age of fifty-eight, leaving Linda a widow. By that time, Melvin had put on a few extra pounds and looked considerably older than his brother.

---

Two years after Melvin's death, Marvin met Linda in a coffee shop, a meeting she asked for. They were alone, discussing their respective families and some of their common memories. Finally, Linda looked down and then back up at Marvin, as if she had decided about something on her mind.

"Marvin, did you and Mel ever swap places with each other when you were with me, either before or after we got married?"

"Why do you ask?" He wasn't sure whether to be amused or frightened by the question.

"Do you remember Diana from high school? She told me that you and your brother had done that to her and she hadn't realized it. I have always wondered if that had happened to me." She held her coffee cup firmly with both hands, waiting. "By the way, she also told me you have a blue dot on your heel."

He stared into her eyes, teasing her with a bemused smile. "Ah, Diana. It was very good of her to be my date for the big dance. I owe that to Melvin—he arranged it. But, unfortunately, she got it backward. It is Melvin who had the blue dot. You might never have seen it because it was fading with age."

"I never saw a dot." She glared at him. "But did you exchange places?"

"It's a possibility."

"But was it? Did you and me ever…you know… know each other in that way?"

Marvin lowered his head and in a low voice, murmured, "Possible, but not quite."

"Not quite? What does that mean?"

"After all these years, what difference would it make? Then, we were hard to tell apart, weren't we? But there were differences—other differences between him and me. I think you knew or should have known. That is all I can tell you."

"You mean that is all you will tell me." Linda stood up, payed for the coffee, and walked out the door without looking back. It was an answer, but not quite.

Photo Essay I.

# How Not to Grow Old

Just play. Dream. Imagine. Let it go and enjoy. Get your feet dirty and hands filthy. Yell and scream; laugh a lot. Laugh again because life is funny, your friends are comedians, and there is no time for tears. Unless it hurts, then cry loud and get it done with.

Play by yourself; play with friends. Make up a new game. Wear a costume or a funny mustache, even if you are a girl. Run hard and fast, keep pace with the wind and climb trees. Be careful, but not too careful. Band-Aids are for bruises and kisses for cuts.

*Children playing in Brücken, Germany*

Pet puppies and cuddle kitties. Ride a horse, feed the ducks. Swim in the water and play on the beach. Make the biggest sandcastle ever. Run barefoot in the grass and reach for the sky as if you can fly. Read a book and take a nap.

Get down on your hands and knees and crawl. Lay on your stomach and feel the earth, the tile floor, the rug. Lay on your back and wonder at the full moon and who lives there. Watch the stars and make a wish when one falls from the sky. You will live forever, child.

# The Color of Remembrance

*Loyalty and memory can and should survive, but each must serve, not rule. Paul Simon sang about Kodachrome and those nice bright colors, but one must acknowledge the harsher world of black and white. They coexist and one defines the other.*

The small shrine at the foot of the concrete wall displayed several burnt-out candles, a few dead flowers, and a soggy teddy bear. Above the shrine, in red letters on a bright gold background, was a single word, shouting to all who passed: REJOICE!

The pizza kid stared at the dead flowers, vowing to replace them out of his next paycheck. He believed, with all his soul, she was still alive. He felt it, smelled it, tasted it. He sometimes heard her laughter, from far away, as if she was inside a house with an open window while he stood a block away.

He saw her in his dreams and when awake. Every detail of her face, her figure, and the way she moved—yes, that was special, as if her body was the rhythm that moved the world. For him, it did, and it was all there for him to replay, over and over, like a favorite film on DVD.

But there was no disc and his mind involuntarily returned to the horrible truth. She was gone—forever. No emotional commitment, no thoughts, however vivid or desperately evoked, would ever bring her back.

Recognition is one thing; acceptance something else. Rejoice? The word was painful as if someone knew how to twist a knife in his soul. Who dared to desecrate his sacred place with such a message?

Around his haven stood a chaotic sprawl of wooden bungalows and a few more substantial but aging brick houses. Carbon grime from a century of industrial spew covered the walls. Streets displayed abundant potholes as if competing for prizes to honor neglect. Most houses needed repairs and some broken windows were covered with paper and tape. The shrine and multicolored wall offered the kid solace and meditation, a place to remember her and what might have been, but joy would never be present.

With hands in pockets, the kid walked quickly from the shrine. It was the last physical representation of her he had, the memorial, intended to be his alone. His dead flowers, her dead teddy bears. One of them, the smallest with a missing ear, had been her favorite. The fresh red-and-gold paint was a violation of his dedication and an affront to her memory. He would obliterate the word and restore the suffering that only prolonged mourning could deliver.

---

THE NEARBY CITY PARK WAS LOSING COLOR, WITH MEADOWS and grass enclosures fading into yellow-brown dullness. Across the lake, dark clouds gathered, accompanied by a low rumble and an occasional bright flash. Rainbow inhaled the storm's approach, a harbinger of relief from the stifling summer heat. Nose to the ground, she continued her patrol along the park's boundary, searching for the troubled one.

Another flash of brightness followed by a long rolling boom. Leaves rustled on branches overhead and a paper bag blew across the field. Rainbow paused, her left front foot raised, ears up, alert to senses that extended beyond the customary five. She could sense his approach, not yet near, but on his way. She turned and sat, facing the street. Today, within a few minutes, they would be together.

---

THE GIRL AND THE KID HAD BEEN INSEPARABLE. GROWING UP on the same block, three houses apart, she had been like a little sister, at first, two years younger than him. They shared birthdays and holidays, always at her house, and played after school—laughing, running, exploring the neighborhood, scheming together like child partners in crime. The kid grew strong and protected her at school and the girl developed the charms and attributes of young womanhood.

The pizza kid earned his name at fourteen, working part-time to deliver pizzas in the neighborhood. His mother was a factory worker and his dad long gone. No siblings, no close relatives—a few casual friends at school, and the girl—his girl. She had a big family, consisting of Poles, Italians, and a few others mixed in for variety or by accident. Her three brothers and two sisters, all younger, made for a riotous household and no privacy.

In contrast, the kid's house was empty by day and lonely at night. His mother kept a bottle of cheap wine company and the red juice relegated mother and the kid to their own realms. The girl filled the vacuum and by the time she was fourteen, they were intimately engaged in the occupation of growing up.

His mother hardly knew the girl existed, even when she spent the night in the kid's bedroom. The teens made plans and schemed dreams—the great escape, they called it. She reached fifteen, ready to quit school. The kid was seventeen and earning a cook's wages in the kitchen. Cooking and delivering, however, was only for the moment. His dream resided in words and music, to create, to compose, to share his internal masterpieces with her and the world. The future loomed bright, ready to envelop them in the eternal promise.

The promise ended on a summer evening, leaving the pizza kid in an existence he didn't recognize or understand. Walking back from the grocery store, almost home, the girl didn't see the dark SUV as she stepped off the corner curb.

She was walking on air, mesmerized by the afternoon she and the kid had spent on his day off. He had saved enough money to rent a canoe and row them around the lake in the nearby park. Putting the paddle down, he laid back and she melted into his arms, the sun cooking them to a romantic simmer. He crooned several of his song-poems in her ear and she smiled. During their walk back to his place, they finalized their plans for their self-styled elopement two weeks hence. It was all she could think about. It was the last thing she thought about.

She was thrown back onto the sidewalk and up against a brick wall, an instant departure from light and life. Such a shame, indicated a witness. Everyone in the neighborhood liked the bright young redhead with a smile for all. The kid didn't know until he saw the lights flashing in the street. By that time, a number of his neighbors had gathered and she was on her way to the hospital and morgue. He was spared the sight of her bloody, crumpled body, but not the overwhelming sense of loss.

He turned away and walked to the park, immersed in a sheet of rain that blurred the world. He crossed streets without looking, not caring. Reaching the bank of the lake, he sat and looked out at the still waters. *How can a few hours make such a difference?* He shook with anger, sobbing uncontrollably, until his emotional energy was spent. Only a dark gray fog remained.

Neighbors consoled him as best they could. Being poor didn't blunt the tragic impact of a family death or the loss of a loved one within a small neighborhood. Many knew the kid and the girl and more than a few were aware of their involvement and intentions. "He is young and will find another," they said, and they returned to the routine of their lives.

The kid took a few days off from work, barely eating or sleeping. His time was dominated by an internal debate—should he join her in whatever afterlife she had gone to? Could he? Suicide might offer a different endpoint, or so the priests had told him.

His mother heard about the accident and told him she was sorry about his friend. She never knew about their plans, but she offered to go with him to the girl's funeral. The kid declined. He shrugged and walked away, as if the girl was a casual neighborhood acquaintance, one of many. Instead, he asked the girl's mother if there was something the girl had treasured from her childhood, something he could keep, to remember her by.

Her mother was sympathetic, aware of their affair, but ignorant of their pending departure. She gave the kid three small stuffed bears, one with a missing ear. Her favorite, she said. He could smell a faint aroma of roses as if the girl had perfumed her furry plaything.

---

Rainbow sat by the curb, stoic as a statue in the heavy rain. A few people remarked about the strange. almost motionless puppy waiting on the corner, fur thoroughly soaked. Must be a new one, someone said. "Poor thing, waiting faithfully for its owner," another remarked. Occasionally, a passerby would reach down to pet her. Rainbow ignored them, senses tuned for the one, the only one.

---

The sky was ominous—dark storm clouds rolling overhead—the wind whipping in sharp, cool bursts. The smell of old asphalt, of wet soil where there was dirt, and the refreshed city streets heralded temporary relief from the prolonged drought of summer. The change in weather brought a smile to the pizza kid and dispelled most of the anger he had felt at the shrine. He welcomed the rain and the drama of a restless sky. His songs could accompany the wind's howling rage, the voices of nature, and his, in harmonious passion.

It was the best he had felt in the three weeks since the accident. The kid rode swift and clean, negotiating sidewalk cracks, extended tree roots, and broken glass, the ever-present hazards of the urban landscape. His rusty blue Schwinn was part of him, an extension of legs and hands that willed the bike in its daily sojourns to work and around the neighborhood.

The shrill of brakes, an unmistakable bump, and the high-pitched scream of something alive reached his ears just as he rounded the corner. The driver of a car in the middle of the block was getting out and a man and woman stood on the sidewalk beside the car. All were looking at a small black bundle near the front right wheel.

The puppy lay in the gutter, rolled up against the curb like a bundle of discarded trash. The kid pedaled quickly to the still creature as the driver explained to the others—he didn't see it and it wasn't his fault. The dog had no collar and the kid had never seen it before. It was a female, a nondescript mixture of multiple breeds. The crouching kid touched her nose. The puppy lifted her head slightly and their eyes made contact. The driver approached and loomed over them, a dark shadow highlighted by the rainbow forming over his shoulder.

The other adults appeared beside the driver and looked down upon the kneeling kid and the injured creature. "Is the dog yours, son?" asked the woman, attempting to console the boy. The kid shook his head but said nothing. "Let it go son, we'll take care of things," said the driver, about to reach for the dog.

"I'll take her; I can save her," the kid shouted over his shoulder. Before the three adults could protest, he gathered the injured puppy in his arms and placed her carefully in the bike basket. She seemed barely alive, but it didn't matter. He rode quickly from the scene as the distraught driver and witnesses called for him to return. Their voices faded as he rounded the corner, passed through a side alley, and completed a circuitous course for home, hoping to avoid pursuit.

A few minutes later, the kid entered an alley next to his house and walked to the small garage set back from the street. He carried the puppy as if she would break at the slightest misstep and placed her in a pile of old discarded clothes in a distant and dark corner. An empty cardboard box was nearby. He picked the clothes and puppy up and gently laid them in the box, covering it with an old sheet, creating a warm and secluded cave.

---

THE CLOTHES SMELLED OF OLD LADIES AND ROSE PERFUME, reminders of a time and place the puppy remembered. Rainbow inhaled the familiar aroma and licked the clothing. Her injuries and pain notwithstanding, she knew she had found him.

The kid brought her water in a bent hubcap and he lifted her head to help her drink. From his bicycle basket, he retrieved a piece of pizza and broke it into small pieces, placing it where she could reach them with her tongue. He kept a vigil that evening, sitting against a workbench and watching her feeble movements and uneven breathing as he spoke word poems of comfort, in soft chants that filled the garage.

Familiar yet strange, as if encountered from some time ago, the garage's mechanical ambience recalled faint memories of oil and grease, engines, and tires. This was a place Rainbow had seen and smelled and she did so again as she slept and dreamt, drank a bit, ate little, and healed. Her appetite returned and the pizza bits were larger, more numerous as the kid attended her daily. A tail wag brought a smile, a tongue lick produced a laugh, and after eight days of rehabilitation, Rainbow stood and walked out of the box to greet the kid at the garage door.

---

Rainbow was jet black, except for three paws, each marked in white, as if she had stepped in something. "Why Rainbow?" asked the kid's mother. "There's no color, just black and white." The kid shrugged and turned away—no use trying to explain. Some things were what they were and not meant to be shared.

It was the most interest his mother had shown in the dog since the accident. She had been mildly amused about his dramatic rescue and initial denial that he was hiding the animal. He finally admitted he was still afraid someone would try to reclaim her, or worse, take her to be put down. She also recognized the difference in her son—he was chanting poems again and smiling, mostly at the dog. In two weeks, the dog and the kid had formed a partnership, a bond that made them one, but admitted no others. His few friends faded into quiet shadows, barely acknowledged. His mother, never a close presence, took her place alongside the other furniture in the house. She had her bottle and her memories of better times, things he neither needed nor wanted.

The park was quiet, a green refuge in a world of gray scenery and white noise. The kid sat back against a large oak, one that was planted when the town was founded. The kid began his rhythmic chant, a song he had composed only a few days ago and the first he had written since the girl's death two months earlier. Rainbow lay at his feet, attentive to each word, sensing the emotional highs and lows as the melodic story unfolded, a tale of love lost but cherished forever.

When it ended, Rainbow crept closer, putting her head between the kid's knees and licking the boy's palms.

"How about that, Rainbow? I have an admirer for my songs, but one without money and one that can't tell others. I guess it's just you and me, huh?"

Rainbow seemed an appropriate name, despite the dog's color. A rainbow had appeared after the accident, like an omen of good fortune. No pot of gold, but a companion was the prize. The kid fashioned a collar out of multicolored beads, staking his right of ownership to preempt any late claims. He bought dog food to supplement the pizza bits and asked one of his friends, a veterinary tech, to look her over. "She's in great shape," he told the kid—no problems from the accident. Something of a miracle, the tech said. *Yep, just like a rainbow.*

---

RAINBOW WAS MOSTLY CONTENT. SHE HAD FOUND THE TROUbled one and he had rescued, fed, and hidden her. They had bonded instantly as she knew they would. But the troubles weren't entirely dispelled. The kid's elation with his new companion was evident, but she could also sense his residual anger and sorrow. His chants were often dirges and much of the time he was sullen, silently replaying the earlier accident, the one in which his world ended. She could usually transform his mood with a wagged tail or sloppy lick of her tongue, but it didn't last. Except for her and his job, the kid's withdrawal from life was nearly complete.

Rainbow followed the kid wherever he went, from home to work and back, to the store, and on rare visits with friends. The best times for both of them were when they relaxed and played in the park. The kid had a pink Frisbee with a pizza ad on it. She never tired when he tossed it and she quickly retrieved it, often catching it in the air.

Once, it landed in the lake and Rainbow swam for it as the current moved the disc farther from the shore. An anxious moment resulted for the kid as he watched the dog paddle out and eventually bring it in. The kid rolled on the lawn in laughter as Rainbow shook off the water and soaked him.

There were two places Rainbow wouldn't follow the kid. He still made a weekly pilgrimage to the shrine, sometimes laying fresh flowers near the wall, at other times just visiting and singing a slow chant, followed by a few minutes of meditation. Rainbow couldn't be coaxed to accompany him, so she waited a block away. When he returned, she walked steadily by his side, as if she had been trained to heel.

The other place Rainbow wouldn't venture was to the girl's house. She would walk by it, as she did almost every day, but would not put her paws on the first front step. The kid occasionally stopped by to say hello to the girl's brothers and sisters or to talk with her parents. He only stayed a few minutes, but always without his canine companion. She waited a few doors down, sitting on the pavement. Although his dog was welcome and the family was curious about her reluctance to enter, the kid couldn't explain it and didn't try.

---

THE PIZZA KID TURNED EIGHTEEN. THE RESTAURANT THREW A birthday party, but it was a small affair. His coworkers, a few faithful customers, and a couple of kids from the neighborhood attended. One of the girl's sisters came—she was fourteen and had taken notice of the kid during the past year. Although she was generous with her flirtations, the kid paid scant attention. She was not the same and never would be. An attractive brunette, she would find someone to charm, but he remained immune. It had been the same with other female encounters. His mother was also there, toasting his newly achieved manhood with a glass of wine, followed by several more.

She was in one of her unpredictable drunken states by midnight, alternating between cheerful pride and teary depression. She wanted to dance and he accommodated her in a slow waltz from the jukebox. She could sense his mood—intractable, uncommunicative. "What now?" she asked him as they slowly moved across the floor. He didn't have an answer until later that night. It was two o'clock, the restaurant had closed, and they were walking quietly toward home.

"I'm leaving next week," he said, without preamble, without emotion. It was a statement of fact, not offered for debate. She didn't hear him, didn't understand, or she chose to ignore the announcement. She was feeling no pain and was not inclined to acknowledge anything that would disrupt an otherwise pleasant evening. They entered the house and he went to his bedroom without a further word. She shrugged and retrieved a fresh bottle of wine from the kitchen. She would discuss his plans the next day when her head and his mood were in a better state.

The kid's mother tried to engage him the next day during lunch, to clarify his announcement of the night before. "

Where will you go, what will you do?" She asked this with a trace of amusement, as if not believing he could be serious.

He said nothing, lowering his head to attack a bowl of lukewarm soup, stopping only to sip on a cup of black instant coffee. She looked at him, waiting for a response.

"You going to keep your job or find something else?"

She bent over the table, lowering her face, trying to make eye contact, but the kid stared through her as if she was not there. She felt it—the cold avoidance, the deliberate effort at non-contact her son was exhibiting.

"Damn it, look at me, you ungrateful little son of a bitch. I'm talking to you and I want some answers."

Any pretense of a smile was gone, replaced by the resentment and anger that had been forming for the past week. He had shut her out of his life and now she was worried. He was more than her son; he was a second breadwinner and she relied on his paycheck to help cover expenses.

"You gonna leave me alone, is that it? Just take off with your damn dog and don't give a crap about me?"

With her hands on her hips, she glared at him, until finally he put down his spoon and looked up at her.

Pushing his chair back from the table, he stood up and met her eyes.

"When did you ever care about me?" He spoke slowly, pronouncing each word carefully. "When Judi died, you hardly knew she existed. She spent nights here with me. We were going to get married as soon as I turned eighteen. You didn't know that, did you? You were immersed in your precious bottle, dreaming about times past, times of your own. Well, now you can dream all you want. I'm off to find *my* own times and I don't need you. My damn dog and I will do just fine. We leave tomorrow morning."

He continued to stare her down and she finally lowered her eyes, gave a sniffle and turned away, walking slowly out of the kitchen.

Rainbow sat by the door, watching the tableau, starting to go to the woman to lick her hand and comfort her, but she went to her bedroom and closed the door. Rainbow looked at the kid and saw his shoulders slump as he backed away from the table. He also needed reassurance and she gave him the "I-need-to-go-out" look that all dog owners understand. The kid knelt and rubbed her behind the ears.

"Sorry you had to see that. I lost it, I guess, but I…I don't know.… Hell, let's go to the park."

He opened the front door and Rainbow bounded through and down the steps onto the sidewalk. The kid followed slowly, still distracted by the confrontation with his mother. Despite their differences and her lack of affection, they had experienced surprisingly few arguments and had rarely exchanged angry words. Mostly, they didn't exchange anything during a lifetime of mutual disregard and neglect.

---

Rainbow could sense, as she always did, that change was in the air. The pizza kid said little and paid scant attention to her. They went for their usual walk in the park and sat by the lake, but the kid was again troubled, a dark shadow isolating him from her companionship. She licked his hand and he looked down at her, not withdrawing but not responding. Once again, he was the lost one and all Rainbow could do was wait and be ready when the kid reemerged from the gray insulating cloud of solitude.

When the kid returned that evening, his mother was gone. No note, as usual, but she rarely left and he felt the first twinges of concern. She had few friends and no interests to take her away. After midnight, her continued absence began to sound an alarm and he decided to make inquiries. His first stop was the restaurant to ask if anyone had seen her. He didn't need to ask. She was there, sitting in a booth, behind a half-full bottle of red wine. The owner looked at him as he entered and nodded toward the booth.

The kid slid into the booth opposite her. She looked terrible, hair strung over her face, her mascara scattered across her cheeks. Her eyes and nose glowed red and she stared at him like a zombie, as if there was no recognition. Her right hand clung tightly around an empty glass and her left hand was trembling. She withdrew it, putting it under the table.

"Mother?" He paused, watching her eyes. "Mom, come home with me. We need to talk."

She looked at him and nodded.

"C'mon, let me help you."

He stood beside her and took her arm, gently helping her stand. She was shaky and leaned on him as they slowly made their way to the door. The owner asked if they wanted a taxi, but the kid shook his head no. "We'll make it, just need to take it slow." Take it slow they did. They entered the house, greeted by Rainbow.

The mother looked at the dog, then at her son. "She really loves you, doesn't she?" She bent down, still holding onto the kid, and gave the dog a gentle pat on the head. He helped her to the sofa and sat down with her. She wiped her eyes and spoke slowly.

"I'm sorry about what I said earlier. I know I haven't been there for you and…I'm sorry about the girl—Judi, is that right?" He nodded and lowered his head but couldn't stop the wetness appearing in the corner of his eyes. "She was somebody very special to you, wasn't she?"

Again, he nodded. *Strange—she is telling me this now. She is about wasted, hardly able to focus, and now she is apologizing.* "It's okay, Mom. She was special and I won't forget her. But I have Rainbow, and she is special too."

His mother looked at him oddly, as if the two statements didn't match. He held her hand and told her he still planned to leave in the morning, but as soon as he had a place and a job, he would send money home.

She cried and he cried, commencing the long catharsis they both needed. He finally released his grief and his mother welcomed him back as her son. Rainbow watched from a corner, shifting eyes from one to the other as if she understood exactly what was taking place. Maybe she did, but more likely she sensed the end of an emotional impasse and the beginning of a renewed relationship. She recognized compassion and love, even if she couldn't explain it.

The next morning, the kid was up early and ready to go. The material contents of his life fit in a large backpack. There was room for Rainbow's food and he was anxious to start the journey to whatever and wherever. His mother fixed breakfast for both of them, a rare but welcome event…rare, because on her days off she usually revived closer to noon, and welcome because it gave the kid and his mother one more opportunity for closure and reconciliation.

"How do you want your eggs fixed, kid?" She hovered over the stove, spatula in hand, hair combed, looking younger than he had seen her in years.

"I'm no longer the pizza kid. I won't be making and delivering food." He looked at her and smiled. "I'm no longer a kid." He stated it with pride, a coming-of-age announcement to finalize the transition that began two days earlier. "From now on, call me by *my* name, the one you gave me at birth—Jeremy. Eggs over easy would be perfect."

The eggs were perfect. She said goodbye to her newfound son. He promised to write and help her out financially. She told Jeremy she would find a better job—perhaps at the restaurant he left. He joked about her becoming the new pizza kid and she could have the pizza shirt he had left behind. She watched the young man and his dog stroll from the house, a confident stride that quickly took them down the street, past Judi's house, and out of sight.

Jeremy knelt before the shrine. The once unwelcomed red letters were fading, negating his need to paint over them. His detailed memories of her, once so fresh, once so alive, were also fading, but her image persisted and her essence remained—he would never forget.

Rainbow sat quietly down the street, like a rearguard providing protection. She was safeguarding his meditation, his holy moment of solitude to recall the girl's fragrance, the touch of lavender that promised eternal spring. Hands folded in his lap, the young man listened once again for her laughter. A slight breeze rustled the leaves of a scraggy bush nearby. Was it her? He couldn't be sure, but it may have been, a farewell message from a distant place. The flaming red hair, the green eyes bright with amusement, an abundance of soft freckles on round cheeks, and lips full with pleasure—all visions that flashed before him as he stared at the fresh roses.

*Who brought them? Another admirer, someone dedicated to preserve her memory?* Only one teddy bear remained, the cut-eared one with light fur that readily displayed the accumulated filth of the year. Around its neck was a bright green ribbon, recently placed.

Slowly he rose to his feet, staring at the ribbon and the fresh flowers. *Someone has continued the memorial vigilance. Family? Friend? Maybe the stuffed toy knows and will be left to guard the shrine. I will never know—I won't be back.*

Rainbow rose and fell in step as Jeremy slowly walked from the wall. The residual heaviness in his heart began to lift as if an anchor was cut and he was adrift, free at last to face an uncertain future, but one with whisperings of promises, of endless possibilities. He looked down at his lop-eared companion. The bright eyes and wagging tail signaled the start of a new adventure together. Jeremy, once known as the pizza kid, began to chant words to a new song forming in his head. Praise for the sunshine, praise for the rainbow. Rejoice!

*This story was entered in a Hackathon contest sponsored by the* Owl Canyon Press *in 2019. The first and a middle paragraph were provided, but these have been modified for this version.*

# Starlight Bernie

*Family can be real or imagined, close or far, short-lived or forever. Whatever form it takes, the requirement is the same: love and compassion for those who need us, for and by those who would care. A simple act of kindness can help dispel the gloom of loneliness and repair the aftermath of neglect.*

She was smiling, kneeling in front of him as he sat forward in his coach section seat. He smiled back, but his eyes wandered from side to side as if he wasn't sure who he was facing or why. A few other passengers on the Coast Starlight looked on, some with curiosity, one or two showing signs of concern.

"I want to go home." The elderly man spoke slowly, in a low voice, not so much to the young woman facing him as to himself.

"Where is that?" she said. "Can you tell me where you live?"

She gently touched his hand, trying to help him focus on her. She was blonde and slightly overweight, appeared to be in her late twenties or early thirties, but had a soft voice and a pleasant smile, projecting an aura of compassionate competence.

"I want to go home," he repeated, but this time with added volume. The words conveyed conviction, as if he had discovered a purpose or reason to communicate.

A connecting door opened and an assistant conductor, a young black woman, entered the car and approached the two. The woman stood up and backed off as the conductor knelt before him. Her name tag said Gabriella. She looked into the man's eyes, but he looked to the side, avoiding contact.

"Good morning, sir. What is your name?" Gabriella also asked him in a gentle voice meant to be soothing, helpful, but the man didn't respond. She repeated the question, a bit louder, thinking he might be hard of hearing.

He looked at her, licked his lips, and once again said, "I want to go home."

He was wearing a sweater that had seen better days and a tweed sports jacket that was noticeably a relic of the past, as if retrieved from an attic. Otherwise, he was unremarkable—a thin, almost frail man who could be in his seventies or eighties. He had wisps of longish, uncombed white hair that stuck up like wild grass in a meadow. He clutched his hands in his lap, rubbing one over the other as if trying to keep warm.

Gabriella looked at the woman who had been talking to him. "Are you with him?"

The woman shook her head. "I'm in the seat behind him and heard him mumbling about going home, so I wanted to see if he was okay."

The conductor checked around his seat, including the floor, and on the railing overhead. "Do you have your ticket, sir?"

He looked at her but didn't say anything.

"Can you show me some identification…something in your wallet?" No response.

A middle-aged white male conductor entered the car and bent down beside Gabriella. He looked at her and smiled. "Do we have a problem here, Gabby?"

"I don't know. Our mystery man here doesn't seem to have a ticket, I don't have any record of him coming aboard, and all he can tell me is he wants to go home."

The eyes of the old man focused sharply on Gabriella, then on the male conductor. "I want to go home," he said as if responding to her for the first time.

"Where is that" asked the conductor. His nametag read Timothy. After a few seconds of silence, Tim asked. "Do you know your name?

May I see your ID?" The man turned to look out the window as if the conversation was done.

The two attendants stood and talked quietly. Gabriella said, "I asked several people in the car, but no one is with him. Should I make a general announcement, in case someone is in the lounge or diner?"

"Yes, go ahead. While you do that, I'll see if he'll let me look at his wallet, if he has one. I hate to search him, but I'll get one of the other passengers to serve as a witness.

Gabby nodded and walked down the aisle to the far end. She picked up the com phone for train-wide broadcast, pushed a button, and announced, "Your attention, please. We have a man by himself in Coach B, the second one after the observation car. He is elderly, thin, wearing glasses and a brown tweed jacket. If you are with him or know anything about him, please come to Coach B. We appreciate any help you can give us in identifying and helping our passenger." She hung up the phone and returned to the front of the coach.

Tim had recruited a man to help him. The passenger stood in the aisle as the conductor bent down once again in front of the mystery man.

"Sir, would it be okay if I looked in your coat pocket?"

The man looked at him for a moment, but his eyes wandered. His hands kept moving and his lips trembled, but he said nothing. Tim looked at the other passenger. "I am going to reach inside his jacket." He pulled the jacket out from the thin body and exposed the inner pocket. Tim slipped his hand inside but found nothing. He looked on the left side, but there was no pocket.

Turning to the old man, Tim asked, "Sir, can I ask you to stand up? We'll help you."

The conductor and the other passenger extended their arms and lifted the old man out of his seat. He rose somewhat unsteadily, but without protest. Tim quickly patted his pants pockets to feel for a wallet, but there was nothing. Not a wallet, keys, or handkerchief.

"Thank you, sir." They carefully seated the old man and stood back.

"I want to go home." The old man looked up at them, eyes better focused, voice clear and louder than before.

"Yes sir, we'll get some help. Sit and enjoy the ride, sir, and I'll be back shortly."

Tim thanked the passenger and met Gabby two rows behind the elderly man. They looked at the connecting door, hoping someone would come from the A Coach in response to the announcement.

"What do we do now?" asked Gabby. She had been a conductress for three months and this was a first for her. "Has this ever happened to you?"

Tim was the boss, the conductor in charge of the train, and he had nine years behind him. He had seen almost everything one could see on the rails.

"Yes, twice before. The first time, several years ago, a homeless man boarded and made it from Oakland almost to Sacramento before we discovered him. The second time involved a small child, about three or four. She was left on the train by her alcoholic mother who got off without knowing or caring her daughter was still aboard. In both cases, we notified the Highway Patrol and they took charge. We may have to do the same here."

"Do you think he's homeless?" she asked, one hopeful eye still on the door.

"Could be. No identification, no wallet, but his clothes are clean and he has shaved recently. Not the usual for someone trying to get a free ride or get out of the cold."

"He must have gotten on, somehow, in Klamath Falls. Our only other stop was Chemult and we dropped two, but I'm pretty sure no one boarded. It's like he appeared by magic. No name, no luggage, just a confused man wanting to go home, wherever that is."

Tim smiled. "Welcome to the magical world of rail travel, Gabby. Stick around for a year or two and this will seem like nothing."

They waited several minutes, but no one came to the car to provide enlightenment or information. Tim knew they still had over an hour before reaching Eugene, their next stop, but he made the call to the Oregon State Police to meet the train when they arrived. At midday lunch was served in the dining car.

"I wonder when the last time was that he had anything to eat or drink," said Gabby. She and Tim were watching the man from the door.

"See if he wants some coffee or a soda. If he does, maybe he'll respond."

Gabby once more knelt before the man in tweed. She put her hand on his left hand and looked into his eyes. He returned her gaze and she said, "Sir, can I get you something to drink or eat?"

His right hand closed over hers and he started to say something but stopped.

"Are you thirsty or hungry?" she said. "I can get you something. Please tell me what you want."

His eyes opened wider and he said, "Yes. I would like a coke. A Coca-Cola." His face relaxed and he removed his hand.

She stood up and said, "We have Pepsi-Cola. Will that do for you?"

He nodded his head slowly, like a little boy not quite believing he was getting what he wanted. Gabby reported back to Tim and he asked her to get one from the snack car. Gabby nodded and went to fetch the drink while Tim strolled forward to the business class and dining cars.

Five minutes later, Gabriella was once again in front of the mysterious passenger. She held the iced cup for him and poured the Pepsi, not quite to the top. He took it with surprisingly steady hands, took a sip, closed his eyes. When he opened them again, she was smiling.

"Does that taste good? I hope you wanted ice."

He nodded and took another slow sip. He was visibly more relaxed, sitting back in his chair, the empty hand still.

"Can you tell me your name?"

He looked at her as if seeing her for the first time. "Bernie. My name is Bernie. I want to go home."

"Bernie. Good. Do you know where home is? We want to help you if you tell me where you live."

He paused as if trying to recall, trying to cut through a thick blanket of fog that made it impossible to see, to know where he was supposed to be.

"It is a big house, with many rooms. Many people, my friends, and other people. Some I don't know." His brow furrowed and he grimaced slightly. "I don't know. I was there." He looked around. "I don't think that is where I am now. " He looked up at her, relaxed when she smiled, took another sip of soda.

Tim returned to the coach car and Gabby joined him at the door.

"Found out his name, or at least *a* name—Bernie. Says he lives in a big house with a lot of rooms, a lot of people, but doesn't know where," she said. "Doesn't seem to know he is on a train. Maybe the 'big house' is a hospital or nursing home?"

"Could be. Well, that's a start. Didn't give you a last name, I suppose?"

"Nope, but he seems content, less agitated than before. Did you contact the police?"

"They'll meet him at the Eugene depot, then it's their baby. Check on him from time to time. We don't want him wandering around before we get there."

"Yes, sir," said Gabby, happy to have helped in some small way.

She walked through Coach B twice before the train slowed for Eugene. The last time she saw Bernie was a few minutes after the train left Oakridge, about an hour or less from Eugene. He was quiet, looking out the window, and was still holding the plastic cup of ice. The drink was gone and she started to ask him if he would like another, but a passenger several seats back put on her call light and Gabriella moved dutifully to answer.

Ten minutes before arrival, the train was moving at about ten miles per hour, with an occasional stop to wait for a freight to pass. Gabriella entered the coach car and glanced at Bernie's seat. Empty. She looked up and down the aisle—no Bernie, no tweed coat. She called Tim to the car to check the restrooms, but no Bernie.

As the train pulled to a stop at the depot, Tim and Gabriella frantically searched the other cars, from sleepers to diner and lounge, to the last coach in the rear. They asked passengers and other crew members if they had seen a frail old man in a tweed coat. The only indication he had ever been on the train was a plastic cup of mostly melted ice on the seat next to where he sat. Tim carefully picked up the cup with a napkin and gave it to the state policeman waiting at the coach outer door.

"That's it, all you got? Maybe there'll be fingerprints."

The policeman accepted the cup and indicated he would ride the train with them to Albany to complete a report on mysterious tweed-jacket Bernie.

Gabriella looked at Tim. "That'd be Starlight Bernie, officer. I'll never forget him."

Tim smiled knowingly. And he thought he'd seen everything.

# Butterfly Memories

It wasn't pretty petals that attracted me
no matter what you think
color can be blinding, confusing, and destroying
not true images in time and place
to consummate my obsessions, your possessions,
that might or might not be mine to claim

It wasn't the flower's fragrance spilling
from your open blossoms
that spun my head in circles, wanton aromas
to steal my ardor, to make me surrender
to perfumes of passion during dreams of eternal slumber,
entrapped in your private bouquet

It wasn't the sweet treat of pollen
tasty to the probing tongue,
that made me wish with full abandon to devour
every bit, every hint, of what you are
what you will be, still in bloom, still with room
to grow and play the siren

It wasn't a fantasy of the earthly garden
where you dwell in innocence
nor my image of perfection, unrealistic and unattainable,
never to be drawn like a moth to the flame
of unrequited desire for one beyond reach,
regardless of my effort

It isn't what you think, my lovely
I am not the discriminate seeker,
selecting the best and leaving the rest, to be content
with only one whose charms enchant
and capture a heart, a mind, a spirit
forever and ever, amen

It is random fate I found you
and like the butterfly I'll leave you,
colored wings in bright traces, a whisper of affection
a fleeting passage of my presence, failing
sustained effort or direction, fading
without a kiss to remember.

# With Open Arms

It's not what you think, is it, mister?
I could be your brother or sister or something in between,
    something you wouldn't acknowledge or care about if you did,
    but you don't, you won't, and I can't help that.

But if you could, just for a moment, give it a thought?
See what you've bought and sold without thinking
    about me or mine or anything in between,
    because that's where it is, between your world and mine.

Can you see it, feel it, know it, what I feel, what I am?
No big deal, nothing to you but something to me,
    somewhere, sometime. I have deep thoughts
    and strange passions, a reality I know you know not.

But where is it, that loose fragment of me and what I was?
What I will be because my future line is not erased, not yet
    by you or anyone in the crowd of blank faces without
    traces of empathy, sympathy, or all those other bullshit words.

I don't have the time, never did, but now it's all too clear.
All the hopes, all the fears of dreams and schemes and best laid
    plans come to this, the precipice, the abyss of existence
    maintained by persistence and random nonsense, such is life.

Look in the mirror with a rebellious stare, widen unbelieving eyes.
Pretend surprise, as if you never knew that it would all come
>   to this, stepping from the edge into the void ahead and into
>   the dark, the depths of eternity, such is death and forgiveness.

The end is an end. Need I say more?

# PART TWO

# Everyday Challenges

◆

Whether we rise with the sun, with the moon, or at some other time suited to our daily schedule, we face the dilemmas and inconsistencies that life offers. Some of the challenges derive from the necessities of life and can only be avoided with difficulty, if at all. Others seem trivial by comparison—inconveniences that promise no lasting scars or consequences.

Many of the problems we face in childhood and adolescence, the mystical and unpredictable coming of age phase, might be regarded as insignificant, or sometimes comical when seen from the advantage of years later. At the time, however, even these have the potential to present formidable obstacles to health and happiness.

There are no supernatural beings or futuristic scenarios in this section. Instead, here lie the all-too-familiar situations, the commonplace events that comprise the majority of our experiences, good and bad, the ones that become integral parts of the fabric of what and who we are.

# The Game

*We all play them, the games of life. The little deceits, to others and to ourselves. No harm, no foul, but others are watching and learning.*

Crosby was wearing a red carnation in his lapel, like a big shot at a wedding. It looked pink, but it was hard to tell under the UV lights and the intermittent strobes. The music was kicking up a few more decibels as if it needed the extra blast. It didn't and neither did I.

He strolled to our table, flashing a crocodile smile. He leaned forward, straight-armed, and placed his knuckles flat on the surface, like a gorilla ready to ramble. Looking us over, he paused a moment on each face to provide the appropriate drama for his proposal. Like him, it was simple.

"Which one of you beautiful dolls would like the opportunity to dance with me? Hmm?"

Cherie was at my left—she looked off into the distance as if Crosby didn't exist. Good for her. She was our stalwart warrior in the hustle games and pointedly ignored his macho come-on.

I was next in line and his eyes locked on mine. "And you? Ready to show these hicks how the big city folks can shake their butts?"

"I don't shake my butt, especially for you." I took a drag on my cigarette, but as usual, didn't inhale.

Cherie gave me a canary-eating grin. "Way to play, Renee."

Nonplussed, the flower man turned to Jeanette. She was the youngest, not quite legal. She had ID but lacked our experience with the wannabe lovers and nightclub losers. She looked at both of us.

"It'd be all right, wouldn't it? If we just danced?"

Her concerned look made Cherie laugh. "Dance away the night, Jeannie, but remember, you leave with us."

Crosby stood up straight and offered his hand to Jeanette, almost like a gentleman. Looking back at us, she followed him onto the crowded floor, walking deep into the writhing crowd and effectively out of our view. We knew that routine and had warned her, but now she was on her own.

Cherie blew smoke slowly out her nose. "Why couldn't he have been someone else? Why Crosby, that arrogant son of a bitch?"

"He's no worse than many of the others. A bit of a show-off, but mostly harmless, not likely to try anything nasty."

For the next number, a slow grinder, we sat in silence. A few guys looked, one almost approached, but no one made a move.

"Think we're getting a reputation?" asked Cherie. She was finishing the last of her second margarita.

"For what? We rarely leave with anyone."

"That's what I mean." She pushed her glass to the center of the table and nodded to a passing waitress for another. I did likewise. "People come here to meet people. We come here to make fun of them."

"And get drunk," I added.

"Yeah, there's always that."

Jeanette waved at us from the floor, smiling and still dancing, but with someone else.

"I like the kid. A lot to learn, but she's coming along and seems to be having fun."

I sipped on my fresh drink and looked around at the crowd. Unfortunately, it was a small nightclub in a small town. We knew almost everyone in the room and had probably turned down every male, and a couple of females, at some time during the past three years.

Cherie suddenly sat up straight and hissed between her teeth. "Don't look around, but there's some fresh meat walking toward us. Never seen him before."

Sure enough, the man, looking to be in his middle thirties and refreshingly professional, came to a stop at our table. He gave us both a nod and smile.

"How are you ladies doing this evening?"

Before we could answer, he continued. "I know that's not a very original greeting, but it beats the hell out of trying to guess your zodiac sign."

He said it with such perfect and natural clarity, lacking phony pretense, we had to laugh.

"Sit down and join us, please," said Cherie, indicating Jeanette's vacant seat. She glanced my way to clue me that her game was on. And when it was on, she knew how to let the charm flow. I was never sure when it was genuine or just a continuation of the barroom singles' drama that played out every weekend. I sat back, taking mental notes, and looking for a cue that would send me to the restroom for a few minutes.

Jeanette came up at that moment with a young man in tow who looked the same age. Seeing her chair occupied, she blushed and said, "Don't get up. I'll just dance some more and…" Looking at her eager partner, she added, "Maybe I'll sit over there with him…. Oh, this is Andrew, and I'll be back a bit later. Okay?"

Cherie looked at her, smiled, and said, "Catch your breath, Jeannie; we'll be here. Remember? We leave together." The girl and boy walked off hand-in-hand.

"Ah, young love—ain't it grand?" I smirked.

Our table guest was indeed a professional—a tax accountant and a CPA, no less. Cherie could already smell the money, but I also noticed a deeper look of interest in her darkly-lined eyes. She had dropped her usual cynical replies and was conversing like a real human. I excused myself and made tracks for the powder room to give my drinking partner some room to roam. I was ready to return to the table when the door opened and Cherie rushed to my side.

In a lowered voice because of others around us, she said, "Renee, I'm gonna break our pact this one time. He has asked me to go to another club with him, that swanky one across town for members only. I can't let this pass. Will you stick around and make sure Jeannie gets home?"

There was a strange glimmer in her eyes, one I hadn't seen in quite some time. Although I hated the thought of returning to an empty table and drinking by myself, I owed her the opportunity to fly. Neither of us scored that often with anyone we would want to take home to mother. So, as a famous song says, "Let It Be." I assured her it would be fine with me, and she told me she trusted him, despite the brevity of their acquaintance.

Jeanette returned to the table after the music stopped and the crowd began to clear. "All done with Andrew and any others?" I asked. She nodded and gathered her purse.

"Where's Cherie?" she asked. I told the sweet thing our friend left with the man who had ridden in on his white horse and swept her off her feet. As we walked for the door, Jeanette sighed and said, "She really knows how to play the game, doesn't she? I can hardly wait."

# The Duck Pond

*When to observe and when to act? Why do we hesitate and what are the consequences? It is not as easy to break through the passive envelope as some would have us believe. It is much safer this way, don't you think?*

Wearing a green medical scrub top, blue jean shorts, and flip-flops, he looked mid-fortyish and sported a full beard, less than well-groomed. He held a cell phone and glanced at it often, as if expecting a call long overdue. It was an early summer evening, still warm on the spacious lawns and among the dense trees in the urban park, but the daytime crowds had left for other places and other events. He sat by himself on a green bench, facing a large duck pond.

I watched him from another bench, partly hidden by the shade of an overarching willow. He knew I was there, but he chose to ignore me, alternating his attention between three ducks cruising the pond and his ever-handy phone. Two of them were snowy white mergansers, a male and a female. The third was a male mallard, following the pair, occasionally submerging his head to nibble at the shallow bottom.

They spent most of their time on the far side of the pool, occasionally entertaining visitors walking the paths around the pond. From time to time, kids or teenagers occupied two of the benches across from Mister Scrub and me. In response, the ducks swam lazily toward the center of the pond, putting distance between themselves and the occupied benches.

*They aren't like most park ducks*, I thought, *usually on the make for handouts*. Two coin-operated dispensers for duck food, one on each side of the pool, allowed visitors to reward the floating menagerie.

Watching their tail flicks and the persistent pursuit by the mallard, the man laughed briefly, enjoying the strange courtship attempt by the green-headed one, always following, but avoided by the pair. Mister Scrub offered no food to entice them closer but seemed content to observe the tableau, as I was to watch the larger drama that included his responses.

The teens vacated the far bench, leaving him, me, and the ducks. A few minutes later, a woman—a blonde wearing a headscarf as if from the nineteen fifties—approached the far bench, looked around for a moment, and sat down. She carried a book in her hand, opened it, and held it in her lap. She crossed her legs, bent her head, and began reading. She was a bit overweight and also appeared to be in her mid-forties. A few jays flew overhead with raucous screams, but the park was otherwise silent.

The ducks began to circle the perimeter of the pond, the mallard still close behind the white ones, swimming casually past me and toward scrub man. He watched them coming, glanced at his phone, then at the woman reading. She didn't look up. The ducks turned toward the center before reaching the man. He uttered a brief chortle as if a joke had been played on him. He looked at the woman and again at his phone.

Ten minutes passed. It was quiet and I remained still, letting the scene unwind: woman, man, and ducks. A man in long pants and a Hawaiian shirt approached the woman's bench from behind her. She looked up, smiled, and closed her book. He sat down beside her, moved closer, thigh to thigh, faces turned toward the ducks. The man with the phone stood up, as if preparing to leave. He turned his head around, glancing behind him, briefly toward me and the couple, then he sat down to again stare at his phone.

The ducks resumed their shoreline patrol and passed in front of the man. He watched them intensely, smiling but remaining still.

The mallard approached the low wall of the pond and clambered out, shook his tail feathers, and waddled slowly toward Mister Scrub. The mergansers passed on by, moving again to the center of the pond. The man leaned forward, his phone on the bench at his side. The duck stopped in front of him, tail in motion, lifting one foot, then the other. The man smiled at his feathered friend in the deepening shadows of evening. The mallard came no closer than an arm's reach, but the eyes of the two seemed locked, as if agreeing to share a few moments.

The couple stood up together and walked away from the pond, hand-in-hand, conversing softly. The man watched them go, then returned to the duck. The mallard quacked twice and shuffled toward the water, hopping over the low retainer and plopping into the pool with a soft splash. The mergansers were halfway across the pond and he swam quickly to join them, once again the third one out, the extra to the intimate twosome. The man watched his new friend go while he picked up his phone, glanced at the screen, and gave a soft sigh. He reclined against the backrest and closed his eyes.

I stood and slowly walked away from him, the pond, and the ducks. Each had their place, their purpose, and their future story yet to be written. As the pond faded from view, I sincerely hoped that someone would call the man in the green scrubs.

# Take Out

*Can one be merely a witness without being involved, even if it's a passive gesture, an affirmation that something is right and good, or that something is wrong and bad?*

We ordered lunch at the busy roadside diner. The booths were filled, but the counter had several empty seats, between where my wife and I sat and the outer door. It was summer 1969 in rural Ohio, the highway filled with trucks and vacationers.

The door opened and a late-middle-aged black man, dressed in a work shirt and well-worn jeans, entered and stood at the end of the counter. He started to sit at the end stool but our waitress—a matronly, overweight woman with red curly hair—moved quickly to the counter in front of him. We could easily hear her tell him, "You can't sit there."

I looked at him and then at the rest of the diners eating, laughing, paying no attention. Until then, I hadn't noticed there were no black people in the diner. No Mexicans, Asians, or anyone else of color.

The black man stood up and mumbled, "Yes ma'am, I just need to get a bite to eat, that's all." He hesitated as she stared at him. "I have money, ma'am." He pulled out several bills from his pocket and straightened them with his hands before putting them on the counter.

"We can fix you a takeout, but you'll need to stand by the door, or you can wait outside and I'll bring it to you. What do you want?"

He told her and then moved to the wall next to the door. A sign above his head proclaimed, "We reserve the right to refuse service to anyone." He leaned back and folded his hands in front of him.

My wife and I looked at each other. We had both spent time in the South, but this was the North, several years after the Civil Rights Act. I looked up at the sign. "I guess they just exercised that right," I said to her.

The waitress brought two ice teas and set them in front of us. With a pleasant smile, she said, "Your order will be right up." I looked at her, probably frowning. "Something wrong, honey? You need something else?"

"The black guy, against the wall. Is he not allowed to sit at the counter?"

She stiffened and backed up a step, looking at us as if we had just landed from a distant part of the galaxy.

"He'll get his food. He wouldn't be comfortable eating in here with…" She glanced around the diner.

"I guess we're not either."

I stood up, paid enough for the two teas, and we walked toward the exit. I could see the reflection of the waitress in the door glass, mouth open, hands on hips. The black man didn't say a word and neither did we, but as we passed him, I detected just the thinnest smile, more in his eyes than in his mouth. It was all he dared give us, but it was enough.

Photo Essay II.

# What People Know

Where are you going? Each of you has a story, a life, connected to millions of other stories and with millions of other lives. Is it an ancient one, recalling the first days of human settlement in Europe, the migrations of Indo-Asians to the West, before there were cities or even the simplest villages? Did you live in caves and keep warm over fires borrowed from nature? What did you gather or hunt? How many did you feed?

Or is your tale a modern one…of winemaking and gourmet dining, of yachts from Italy and ski trips in the Julian Alps? Do you worship the dragons on Ljubljana's bridges, prowl the corridors of your ancient castles with today's tourists and their clicking cell phones? Do you swim in the sea and expose your semi-naked body to the sun and curious onlookers?

Where will your children go and what will they tell their children? Will the stories be old ones, passed down the generations and venerated by tradition? Will they be new ones, gathered from today's stage and tomorrow's performances, or something never seen or heard before?

*Adriatic Sea harbor and embankment in Piran, Slovenia.
Croatia is the far shoreline at right.*

# The Dance

*Fear of rejection, a major obstacle to the self-esteem of an individual, comprises a special torment for adolescents. This is a modernized revision of a chapter from my novel (2019)* The Home, *originally set in the 1950s and the early days of rock 'n' roll. Some things, however, never change.*

Most of my ninth-grade classes at Fisher Junior High were terminally boring and ultimately forgettable. My attention was often targeted elsewhere, anywhere except on the teacher or lesson. I spent lunchtimes either by myself or with Brad, my best and only friend. We shared our disdain for adolescent academics and education, in general, but I did have two classes that aroused Brad's interest and envy. One was an orientation session that planned the school's social and student body activities and the other was drama.

"So, you get to hang around with some real dolls, I bet."

We were eating our sack lunches on a bench near the football field. He knew I enjoyed performing on the stage, and I had convinced him the orientation class was a better alternative to an hour of study hall. I had a mouth full of peanut butter and jelly and could only mumble an indistinct "yeah."

He looked at the banana I had in my bag.

"Wanna trade that for an apple?" he asked.

I shook my head no, swallowing the last of the sandwich. "I like bananas. Keep the apple; it's good for you."

"Okay, Doctor Walt, but what about the girls? You thinking about asking any of them to the hop in a couple of weeks?"

I knew about the sock hop in October. I had been helping prepare posters for the dance that would take place about ten days before Halloween. Although it was informal and I didn't need a date, many of the ninth-graders were pairing off. I hadn't given it much thought. I didn't know anyone to ask, and I wasn't sure if Brad and I could attend a Friday evening dance.

We lived at The Children's Home, a residence for kids with working parents. Some of our friends didn't have parents or they were in transit to and from foster homes. I had only been in The Home for two months and still didn't know all of the rules and restrictions.

Brad enlightened me. "The older guys and girls can go to an organized dance or game at school if we aren't in trouble and we get permission in advance."

"Am I considered an older guy?" The thought amused me.

He nodded and said, "Yep, they'll let the ninth-graders go. You're a bit young for the ninth—did you skip a grade or something?" He knew I wouldn't turn fourteen until December.

"No, I just started early—my mother's idea. Are you going to ask someone?"

I hadn't thought about Brad dating either, although I knew he was further along in chatting up the girls than I was.

"Maybe you can fix me up with one of your drama dolls, Walt. You'd do that for a buddy, wouldn't you?"

"Me? You think I can fix you up? Most of them don't know my name. They don't know I'm in their class when I see them in the hall. Besides, I wouldn't know what to say to them."

"Hey, you're supposed to be learning to act, aren't you? Put it to work. Pretend that you're Johnny Depp or Brad Pitt. Come on to them and then tell them you got this really cool friend who would like to meet them. We can double date."

"I'm not Brad Pitt," I said. "I'm more like a goofy comedian. I get laughs, sometimes, not dates. Besides, what's wrong with *you* asking for both of us? It would probably be no sweat for a smooth talker like you."

He shook his head and chomped on the apple. I peeled the banana and we stared at a bunch of jocks on the field, practicing hikes and football formations. We finished and walked back to the main classroom building.

Before we parted, he said, "Don't worry about it, Walt. I wasn't that serious."

"If I find someone for you, I'll let you know." I thought about it as I walked into the main building. He just didn't have the right friend to find him a girl.

---

Two weeks later, I still hadn't done anything about finding a date for Brad or myself. I told Brad on the Wednesday before the dance that our only options were to go stag or to not go at all. I was leaning toward the latter because I remembered how much fun it had been on a couple of occasions at a previous school, standing against the wall and watching others pair off while I tried to overcome my fear of rejection. It was a toss-up as to which was worse—asking someone to dance and have them laugh and walk away, or having someone accept and then making a fool of myself because I never learned to dance. Brad was not as reluctant to face failure.

"It goes with the game; you just have to keep asking until someone says 'yes' and lets you shuffle feet with her," he said. As if it was something he did every day.

"Shuffle feet? Brad, when was the last time you went to a dance?"

He started to answer.

"At school, not at The Home," I interrupted.

We had a recreation hall and the kids danced to music on the weekends. The girls often danced with each other while the guys shot baskets on the adjoining court.

He lowered his head. "Last year, during the spring. They had a sock hop for the eighth- and seventh-graders. I went with Burt."

"With Burt? Your brother?"

He nodded.

"Did your brother dance? I mean, did he actually ask a girl to dance?"

Brad smiled. "No, he didn't. But some of the guys and a few of the girls danced by themselves, kind of in a circle. They moved to the music and no one seemed to mind."

"And what about you—did you ask anyone to dance, besides your brother?"

He looked at me strangely but laughed. "I did. There was a girl by herself and after the music started, I walked up to her. She had her back to me, so I tapped her on the shoulder. When she turned around, I realized that she was probably one of the nerdiest girls at the dance."

"What did you do?"

"What *could* I do? I asked her to dance." He paused, then closed his mouth.

"And...," I prompted.

"Well, she looked at me as if she didn't trust me or something. She didn't actually agree, but I figured, what the hell—what is the worse that could happen? So I took her arm and led her to the edge of the dance floor and we started moving to the music, doing our own thing. I didn't have to hold on to her and we didn't talk."

"Then what?"

"Then, nothing. When the music stopped I said 'thank you' and we walked back to the wall. She went her way and I went mine."

"So, you didn't get her name or find out anything about her, huh?"

"C'mon, Walt, I didn't want to know her name. I didn't want her to know mine. I wasn't going to date her or anything."

"Is that it? Is that your entire 'I know my way around the dance floor experience'? Sounds like a lot of fun. I can hardly wait until Friday night."

"Cool. That means we're going, right?"

His face lit up like I had announced we had found a thousand dollars. Despite my foreboding, I reluctantly agreed. I was hoping the event would be merely boring and not a monumental disaster. That evening we talked to Mrs. Troillet, our housemother for the week, and she filled out a form. We could leave the grounds after dinner, go to the school dance, which lasted until eleven, and then we were to return directly back to The Home. We were to check in with her no later than eleven thirty and we were to stay together.

She laughed. "You don't have to dance with each other, but you can't leave the school without the other, even if a beautiful girl wants to invite you to go out and party."

"Fat chance of that," I mumbled. Brad hit me on the arm and told me not to be negative. Mrs. Troillet was amused about the whole thing, but then she got serious and told us to have fun, stay out of trouble, and to be back on time.

"I don't want to fill out any more forms," she said, holding up the ones we had just signed.

At least we didn't have to wear a coat and tie to a sock hop. Casual clothes were in and dressing down was even better—raggedly clothes, jeans with kneeholes, and well-worn shirts. Many of the girls wore knee-high socks in bright colors, crazy hair ribbons, and outlandish beads. The dance resembled an early Halloween party, but actual costumes were not permitted. Still, it didn't stop many of the students from improvising. By contrast, Brad and I could have been wallpaper, wearing the same clothes we had worn to school that day.

We left the dormitory at 7:10 and walked to school. The doors opened at seven-thirty and the recorded music started at eight. I was already regretting my decision to attend, but Brad was relaxed and looking forward to the evening. I could picture him dancing at will and me making excuses to go to the punch bowl, the bathroom, or trying to engage someone—anyone—in idle conversation until the last song played.

We approached the gymnasium just as the doors opened. Only a few students were waiting, some stag and some couples. Groups formed and reformed as individuals mixed and socialized while they entered the nearly empty gym. Several Halloween-inspired decorations hung from the rafters and a row of tables with snacks and three different punch bowls lined one side. As usual with dances held in gyms, the faint aroma of sweat and dirty gym socks drifted here and there, especially in the corners near the locker room doors.

Brad and I made our way to one of the tables to get a few pieces of candy. We each filled a paper cup with red punch, better known as strawberry Kool-Aid, and walked back toward the entrance. A stage at one end of the gym floor held a player and several boxes of CDs. Two guys hovered over the boxes, selecting and placing the discs in a pile. As I looked around, I recognized very few faces. I wasn't sure whether that was bad or good, but Brad kept asking me if I had seen any of the girls from my drama class or orientation group.

"Not yet," I said. "I don't know anyone, not a soul."

"Me neither," he admitted, "but it's still early."

Indeed, it was. It would be another twenty minutes before the music started and the room was still mostly empty.

"Maybe the girl you asked last year will come," I said, not without malice.

Brad looked at me and for the first time, I saw some of the despair in his eyes that I had been feeling all day.

"Oh, God, I hope not. I hadn't thought about that." He put his head down, but then he lifted it, a smile creeping across his face.

"Hey, Walt, I could introduce you to her. You'd have someone to dance with."

"You idiot, you don't even know her name. You can't introduce anyone to anyone." I looked at him with some satisfaction, as if I had foiled his most evil plans.

"Just a thought, Walt, just a thought."

Then I saw her. It was Phyllis, the sexy jazz dancer of my most secret romantic fantasies. She was wearing a short black skirt and red-and-white striped socks. She was also wearing a gold tiara as if she had won a beauty pageant. My eyes followed her across the gym and Brad noticed.

"Is that one of them? From your drama class?"

"No, she's not in my class." I told him about the talent show rehearsals and my backstage management of curtains and lights. She was fourteen and her choreographic moves were the embodiment of all I found desirable in a girl. I didn't have to tell him that I worshipped her—it must have been all too apparent. She was with another girl and they were talking by the central punch bowl.

"Are you thirsty, Walt? Think we should go get some more Kool-Aid?" Brad downed his drink and looked at mine.

"I still have some. I'm not ready yet," I said as I looked down at my half-filled cup.

Without a word, he grabbed my cup, drank it in one swallow, and gave it back. "You're welcome. Now you're ready."

My mind was running at full speed, as it always did in these situations. I knew Brad was going to do his best to get us close to Phyllis and her friend. I could foresee two distinct, equally unpleasant outcomes. Most likely, Phyllis would ignore both of us and we would be starting the evening on a dismal note. The other possibility is that Brad would somehow manage to hit it off with her, and I, unable to intervene, would see my unrealistic and unrequited hopes shattered.

"You talk to your dancer and I'll chat with her friend," he told me as we slowly walked toward the punch bowl. "What's her name?"

"I don't know. I've never seen her before."

Her friend was cute and Brad could probably engage her, but that still left me with the dilemma of what to say to Phyllis. *Remember me, Walt, your light man? I pull the curtains for you. I really like the way you dance.* It all seemed so hopeless, trying to say something that wouldn't be obvious or lame. Their backs were to us as we approached. They were laughing but hadn't gotten anything to eat or drink yet. That was all Brad needed—he walked around Phyllis and smiled at her friend.

"Can I pour you a cup of Kool-Aid?" he said. Just like that, nothing more, nothing less.

"Sure," she said. "My name is Sandra." She held up her hand and gave him a petite wave of her fingers.

"*The* Sandra? Sandy—Walt's friend?" he asked.

"Who is Walt?"

Brad looked at me, still standing behind Phyllis. "That Walt. He told me about you and the orientation group.

Phyllis smiled at me and said, "Hello, Walt."

I looked at her friend and at Brad. "No, that's not the Sandy in the orientation group." I was not sure where this was going and I stepped back, ready to retreat fast and far.

Phyllis continued smiling at Brad and me. "Walt works with me when I do my dance numbers, the ones I'll be doing for the whole school in two weeks."

I wished I felt as relaxed as she looked.

"I'll look forward to that, for sure," Brad said. "Would you like some punch too?" He gave me a look of expectation that I would do my part and get Phyllis a cup. I misunderstood.

"No, I'm not thirsty right now; thanks anyway," I said, amazed that Phyllis was still smiling.

"We'll get some later," Phyllis said to Brad, "but thank you for asking. You're sweet." She giggled and the two of them walked away, leaving Brad and me with our empty paper cups. Brad looked at me as if I had crawled out from under a rock.

"What the hell were you thinking? 'I'm not thirsty.' Damn, Walt, I wasn't asking *you*."

"Oh." I shrugged, watching Phyllis across the room. All of a sudden it seemed the only thing I wanted was to grab another cup of Kool-Aid.

The floor was filling up and the noise level rose accordingly. I still didn't recognize most of those around me, but Brad indicated several of his classmates here and there, guys and girls. The first sounds shook the gym as a fast rock number poured from the speakers. Brad and I looked at each other and moved to the wall where we could survey the scene. The crowds mingled, talking and moving, but very few danced.

It was the usual routine, most of the kids waiting for the first few to get on the floor. These were usually couples, not afraid to dance or of what others thought of their moves. Slowly, more students would join them until most of the dance floor was occupied.

The same would occur when the first slow numbers were played. A few couples would start and others would join in after initial shyness dissipated. It was one thing to bounce around and swing, dancing apart or holding only each other's hands, but something else to dance slowly with arms around waists and hugging close. I was waiting for Brad to make his move. I wouldn't try until after he was distracted.

The chance came sooner than I expected. It was the third song, a fast dance, and Brad asked a girl standing with two others. She said yes and her two friends looked over at me as Brad and the girl walked away. I pretended like I didn't see them and edged into the crowd to stand behind a couple of overweight guys. I looked around to see if there was someone else I could ask. I didn't want to risk a refusal from the group Brad had approached—it would be embarrassing if one of them refused.

A younger girl was standing by herself. *Probably a seventh-grader*, I thought. I took several steps to get near her left side. I looked out at the floor and spotted Brad and his partner bouncing to the music. He wasn't particularly graceful or good at it, but they were enjoying themselves. Finally getting my nerve up, I looked back to the girl, but she was now standing to my left, peering out at the crowd. *Looking for someone she knows. I know that feeling.*

The number was almost over, so I waited for the next one to start. *No sense in risking humiliation to dance for only a few seconds.* The song ended and the next one immediately started, a slow song. My heart dropped. I had never slow danced in my life. I didn't know how. I would have to wait for the next fast one.

The girl looked at me, took a step closer, and asked in a soft voice, "Do you want to dance?" She was about four inches shorter than I was, slim, not beautiful but attractive in a wholesome manner. She was wearing a semitransparent white blouse and I could see her bra. She was not wearing big bright socks.

"I'm not very good at slow dancing," I confessed. "In fact, I have never slow-danced before. Sorry."

"That's okay, I just thought maybe you were by yourself and would like to dance." She started to walk away.

I thought quickly. "Would you like some punch? We could get something to drink and wait for the next fast dance."

She turned back toward me. "No, thanks. I really want to dance. Maybe later." She turned and disappeared in the crowd.

I looked again toward the floor and didn't see Brad. *He probably has the same problem I do—can't slow dance. We are the real lady-killers.* I turned my head to where the other two girls had been and there he was, with all three of them, laughing like old friends at a reunion. *Should I join them or stay here? Would it help Brad or ruin things for him? He's doing great without me.*

I put my head down and shuffled a little further into the crowd, out of sight. I decided I would wait for the next fast dance and find someone, anyone. Once that was accomplished, I would be able to join Brad and his friends, almost as an equal, without embarrassment or apology. However, as was usual, a second slow number followed the first, a concession to those with the courage to try the moving embrace—they could stay on the floor and continue the game. I would recognize that and much more in later years.

Finally, a fast number came and I decided to act before the next wave of cowardice overwhelmed me. Two girls were standing nearby. A guy stepped up and asked one of them to dance, leaving her friend alone. She was slightly overweight but seemed pleasant and energetic. She moved her feet and her hips swayed to the upbeat tempo of an R.E.M. classic.

Stepping in front of her, I nodded toward the dance floor. "Give it a try?" I asked, trying to sound casual and confident.

She stopped moving, looked at me for a brief second, and said, "Why not?" She took my hand and led me onto the floor, right next to Brad dancing with one of the other girls in his trio.

"Hey, Walt, way to go. This is Frannie," he said, nodding to the brunette in front of him.

My partner looked up at me. "Walt, huh? Great name, I'm Sue. My friends call me Susie, but I usually prefer Sue."

We were dancing in a swing style, with both hands held, and I was barely moving my feet back and forth. She knew the moves, when to break and when to turn. I kept looking at others, doing my best to follow their example. On one of her turns, she twirled in close to me so that my arms were around her waist.

"Relax, Walt, I only bite on Mondays, never on Fridays."

That was when I put my right foot firmly on her left foot. Her open-toed sandals caught the full force of my weight, bringing a gasp of pain that didn't go unnoticed by those around us.

"Sorry, Sue, I'm really sorry."

We stood there facing each other and I was sure she was going to walk away, but she didn't. She shrugged, took my hand, and we finished the number, but she kept her feet well out of range of mine, preferring a wider stance and less ambitious spins. When the number ended, I walked her back to the side and went to join Brad and the trio. They weren't there.

I knew he wouldn't leave without me, but the four of them had disappeared. I looked around the table area, thinking that they were getting some refreshments, but at the entrance, I saw the three girls, without Brad. They were greeting two other girls who had just arrived. I felt an arm on my shoulder and turned to see Brad, grinning up at me.

"Where have you been?" I asked.

"Whiz break. Gotta take a whiz break every now and then. What do you think of the three fair maidens?"

"The three are now five," I said, looking toward the door. They were walking our way.

"Ooh, now what do we do?" he said.

"Should be easier, Brad. With three, it's hard to pair off. It leaves one alone. With five, we can take the two we want and the others still have company."

I said this with complete confidence, as if this was an arrangement we made every day and there could be no doubt about our ability to make it so. Actually, I had worked out the numbers game sometime before this but had never acted on it.

"Wow, Walt, sometimes you amaze me." His mouth was partly open.

The girls neared and we turned to them. All of them were cute and friendly. Their eyes, however, focused on Brad. He had obviously made an impression on the three and they had relayed it to the new ones.

We introduced ourselves and took turns, along with other guys, in dancing with the girls, but only to the fast numbers. One of those guys, a football player who I had met during the orientation sessions, invited the five girls to a party that was starting before the dance ended. Frannie asked Brad if he and I would like to join them, but Brad said we had other things to do. He never told them where we were from. Since very few students at our grade in school could drive, it was assumed that most kids had a ride with someone older or lived nearby.

A little after ten, the group said goodbye and left. We hung around for a few more numbers but didn't dance.

"Ready to go?" Brad asked. The crowd was beginning to thin out and the number of slow songs was increasing at the expense of the fast ones.

"Aren't you going to wait for your partner from last year—you know, the one whose name you never learned?"

"Walt, I'm saving her for you, remember? I'm sure she would like to slow dance with you."

"Yeah, let's head for home."

Under the full moon, we walked back slowly, discussing the great time we had with the five girls. I started calling them "Brad's harem," a reference he didn't seem to mind. I had to admit that Brad knew how to talk them up and they responded in kind. We speculated on what might have happened had we been able to join them at the party.

"I wonder how late that will go," I said.

"We will probably never know. Maybe we'll run into some of them at school and ask."

"Maybe there is a future where we can get dates with someone from outside the home."

We were tired when we entered the dorm. We checked in with Mrs. Troillet, who noticed we were early, quarter to eleven.

"Did it go that bad?" she asked.

"No, ma'am," Brad replied. "It went well. We decided to quit while we were ahead." His smile reassured her and also preempted her from asking further questions.

Our evening strengthened the friendship between Brad and me. He was more confident about girls than I, but I was learning to overcome my fear of rejection. The problem was the lack of sufficient opportunities to learn the game. The rules of engagement were different on the outside than they were at The Home, but the goals weren't all that different.

We did see a couple of Brad's harem in the halls and on the fields of The Fish, but Brad and I were not able to follow up on our initial interactions. Dating was too difficult and awkward for Homies and we could never bring them to our place. Better to let it slide and keep our ambitions tucked inside the fantasy shelter we dreamed and lived in.

# Relay

*Communication is one of the most important keys to our social structure and existence. Sometimes it isn't what we say, but what we mean.*

"I might not make it."

"You'll make it; hang in there." I inserted the needle in the IV port to draw blood.

Dana was scared, the tears running down her cheek, but that may have been pain. The morphine drip had just started, and the last tube was filling when the ER nurse nodded to the attending physician about her falling blood pressure. The monitors were doing backflips as her ECG traces became increasingly rapid and erratic. She grabbed my arm as I withdrew the needle.

"Tell my mother, please…" I had to bend close, her voice a whisper lost in the ER clamor. "Tell her…." The drug was doing its magic.

"She's not here yet, Dana, but she will be soon. I have to go. You'll be fine."

"I won't. I can feel it." Her hand gripped tighter, the fingernails leaving a red mark. The ER physician prepared a cardiac stimulant. "Please…tell her I'm sorry. It was my fault, not Billy's. Don't blame him. I'm sorry… I…"

Her eyes closed, she convulsed briefly, and her hand relaxed.

The doctor and nurse converged on the battered teen as I hurried to the laboratory to prepare blood for a transfusion. If Dana survived the immediate crisis, she would need several units. She didn't know her brother had been pronounced dead at the scene. I was just starting the crossmatch when the ER called.

"Dana expired; we won't need the blood." The nurse said it matter-of-factly, but we never got used to the death of a young person. Dana was fifteen.

When I returned to the ER to complete the paperwork, the nurse was talking with a distraught middle-aged woman, Dana's mother. The nurse introduced me to the woman and left me to talk with her.

"I am very sorry for your loss, Mrs. Starlett. Have you talked to Doctor Rao yet?"

She looked at me before answering. "No, I haven't. I'll see him in a few minutes. The nurse told me you were the last person Dana talked to before she… I didn't make it in time…." Her tears were flowing freely and she was trembling. "What did she say?"

I helped her to a chair and brought her a cup of coffee. I waited while she regained her composure. My eyes were also a bit misty and I took a sip of my coffee. I suddenly realized I was the final messenger, the last stage in the relay.

"She said she was sorry. She said it was her fault, not her brother's."

"No, it wasn't. It wasn't her fault—it was mine. She had a learner's permit. I should have been with her, not her fourteen-year-old brother."

She said this while looking at her lap, hands folded around the paper cup. She looked up at me. "Did she say anything else?"

I hesitated. Looking into her eyes, I spoke slowly, "She said to tell you… to tell you, she loved you."

# Fig Newton

Carl Newton and his lovely wife Loretta, also bearing the name Newton for almost two years, received the happy news that they were to produce their own little Newton. Sonography revealed it was now officially a boy.

A few weeks before the blessed event, the parents engaged in a friendly but intense contest over what name the firstborn would possess. The father leaned heavily toward his ancestry, citing precedents such as Andrew, Charles, and, not unexpectedly, Carl. Loretta was more inclined to a fresh namesake. She was firm in not wanting the child to end up with a junior tag, so Carl, at least in her opinion, was a no-go. She wasn't especially thrilled with Charlie and Andy either.

"Why reduce him to nicknames? Charles and Andrew are distinguished first names and we don't need to revert to the cutesy monikers everyone else uses."

Carl folded his arms in front of him, as he usually did when he believed his case was made and no further debate would matter. That is the way with some lawyers, even those who don't appear in court. He pleaded his case further, another known trait of the persuasive set.

"In fact, both names would be perfect: Charles Andrew Newton. With a name like that, he could grow up to be a lawyer—a great lawyer—become a judge, rise to the Supreme…"

"We haven't agreed on a name yet and you have him on the Supreme Court? Ambitious, my love, ambitious you are. I had in mind something a little less exalted, more down to earth, if you will." She looked at him with his arms still folded and waited.

He knew the signs. It didn't take twenty years of marriage for a clever chap like him to read the opposition and realize he had to at least give the appearance of considering her opinion. He dropped his arms to his sides, smiled, and leaned toward her.

"What'cha got in mind, sweetie?" It was the same voice and intonation he used when inviting her to the bedroom for a foray on the flannel sheets.

She wasn't falling for it. Instead of providing the expected flirtatious response, she folded her arms and fixed him with a serious but not hostile stare.

"Isaac Foster Newton," she stated firmly as if reading a royal proclamation. Isaac was the name of my favorite uncle."

"Isaac? You want to call our boy Isaac Newton?"

"Hmm, my uncle's name was Isaac Greenspan. I hadn't thought about that, but it is a distinguished name, right?" She relaxed, and any traces of belligerence vanished.

"Maybe he'll grow up to be bright and creative, discover one or more of the great truths of the universe."

"More likely he will be the butt of endless jokes and teasing from his classmates. And what about his teachers? What will they expect from a kid named after one of the most famous scientists ever? Why not call him Albert Einstein Newton?"

He paused. "Where did you get Foster?" He was thinking about Australian beer but decided not to open that door.

"I just like the name. Sounds refined, elegant. Don't you think so? If you don't want Isaac, at least let me have Foster."

So it was decided. Charles Foster Newton would be the next Supreme Court justice or academic physicist or something else in the world, the pride and joy of the Newton family. With a distinguished name like that, what could go wrong?

Charles Foster was born, babied, learned to walk and talk, and grew in size like any normal child. Despite repeated efforts, Carl and Loretta only produced the singleton, the one son to carry their banner forth on life's battlefield.

Being of substantial means, though not wealthy by contemporary American standards, they were able to indulge the maturing lad with all of the material benefits and accouterments of childhood. He had the best bike in the neighborhood, frolicked on a grand backyard playground set, enjoyed vacations at beaches and mountain resorts, and performed notably well in school. Carl and Loretta were convinced that Charles Foster would indeed become a great lawyer or scientist, depending on which parent you asked.

Foster, as the ten-year-old was now known, avoided the dreaded "Charlie" for his mother's sake. Poor eyesight, like that of his father, necessitated eyeglasses. He was quiet, an avid reader, and spent a good deal of time alone.

But what set him apart, even from other kids with a geek streak, was his collection of about two dozen common spiders: colorful orb weavers, speedy ground-running wolf spiders, delicate and camouflaged crab spiders, and a trapdoor spider he had bought from an exotic animal dealer.

But his favorites, without a doubt, were the tarantulas he had obtained, one by one, from a local pet shop. The first large spider was a Mexican red-knee tarantula, a common species that was notable for being docile and easy to handle. Handle it he did, carrying it about on his shoulder, showing it to his few friends and taking photographs of his hairy pet on different backgrounds.

"Why don't we get him a dog or a gerbil, or something a little less creepy?" asked Carl one night as Foster was on the living room rug with Pedro, the eight-legged one.

"What's the harm? He likes spiders, at least for now. He'll grow out of it and want something else. You know how boys are." This was offered with the entirety of sympathy, compassion, and understanding of a mother who sees her son, regardless of the path he follows, fulfilling all of her dreams.

"No, I don't know how boys are. I wasn't like that. Spiders were something you stepped on and avoided if you could. I can only hope they are as harmless as Foster tells us they are."

Carl wasn't afraid of his son's companions, but neither was he thrilled by their presence in the house, especially when outside of the terraria they occupied. The tanks and cages were kept in a corner of the boy's room, so they were usually easy to ignore, but the tarantula was a large, bright red presence that seemed to dominate the living room when Foster let him "exercise." Loretta didn't like to watch when Foster fed his charges live insects, but otherwise, her son could indulge in his interests to his and her heart's content.

The predicted shift in interests did not occur. When Foster turned eleven, his spider collection grew with him. Freckle-faced, wearing his thick-lens glasses, and inclined toward a thin and short stature, he continued to read and indulge his love of natural curiosities. As a younger child, his strange pets made him popular with the snake-and-lizard set—boys who followed their fancies for the strange and exotic. But as most of his companions grew older, they traded reptiles for baseball gloves and a few of them whispered about learning a dance step or two.

Foster had achieved the status of a certified nerd, a quiet kid with only two equally geeky friends with whom to share lunchtime and interests. It was bad enough that Foster was bright and excelled in school, but his disinterest and ineptitude in all sports, except running, made him an easy target for boys who culled the herd of the weak ones. Running had become a survival skill. Frequent verbal jibes, occasional hallway pushes, and a few humiliating pranks became the daily expectations as the fall term of sixth grade progressed. Matters reached a critical point during a late October week, two days before Halloween.

Foster's social studies teacher presented a lesson on pagan traditions and the evolution of Halloween as a celebration. Students were invited to bring a show-and-tell item for the class that week and Foster knew, without a doubt, what he would present.

On Wednesday morning, he placed Pedro, the red-kneed one, in a special carrying cage, put the cage in a paper bag, and proudly brought him to class. By this time, the boy had acquired two other species of tarantula, but Pedro was still his favorite and the spider was accustomed to being handled. Foster didn't think the potential chaos of school and a noisy classroom would be a challenge.

After several students demonstrated costumes and their symbolic significance, a few passed out themed candies or cookies, and a couple of girls read Halloween poems, Foster stood at the front of the room with his paper bag. He lifted the cage out of the sack slowly, teasing the expectations of those who suspected, and delaying the revelation to those who didn't. Many of his classmates knew he raised spiders, but only a couple of them had ever seen one or more.

He held the cage up, the thin wire mesh revealing Pedro in all of his glory. And now the dramatic moment that Foster had been anticipating for the past two days. He opened the top of the cage and, as if on cue, Pedro hopped onto his outstretched arm and begin crawling slowly toward his elbow.

A few girls shrieked, some of the boys expressed sounds of amazement or disgust, and their teacher, Miss Folsom, looked concerned, not sure whether she should cancel the rest of the performance. Foster held his hand out and the three-inch arachnid turned and crawled onto his palm and sat, as if waiting to be stroked, which Foster did, slowly and gently so as not to alarm his pet to discharge irritating hairs.

Foster explained this as the students watched, fascination overcoming fear in most of the audience. After a few minutes, he offered to walk around and let them touch Pedro, but the teacher decided that Foster had used his allotted time and asked him to put the hairy one back. She thanked him and most of the kids applauded, acknowledging Foster for his effort and expertise.

One boy, larger and a bit older than the rest of the class, was not appreciative. Ralph, better known on the football field as "Big

Bad Butch" or "Triple B," sulked near the back wall of the classroom. He especially resented the attention bestowed on the spider man from Darla, one of the cutest girls in the class. She displayed a new respect, perhaps an admiration, for the pale freckled kid who deserved nothing of the kind. Butch had renamed Foster two years ago, when his crusade of personal torment for the boy had started.

"Fig Newton should be your name. You eat them all the time and you are ugly like a fig. Figgy, Figgy, that's who you are."

Butch and several of his teammates followed Foster home, chanting the nickname then and whenever the opportunity arose on the playground. The taunt had become repeated often enough that it assumed an informal status, one that his friends had also adopted. Foster didn't mind. He liked the cookies and there were worse names he could be called.

Butch was waiting on his bike when Foster walked out of the schoolyard with his paper bag.

"Hey, Figgy, that was a pretty cool thing you did in class today. Can I get a better look at your spider?"

Butch had a grin on his face and he stood over the bike relaxed and welcoming as if greeting a buddy. Foster approached cautiously, clutching the bag, uncertain whether to walk away or to find out if the two-year cycle of bullying would finally end. Some of his other classmates were noticeably friendlier and there was always hope for a better day. Foster opened the sack and pulled out the cage, holding it in front of Butch.

"Amazing, Figgy, just friggin' amazing. Do you think I could hold it in my hand like you did? How about it, I'd like to do that."

Foster opened the cage and Pedro jumped onto his wrist. Extending his hand toward Butch, he held his breath while the older boy reached toward Pedro. The spider slowly crawled onto Butch's upheld palm.

Suddenly, Butch's other hand swung up and slapped hard onto the palm and spider, a loud clap that was partly muffled by the soft squish of spider flesh. It was over in a heartbeat. The grin that Butch displayed as he wiped his hands on Foster's shirt was no longer benign. It was a sneer that left no doubt about what had been a planned assassination, an assault on Foster that was worse than any physical beating he could have suffered.

"Well, Figgy, you'll have to tell all his spider friends about his misfortune. Just show them your shirt and they'll understand."

With a laugh, he was off on his bike, down the street, leaving Figgy with a cage, sack, and a bloody shirt.

Foster still had a robust collection of arachnids at home, but he had one very special friend, a wandering spider, a specimen from Panama that he had acquired from an exotic animal supplier. The spider had a five-inch leg span and a large body, the biggest in Foster's collection. He didn't handle it like he did the tarantulas. Sometimes called a banana spider or an armed spider, *Phoneutria bolieviensis* was the pride of his collection, but it had significant, although not necessarily fatal, venom. His parents were kept blissfully ignorant of the potential medical dangers.

The spider had a relatively large terrarium to wander in and she was provided with fresh mealworms, crickets, and other bugs. Foster delighted in the defensive posture that Annabelle assumed, rearing back with her abdomen pressed to the ground, two pairs of forelegs raised, jaws displayed and ready.

The next day, Foster brought his lunch pail to school instead of a usual paper sack. It contained a peanut butter and jelly sandwich, a small carton of orange juice, a banana, five fig newtons, and a small cheesecloth sack. During the morning recess, while Butch was promoting his basketball prowess on the concrete court, Foster cautiously approached an open shelf-locker where Butch's lunch pail sat.

He opened the pail and placed one fig newton on the top of a wrapped sandwich. He carefully placed the cheesecloth sack at one side in the pail and opened it, allowing Annabelle to crawl out. As her kind often did, especially during the day, she sought refuge, crawling under a napkin lying beside the sandwich. Removing the cheesecloth, Foster closed the pail and withdrew.

Lunchtime was usually spent with one or both of his nerdy friends, but the classroom demonstration had resulted in an invitation to join others at one of the lunch tables. Darla was among the group who was anxious to learn more about Foster's hobby. Sweating profusely, Butch joined the table, forcing a place on the bench between Darla and Foster.

Butch grinned at his victim. "How are your spider friends today, Figgy? Doing well, I hope." Butch was not overly endowed with smarts and he couldn't keep the evil tone from his poorly disguised remark, as several of the others noticed while they watched both boys.

"Everything is well that ends well," answered Foster, casually chomping on his sandwich.

"Got your figgy newtons there, dontcha?" said Butch, as he opened his lunch pail. He paused at the sight of the lone cookie on top of his sandwich. "What the hell?" He turned to Foster, a scowl replacing the smile. "Where in the hell… what do ya think you're up to?"

Foster looked straight ahead, munching slowly on the last of his sandwich. The others at the table were silent, waiting for whatever drama was going to unfold. Butch stared hard, trying to unnerve the smaller boy. Getting no reaction, he reached down into the pail, picked up the fig newton, and ground it in his hand, letting the crumbs fall to the ground.

"That's what I think of your stupid cookie, you stupid fig."

Butch reached down again into the pail and picked up his sandwich without taking his eyes off of Foster, still sitting patient and nonchalant. A gasp and shriek from two of the others pulled Butch's attention away from Foster. Still holding the sandwich in his left hand, he looked into his pail to see a large brown spider with a purplish abdomen and white spots staring up at him. Its forelegs were raised high overhead, pointing toward the snarling face above it.

Butch growled and turned toward Foster. "You think I'm afraid of that. Your shirt is about to get messed again, you little freak."

He reached for the brown one and it jumped, landing on his wrist. Before Butch could put the sandwich down and repeat yesterday's arachnicide, Annabelle sank her chelicerae into the underside of Butch's wrist. She hopped off almost immediately, retreating into the pail and under the paper napkin. But the fangs had done their work, injecting a small amount of venom into Triple B, the big bad boy who was now rolling on the ground, holding his arm and crying in terror.

"It bit me, it bit me; the damned thing bit me," he repeated over and over.

While one of the students ran for a teacher, the others gathered around Butch trying to console him. Only Darla watched Foster carefully prod Annabelle into the cheesecloth and put it back in his lunch pail. Closing the lid, he looked up to see Darla's eyes fixed on him, a slight smile on her lips.

"For Pedro?" she asked.

"Unfortunate accident yesterday after school," he said.

"We heard. Butch was bragging about what he had done. I'm so sorry." She put her hand on Foster's arm. "Maybe you should go home and take care of your friend there." She nodded at his lunch pail. "I'll tell the teacher you weren't feeling well. Will Butch be okay?"

"He will probably have swelling and some pain and might not feel well for a day or two, but it won't kill him. I hope." He smiled and stood up. "Thanks. I'll finish the rest of my lunch later."

"Do you think you'll get in big trouble?"

"Nah, my dad's a lawyer."

"Someday I'd like to come and see your spider collection. Would that be all right?"

"Sure, that'd be great. Later." He walked away, whistling and carrying the lunch pail as if it contained a fragile treasure—that is, in addition to four uneaten fig newtons.

# The Trove

It was a bright sunny day, punctuated by a steady but soft breeze from the nearby ocean, one of those "you-can-taste-in-your mouth" mornings that signaled a day off from school. We both knew it before we conferred on the phone.

I guessed it was Robbie before I picked up. He and I had been hoping for some hooky time during the last semester of school, a day to hit the beach and worship sand and surf. It had arrived with April promptness.

"Walt, you ready, man? This is it." His voice was usually subdued, casual, but not today. Enthusiasm poured from the earpiece and I inhaled it, grew it like an inflating balloon, and pushed it out with my answer.

"See you in a few minutes," I answered, not wanting to delay the trip with an extended conversation.

"I'll be there, buddy, with my conga, some sandwiches, and snacks. Bring your bongos, a blanket, and..."

"And?" I knew what was coming.

"Got any beer or wine?"

It was more an affirmation than an open-ended question because I could almost always put my hands on one or the other. Today, I had both.

We were seventeen, but it wasn't hard to score a bottle of Boone's Farm strawberry wine and I usually had some around the apartment my dad and I shared. He went to work at seven and didn't mind if I imbibed at home, but he was less approving about my drinking out and about.

"Don't call me if you land in jail," he would tell me. "You'll have time to think about it before I bail you out."

I didn't drive, one of the few California kids over sixteen who didn't have a license, so he was more concerned about my friends going DUI than about me. He knew some of my earlier pals and I had cut a few corners close at times. But that had been last year and this was different. Robbie and I were pretty straight, didn't smoke, and didn't hang out on the street. We embodied the image that many mothers wanted to see their daughters date—somewhat nerdy but trustworthy.

Ah, yes, that trust was not necessarily a mark of self-imposed discipline and decency. We just weren't part of the popular cliques that seemed all-important in high school. It was spring and I still didn't have a date for the Senior Ball, only a few weeks away. Robbie wasn't doing much better. Our lame jokes about going to the big dance and last hurrah together weren't consoling, as our failure to connect with the fairer sex made evident.

But we had the beach, our drums, and a casual attitude toward life that made the angst of teenage social failures tolerable, barely. We had other friends, but the two of us shared a special rapport. I was heavy into reading, especially science fiction. Rob was an artist and we both grooved on West Coast "cool" jazz: Dave Brubeck, Shelly Manne, and Gerry Mulligan.

Rob sometimes wore a beret and we would sit in my kitchen at night, lights out, listening to the vibes broadcasting from San Francisco. We were 1950s beatniks before they became 1960s hippies.

"I can also bring a six-pack—that should set us up," I informed him.

"Cool, see ya in a few."

He hung up and I grabbed my suit, a towel, and six cans of Hamm's from the fridge, replacing them with warm ones from the pantry. I was waiting by the front gate when he drove up in his '50 Ford convertible, a puce yellow rod with a bad top. We usually left it down.

Rob had flaming red hair, lots of freckles, and wore glasses. On the thin side with a weak chin, he would never impress anyone on muscle beach. But we weren't going to a boardwalk or popular resort.

Between San Francisco and Half Moon Bay was a small fishing town named Princeton and just north of that was a secluded spot, a beach between headlands that we needed to climb down a steep path to reach. There was rarely another car when we arrived, especially on a weekday and a school day. Besides, it was still a bit nippy for casual swimming and the surfers were farther south at Pescadero and other beaches with easier access.

We arrived at nine and were alone. Both of us were wearing Hawaiian shirts, swim trunks, and sandals. The latter were a bit risky on the steep sand-gravel slopes, but we grabbed our stuff and made our way carefully to one end of the brown sandy strip, where numerous large rocks projected from the surf. I liked the tide pools, and the overhanging cliffs made a dramatic setting for Rob to render a few pencil sketches. I brought a Brownie camera to properly document our Skip Day. We tied the beer pack to a stake and put it in a tide pool to stay cool.

After a bit of wading and hiking along the beach, we settled into munching and drinking. We each had a few hits of the sweet wine, but it was the beer that satisfied the cold water and hot sun exposure. Laying back on the blanket, I watched the gulls circling overhead, squawking for a lunch handout.

Rob sat facing the cliffs with a pencil and pad. We had both worked in factories for summer money, but he was serious about being a professional artist. His bedroom walls were covered with his pastels, line drawings, and a few acrylics. He had the eye and the imagination. Much of his work was surrealistic and that appealed to my sci-fi and fantasy passion.

I had also brought a transistor radio and we turned it up to blast level. Sitting on the rocks, he and I beat out the rock rhythms on our drums, interspersed with a few Latin numbers designed for the conga. We both brought bongos and I had sticks, pretending I was Buddy Rich or Shelly as I rapped the four skins. More beer, more sun, more cool splashes as the day wore on.

By noon, a few other people had arrived, but they spread out, leaving the two crazy kids alone at the end of the beach. By two o'clock, we had finished the beer, decided to leave the wine for another day, and commenced to pack up. There were probably a dozen or more people on the beach by then and a few adults strolled by us. One man, in his mid-forties or so, stopped to ask us if we were old enough to drink and why we weren't in school. Easy to ignore after a few cans of suds, so we did.

Gathering our stuff, including the lighter empties, we slowly crawled back up the hill. It seemed like a lot longer trail than earlier that morning, but we loaded the car and decided to take a last look at the Pacific expanse and crashing surf. It was a sight I never tired of and that would have ended a pleasant and successful day of freedom and irresponsibility, if Rob hadn't spotted the magazine a few feet from the car.

Curious, he picked it up and whistled in astonishment. "Walt, check this out." He held it up and even from several feet away, I recognized what he had found.

Several men's magazines were available in the 1950s, ranging from the typical sports rags to the naughty under-the-counter types. *Adam*, *Penthouse*, and *Playboy* were among the popular titles, but it would still be several years before these soft-porn journals would feature full-frontal nudity.

The exceptions were the magazines devoted to sunbathing and naturism. Although not as lavish or sophisticated as the purely commercial titles, they presented family nudity, usually engaged in recreational settings. The subjects ranged from infants to the elderly, with a goodly helping of young girls and women scattered among the pages. We knew about them but had only seen them once or twice, usually in someone else's hands. Here, we had one of our own.

I was the one who spotted the second one, a few feet further away, at the edge of the cliff. I walked over to retrieve it and looked down the hillside.

"Rob, get over here. Look what we have!"

My excitement brought him on the run, still clutching his prize. It was like a man with a single gold coin looking at a room filled with treasure. Before and below us, across the top of the cliff, were scattered dozens of magazines, all apparently of the same ilk. We were in teen boys heaven!

We weren't sure if they had been there earlier or had been dumped after we arrived in the morning. Our trip down the trail with a full burden may have prevented us from noticing, but we were all eyes now. We threw the two magazines we had in the car and started our scramble, grabbing the ones we could easily reach without descending very far. The sandals were a problem, so we shed those and started again, descending lower and lower as the piles of magazines in our arms grew bigger.

The cliffs consisted of hard-exposed rock and loose scree. It was the latter that gave us some purchase as we dropped down the cliff, but with an armful, it was almost impossible to climb back up. Rob and I were about twelve feet apart when we decided we had reached our carrying capacity.

"We can always make a second trip," he said, shouting over the afternoon wind now buffeting the cliff.

"Rob, we'll have so many we can afford to sell a lot of them," I shouted back. "After reading them, of course. We'll be rich."

"Reading them? You're going to *read* them?" Rob was always a man of few words. Whether talking or reading, he cut to the chase.

We nodded and started upward, taking tentative steps while trying to balance without the use of arms or hands. It was no go. One step up, slide one down, sometimes two steps down.

"Looks like we'll need to go down to the beach," he said.

We looked below us and two things became immediately apparent. First, the way down was a lot more vertical than the path we had used earlier. There was at least a twelve-foot drop to the beach and we were about one hundred feet above the drop-off. It was going to be tricky to negotiate, even without two armfuls.

The second problem was the people. It seemed that everyone on the beach had gathered under us, looking up at the two crazies stranded on the cliffside. They probably could see that we were carrying something and might have seen some of the other scattered magazines, but, hopefully, they didn't know what they were.

"We can throw them down and pick up as many as we can afterward or we can try to get down with them." Rob looked at me for an answer.

"Let's hang on to them as long as we can. If we throw them, those clowns might get them. This is a fortune, man."

He nodded, apparently convinced by my resolute logic if not my mournful pleading. He was several feet ahead of me and started down, carefully placing each foot, testing it with his weight before proceeding. I followed, but not exactly behind him.

We made it to within about twenty feet of the drop-off before I heard him yell. I looked up in time to watch him sliding down the slope feet first, on his butt, magazines flying in all directions. He disappeared over the edge of the drop-off, then came into view, rolling head over heels on the beach. Several people gathered around him, but he quickly stood up, shook dirt and sand off, and walked away from them. I could see that a few of them were laughing and pointing as he retreated toward the cliff.

Now it was my turn, hoping not to repeat his dramatic exit from the cliff, but not wanting to forfeit the trove of naughtiness in my possession. It only took a few steps for fate to play its hand. I stepped out with my left foot, thinking it was a solid base, only to slide dramatically in the scree. I wasn't prepared to do a leg-breaking split, so I followed my left foot, dropping the magazines for a frantic grab at anything.

Anything was a small shrub projecting from the gravel and my hand closed on it in a desperate bid to stop the downward slide. The bush detached immediately from the hillside and I proceeded toward the drop-off at full speed, bush in hand. I had just enough time to remember Rob's roll across the sand, so I tucked into a ball before hitting the beach and performed a double somersault across the sand.

The people were still there, most of them laughing by now. I stood up, bruised, scratched, and a bit shaken. Rob came over to me, several magazines in his arms.

"You okay, Walt?"

I nodded and said, "How about you?"

"I'll live. There's still a few mags that made it to the bottom. Get some and let's get the hell out of here."

I walked to the cliff bottom, picked up several magazines, and followed Rob back to the upward trail. That was when I noticed that my rear felt both hot and cold at the same time. I put my free hand behind me and discovered that a large portion of my swim trunks was no longer there. The Pacific breeze was cooling a hot blistered butt. A glance ahead showed that Rob was enjoying a similar outcome. Loud guffaws followed us as we plowed up the hill, our humiliation somewhat tempered by the partial recollection of our treasure.

The car at last. We threw the magazines into the trunk, wrapped towels around our battered and exposed posteriors, and started for home. We didn't say anything at first. I was replaying the day in my mind, the delicious excitement of skipping school, the bracing environment of a Pacific beach in the spring, and the shared comradery of two good friends.

The day could have resulted in a lot more than a bruised butt—we might have been lying on the beach with broken necks, surrounded by magazines. The newspaper headlines would tell the world about the two skinny teens who DIED FOR PORN.

"Who do you think dumped them there?" asked Rob.

"Don't know. Probably some mother who discovered them in her son's bedroom."

We both laughed and I turned up the radio. Later, it occurred to both of us that we were cold sober, without a trace of beer or wine after-effects on the way home.

We spent the next Saturday afternoon at my place, looking at each magazine. We kept a couple of our favorite issues for a couple of months, but sold the rest to a high school junior and his "Men's Club." Rob and I made enough money to take two sophomores to the Senior Ball in May and, best of all, we had enough money left over to buy new swim trunks for the year-end swimming party in June.

*Princeton Beach, California in 1960 (photo by L. Wade Powers)*

# Renewal

In a moment of delicate interlude, a cloud whispering
a promise of mist, she appears unbidden,
not forbidden, not my will to resist her promised kiss,
a gift bestowed on lips that need more than dew.

Thunder too reveals the purpose, the dramatic lighting
of a landscape parched, devoid of life,
the desert of dreams only awakens with a violent shiver
from a raging river of churning mud, stirring hopes.

Again the sun and heat, a relentless beat, warms the
earthly seeds and flowers adorning heads of weeds,
worthless weeds in watered places, but you don't live
in forsaken spaces, do you?

It is not the cycle, a wise man said, not an awakening
of the dead, but the living breath, a blessing blown
from above. A trickle, a storm, brings salvation to the sand,
color to the land, slakes our thirst, renews our faith.

# Lingering Leaves

Trees trimmed with life maintain peace with destiny,
speak of eternity in low windy whispers,
soft and persistent messages of green growth, slow growth,
always reaching the sky, seeking earth's depths,
fulfilling the buried seed's promise.

Water sought, moisture found, deeper than before,
cool clouds foreshadow change,
dry days ahead, shorter days, green remains.
Struggle persisting, persevering, reoccurring
photosynthesis, lighter than before.

Curled edges, spotted surfaces, not so green as before,
trembling leaves caught in autumn breezes,
reluctant to leave, willing to serve, maintain integrity
and loyalty to towering titans standing straight,
parental source of foliage, unaware.

Less light, colder days, hormones have their ways,
signals sent and leaves must go, preparing for
the coming snow, the coming cold, when
trees sleep and willows weep, and leaves release,
forming colored blankets on forest floors.

Lying they linger, deep layers of silence, intimate
substrates of molds and soil creatures,
waiting and abiding, the layer of ice and snow
arriving. No longer pretending, only descending
into blackness, winter's promised end.

# The Parade

A long life, if one is lucky,
from the dark side alley through the side streets
onto the main boulevard, and finally to the park
riding, gliding to the end

Off the float, off your feet on a bench
to rest, recalling the trip and marking the miles,
the moments passed, the people passed
waving, calling to the end

Waiting crowds line the sidewalk,
children's faces turned upward seeking
trinkets and candy raining down, producing
laughter, the scramble, and on you go

To the next block, the next throw,
next stage of your big ride in the big show
from dark shadows to bright street lights
your first deep breath and your last gasp

Life is a carnival you were always told,
believe it or don't, the parade will start with
or without you, your choice to play your part,
an appearance, a role, a place to go

Wear a mask to a masque
strut and stroll in the grand parade of
glittered faces, littered traces on streets
of busy places, always a place to know

Ponder this upon your bench:
was the ride what you expected and
were your companions who you wanted,
how did they come and go?

On the ride of life, the festive float,
are memories gay, future shining bright?
Is the trip completed, reaching journey's end
with business still unfinished?

Can you grab some beads and find a Krewe,
hitch a ride down Mississippi Avenue, grab a brew?
Is it Mardi Gras or life's last chance to celebrate
Oregon spring before winter's chilly grasp?

Events in life pass like city blocks,
a carnival parading in beads and feathers,
life's many moments tick like clocks, passing
time, passing by, passing away.

"The Parade," written by L. Wade Powers, originally appeared in *Carnival*, the 2018 anthology published by the Northwest Independent Writers Association (NIWA).

PART THREE

# Ultimate Boundaries

◆

THERE ARE FAMILIAR vistas and events, ones we grow up in, occupy, and in which we participate. They do not require much of our imagination to identify or understand the challenges and limitations they impose. There are also other possibilities, or perhaps, impossibilities. The human mind is not confined to mere observation and defined by experience. We can extend the horizon to far-flung vistas we haven't seen and sample events that might never occur.

Fantasy and science fiction allow us the freedom to speculate on what might be and what could have been. Some tales are based on realistic projections of what we know and others are purely imaginative, conceived without reference to what we perceive as the real world. But be cautious about what we define as real or imagined. All of our history is a constrained fiction and all fiction possesses a reality once it is created and presented.

A few of the following stories cross into uncharted waters, although they vary concerning believability. Others do not require as large a leap of faith, but may still require one to leave behind the comforts of presumptions and assumptions. Are you ready?

# Incommunicado

*Confrontation can take many forms, including anger, passive resistance, deceit, and persistent competition. The outcome is not always what one hoped for. What are you hoping for?*

I know what's wrong with the world. Not the world, as such, but the people in it, the human species. Many of them are weak and wouldn't meet Darwin's minimum criteria for survival and reproductive success. Many others are nasty, despicable, horrible individuals who the rest of us would be better without. I know I would.

The biggest problem, regardless of the merits or attributes of any one person, is that there are just too damn many of them. Polluting the earth, fouling our air and water, killing off multitudes of species, getting in the way. Their urban lights fill the night skies and their noise, that insufferable noise, is everywhere. Radio and television now seem like mild background murmurs compared to the computers and cell phones that chatter endlessly, filling our lives with nonsense and unnecessary disturbances. What is a sane person to do?

I am superior to most of the people I encounter. I never used to consider myself above others, until recently. Now, I know better. Not that I have received recognition or support from any of my acquaintances. I will never be the *Time* "Person of the Year." No Pulitzer, Oscar, or Nobel Prize in my future. I have zero Facebook "likes."

But I can see things. I know what's coming and I know how to change it. I see and navigate a path through the maze, using my highly developed intuition and accumulation of experiential hard knocks. I have experienced all the bruises that other mortals suffer.

If I was on an island by myself and had adequate food and water, I would survive. Not just physically, but mentally and psychologically. I can communicate with me, make decisions, plan for contingencies, and analyze consequences.

But humans are social animals and most of them need the words and reassuring touches of their fellow beings. They don't rely on themselves—isolation results in vulnerability and produces suffering. They require acknowledgment and recognition by others, and most people desire to give in return.

However, it is a cluttered mass of humanity we live with—a Tower of Babel with too many words, too many voices—and we lose our precious status as intellectual superiors. We cannot hear the voices we want and need to hear. Worst of all, we cannot hear ourselves. We pay a price for constant contact and reassurance. When everyone speaks, no one listens, no matter how important the message. Even my superiority can't deal with that.

That's why I decided to get rid of the other voices, or at least, most of them. I perceived this was the best way, not necessarily for them but for me, the one that counts. My plan wouldn't have worked forty years ago or even ten. It required a critical development of technology. Paradoxically, the final solution is dependent on advances in communication technology, the breakthroughs that allowed everyone to contact everyone else, all the time and at any time.

Countless millions of people are linked to a vast network, completely dependent on and addicted to the psychological need for continuous contact. From preschool to deathbed, they punch, tweet, text, ring, listen, and wait. But not for long. Waiting doesn't earn popularity points. Fulfillment only comes with contact and validation. One must be important to live and dream.

However, *you* are not important—*you* are disposable. I don't care about your dreams.

The plan is so simple that it seems almost inconceivable that others haven't already tried it. At the very least, one enlightened individual, a rare example with my insight, should have proposed it. Maybe he or she (never underestimate the wicked intents of the fair gender) did propose it but met too much resistance. Perhaps they paid the ultimate price for their daring solution. I know better—I won't forewarn. I'll just proceed with my project and surprise everyone, take no prisoners, and show no mercy.

It won't be everyone. Complete extermination is not needed or wanted. There are a few primitives who don't use cell phones or similar devices. Some of them live in the outback, isolated, off the network. That's okay. They don't count. I didn't hear their voices before and I won't hear them now. Tend to your goats or go hunt and gather; see if I give a damn. You didn't have any "likes" anyway. You will survive, just like you have for thousands of years. It's the cities and suburbs, the developed hustle and bustle of humanity, overpopulated and suffocating, that constitute my target. They will bear the consequences of my frustration and fury.

The guest bed and drawers are gone from the spare bedroom, replaced by shelves and tables of electronic gear, including one wall of servers and computers. The machines are glowing with life, pulsing with their virtual interface to the civilized world. My ingenuity has linked all of the social media, plus the stock markets, weather services, aviation communications, the Pentagon, NASA, energy production sources, university systems, medical facilities, and all major computer networks. All of their input and output channels are accessible in my bedroom.

I'm especially proud of the discreet hacks into the global satellites, military, and communication systems of every major nation. Whenever I am ready, when I flip the master switch, it will all end. Every networked computer of importance will freeze. All orbiting relay systems will fail as if a strong solar flare reduced the satellites to smoldering embers. Beautiful silence will ensue as the civilized world crumbles, becomes quiet and dark, as populations starve, medical care terminates, and chaos reigns everywhere. But it shouldn't last long.

I remember a brownout in New York City many years ago. Not even a blackout, just the threat of a sustained power loss, a delay in traffic bringing food and other vital resources into Manhattan. It had been enough to ensure panic and a mad rush to empty grocery and drugstore shelves. Order was restored because the emergency was local.

This time it will be different. There won't be any outside providers, no one to come to the rescue. The hysteria will be universal. The little plastic panels with the touch screens will be useless. There are no apps to restore civilization. Welcome to the worldwide dead zone!

---

Brenda is impressed. "You assembled this and built it by yourself?" She is standing in the doorway, looking at my laboratory of lights and dials. She has not been in the room since I started refurbishing it.

I am also impressed, by two things. The room, of course. It has taken me three years to find what I needed, purchase it, and make the appropriate modifications and connections. It took the best part of a year to hack into each system and implant a permanent link, one that automatically updates. Program changes cannot alter or remove my virus. Any transfer of existing programs to a new platform retains my latent receiver.

The other thing is Brenda. She had always been an exception to my elimination scheme. It will be her and I, the ultimate survivors. She doesn't know this—not yet. No one knows about the master switch, and I am certain she would not approve.

Brenda actually likes many people—our neighbors, her coworkers, relatives, even many of the strangers she encounters during her daily activities. Why would anyone like a snotty-nosed preteen girl texting to her friends while shopping for clothes? Brenda doesn't even know these people, but she has a kind heart and tolerates my opinions. And she doesn't own a cell phone. She has a computer and uses it to create graphics for commercial purposes.

*Sorry, Brenda, once the power grid fails, there won't be any commercial businesses.*

"What does it do?" she asks. "I knew you were working on something big, but I had no idea that it involved…all of this."

"It keeps me in touch with a lot of things going on," I reply, putting my arm around her waist.

She knows I'm a newsie, a current-events freak who often watches two or three news channels on television at the same time. This is in addition to print media and computer sources from around the world.

"If World War III breaks out, you'll probably be the first to know it," she says, grinning and turning to face me, her arms around my neck.

"Believe it, honey, I'll know it. And I'll be prepared."

This is the other thing that makes my plan realistic. I prepared our rural house with my self-sustaining technology. Solar power, a small stream hydro generator, water supplied by a deep well, a well-stocked garden and seed store, some livestock, a library of useful information—I am the supreme survivalist. I have the power to operate our computers and electric appliances and keep an electric automobile charged. I also have weapons, the best that money can buy. Not just firearms, but explosives, surveillance equipment, and poisons that can eliminate any conceivable threat. I am very good at conceiving, in the mental sense.

I am ready. Everything is in place and my plans only wait for the right moment, the most advantageous time to strike. Although I'm not sure how long it will take for the calamity to spread, the initial effects should be almost instantaneous. Power off, phones dead, hampering any attempts at repair. Disorganization should lead quickly to immobility and impotence, guaranteeing that the end of life as we know it will not be reversed. The fight for basic survival should rapidly replace the ability to reestablish the technology in which the world has placed complete trust.

During the beginning, I want Brenda to be at home with me, preferably starting a long weekend. She has her own place and we usually spend weekends together, at her apartment, or my sprawling ranchero.

But I don't want her to know what has happened until the initial events pass and the turmoil is well underway. *Regrets, maybe, but no going back.*

I propose a quiet weekend for us, a romantic dinner on Friday at home, late sleep-ins in the mornings, leisurely brunches, some outdoor strolling, perhaps a Sunday picnic. There will be no television, radio, or computer news. I will forego my customary habits and listen to music, read a book, and share sweet nothings with my lover.

And Monday? Monday will be a special day. I will begin it with an attempt to intercept a broadcast. Either the news should be monopolized by the global catastrophe or, better yet, there will be no news, no broadcast of any kind. Ideally, the outside world will be silent, leaving Brenda and me to pursue our version of utopia unmolested by the rabble. I am mindful of the Biblical account of paradise preceded by an apocalypse. So, shall it be.

Friday evening, just before dinner, I enter the spare bedroom and sit down in front of the switch. Not a button, not a preset or timed program—an old-fashioned toggle switch with electric contacts. It seems like poetic justice to eliminate high technology from the rest of the world using a device from the nineteenth century. There is a scripted delay of twenty hours from the time I activate my program until all other programs fail. This ensures that the coming calamity is synchronized and produces the desired collapse. I stare at the switch for almost a minute, fully enjoying the significance of the moment.

Finally, the moment. I reach out and push the toggle forward, producing a distinct, purposeful click. The computer panels erupt in a flurry of colored lights, and a low hum pervades the room. I stand up and look over the servers. It seems a bit anticlimactic, after all of the time, effort, and no small amount of money expended. All of this for a simple movement of a metal switch. I leave the room and close the door.

◆

THE WEEKEND GOES AS PLANNED. BRENDA AND I DINE BY CANdlelight on Friday. We sip Old-Fashioneds on a plush rug by a roaring fire. The pillows, the warm glow of the liquor, and comfort from the burning logs contribute to a living room slumber party. We wake the next morning in our pajamas and robes, prepare Dungeness crab omelets and Panamanian coffee.

*We'll have to sacrifice a few things when the shit hits the fan*, I think, *but the coast isn't that far and I can handle a crab trap.*

Brenda asks me once about the news. "You really going cold turkey, huh? Sure you don't want to grab a headline or two?"

"No, I'm satisfied to focus on you for a change." My reassuring smile is immediately returned.

"Hmmm, wish I could bottle that." She turns back to cleaning up the kitchen while I ponder what is happening beyond our property boundaries.

I don't want to think about the details—I'm not a cruel man and the inevitable fear and pain isn't my objective. If I could have done it with a "magic button"—the old science-fiction contraption—I would have. Silent, instant, no misery, just annihilation. *Sorry, this is the best I can do.*

Saturday and Sunday pass in the same idyllic fashion, just the two of us, as if we were newly star-crossed lovers, in the throes of an early affair instead of a four-year relationship. We talk about our future, whether we want to seal the deal with a formal marriage, whether children should be considered. We had both been married and she doesn't consider children to be an imposing priority. "Maybe someday" is the way she expresses it. She is twenty-nine and feels she has plenty of time to make a decision. Only I know that time is running out, that alternatives and options are leaving the table.

My next big decision is whether to turn the television on Sunday night or wait until early the next morning. I am curious, of course. If all goes as planned, I won't be able to witness the finale. Since we are off the grid, there have been no power interruptions. I still have an option on external electricity, but I chose to isolate our love nest, creating an enclosed sanctuary for the weekend. I decide to wait and enjoy Sunday night, our last normal one before the New World dawns.

Brenda wakes at seven. The house, inside and out, remains quiet. It usually is. Located well away from ground traffic, there are also no direct airline routes above. The tranquility will remain uninterrupted until I turn on a TV or the radio. She makes coffee as I dress. I take my time, anticipating the moment of discovery.

Fortunately, Brenda's job is mostly self-directed, with flexible hours. However, she likes to get an early start at the beginning of the week and will probably be out the door well before nine. I need to stop her before then. We must stay isolated from everyone else for at least two weeks. We have resources that others want. They will be desperate and I need all of the advantages I have created to prevail against the mob. Brenda and I will be safe as long as we avoid contact with others, until after the collapse is complete.

I walk into the study, out of earshot from Brenda. I decide to try the radio. It will be more likely to operate on an emergency basis, even if massive power failures have knocked out television and communication satellites. I turn it on and a low hum confirms power. But, there is no voice, no music. I scan through the AM and FM dials, picking up a few zones of static, but no active channels. The radio world is gone. I walk back to the spare room where I keep a shortwave radio. Again, a band sweep reveals no activity.

I find this strange because I expect a few survivors will be communicating by emergency broadcast, trying to organize some response to the disaster. Surely a few of the hobbyists or hard-core survivalists have generators or backup power supplies just for such events. I keep moving the dial, listening, but there is nothing except for random bursts of noise. I also try the CW channel, listening for Morse code signals. Nothing. The world is off the air.

"Charlie, coffee's ready, and the eggs are about to hit the plate." Brenda's voice rings through the house, carefree, anticipating a casual breakfast before her weekly routine starts.

*Won't be routine, today, babe. I'm certain about that.*

I close the door to the study and walk down the hall into the dining room. I turn the television on in the breakfast nook as if it is my first news attempt of the day. The screen remains black—no transmission on any channel.

"That's odd," she says. "The power is on; what's wrong with the TV?" Brenda sets my plate in front of me, gets hers, and we sit side by side, looking up at the small flat screen mounted above us.

"Don't know," I reply. I say it casually as if the television is unreliable and this isn't an unexpected outcome. It is hard for me not to grin, to exult in my triumph, but I suppress it.

Brenda gets up and walks over to a small radio on the counter. She turns it on, but again, there is silence except for a low level of static.

She turns and looks at me. "Charlie, what the hell?"

I motion to her. "Come and sit, Brenda. Your eggs will get cold. And this coffee, just can't get enough of…"

Her voice is louder, fearful. "Charlie, what is going on? Are any of the TVs and radios working?" She knows I have several, but I ignore her question.

"Brenda. I have something to tell you. Two things, actually. This won't be easy, but I need to let you know about my big project in the bedroom. But first, I need to tell you I love you and that no matter what happens, I will always love you. Please, darling, believe that and everything will work out."

I give her my best smile and reach for her hand. Her eggs *are* getting cold as she stares at me, her eyes wider than usual, her mouth slightly open. She withdraws her hand and folds her arms in her lap.

"Charlie, what are you talking about? What does this have to do with the television and the radio?"

"Honey, there has been a global power failure. It affects everything, including computers, satellite transmission, everything." I pause, not sure how to continue.

Then I tell her how I spent the last few years meticulously planning the disruption—how I was able to consolidate access to computer systems and hack into databases and operational controls around the world. At first, she doesn't believe me and thinks I am pulling an elaborate prank.

When I share the expected outcome and the need for us to remain here, she begins to cry. It doesn't go well. From disbelief, she cycles through distress to anger. She accuses me of being selfish and uncaring. If I had known how badly she would take it, I would have stopped with the global power failure and not rationalized my role in it. *Hindsight, you idiot.*

"If what you say is true, you are a reckless egomaniac. You are a heartless killer, you son of a bitch."

Brenda leaves the table and rushes to the living room to grab her purse. She doesn't collect her clothes or other personal items scattered around the house. I try to stop her, to tell her what will be waiting for her in town and that she will only be safe here with me. I tell her I did it for us. That seems to be the final seal of doom.

She stops and glares at me. She spits the word in my face, as if "us" is the vilest thing I might have said. Then she is gone. From the kitchen window, I watch her car turn on the lawn and race down the long driveway, disappearing over a rise about fifty yards from the house. The black TV screen is still humming as I finish breakfast.

---

"Miss Ellison, this is unusual, to say the least. Do you believe Charlie Dennison is mentally ill?"

"I don't know. It all happened so suddenly. He has the equipment and he is a gifted computer programmer. He can be strange at times, but I never suspected he would want to do something like this."

Brenda had stopped crying and was slowly regaining control of her emotions. After the nicest weekend she could remember, the nature of his revelation was overwhelming and disgusting,

"Well, as you can see, it didn't work, whatever 'it' was." The sheriff smiled, shook his head, and stood up. He had written it all down—her incredible story.

The TV in the background displayed a network morning show. Everything was normal, another Monday morning, with no sign of a power failure. Brenda had passed several people talking or texting on their cell phones. Her car radio worked, but she hadn't thought to turn it on until she was almost in town.

As Brenda stood up to leave, the call came in from the deputy. He had been sent out to talk to Charlie, to assess his behavior. The sheriff listened on the receiver and asked the deputy if he was sure he was in the right place. Satisfied, he slowly put the phone down.

"Brenda, I… well, I don't know what to say. Roger is out at the Dennison property. It seems the fence and mailbox are there, and the road goes up to the house like it always did. But…" He paused. "There isn't any house. No foundation, nothing. Just an empty spot where the house oughta be."

"What? That's impossible. I was just there, about an hour ago. We were having breakfast…" She sat down again, trembling as if exposed to a freezing blizzard.

"We tried to call him first, but there was no answer. In fact, there doesn't seem to be any service, as if the phone has been disconnected."

"I shouldn't have left him. Even after what he told me. He must have needed me and I deserted him. Now he is…where?"

The sheriff looked at her sympathetically and gently touched her shoulder. "I don't know. I'm afraid he got what he wanted. Wherever he is, he's probably alone."

# Threshold

*Some boundaries are arbitrary, a time and place that blends into others so that we know we have crossed over only by comparing past and present. Other boundaries are distinct—day and night without an intervening dawn or dusk. And what role does curiosity play in decisions to pass through the portal?*

She had been there twice and beyond it once. It changed her... didn't just frighten her, like a bad dream or an ominous warning. It possessed and manipulated her and, by doing so, transformed my Marie into someone else.

Physically, she looked much the same, an innocent woman of twenty-six given to reassuring smiles, a subdued voice, and a soft caressing touch. But a look in her eyes that had not been there before. Her hands moved more and her lips trembled slightly when she wasn't aware I was watching. Marie cried more and occasionally shivered during a warm sunny day, as if something cold was touching her, something from within that produced a chill she couldn't dispel.

I first noticed the changes about a week ago but said nothing. I knew she would eventually confide in me. We were engaged and shared everything, the good and the bad.

Last night she told me about the cave she had recently discovered. Her description started as if it was an ordinary, though unexpected, event. I waited and we relaxed. Her hesitation was apparent and she avoided looking directly into my eyes, quite unlike her usual behavior. We were in front of a roaring fire, a friendly haven of warmth in my upscale apartment. Marie shivered and leaned in closer so I could envelop her with a blanket. She clutched her arms as if the fireplace was full of ice instead of burning logs.

"I can show you," Marie said. "I can take you there; it's close by. But, Rod, you won't like it."

"Why not?"

I reminded her that geology was a hobby of mine and caves ranked high on my list of places to visit. I was also unaware of any caves nearby. Both limestone caves and lava tubes were common in various locales throughout Oregon, but not near our town. "How did you find it?"

"I decided to visit the cabin on my uncle's property, the land I inherited when he disappeared three years ago. He was presumed dead and the court finally issued papers to transfer the property to me. I knew about the old bungalow there, built sometime in the mid-nineteenth century, but I also knew the structure was a worthless derelict. The forty-acre property, however, would probably bring a decent price and I wanted to get a good look at it before listing it for sale."

---

THE SINGLE-ROOM CABIN POSSESSED AN OLD MATTRESS, A SMALL wooden table, and two chairs. The roof leaked in one corner and the wood underneath it was rotten. The door was ready to fall off its hinges and nearly did so when she opened it for the cursory inspection. The room gave no evidence of her uncle's presence.

It was on her way back to the road that the dark crescent in the rock caught her eye. An old pine had snapped and fallen, flattening a large blackberry bush and exposing the top of a dark entrance into a basalt cliff.

*Strange,* she thought. *No one in the family ever mentioned a cave in the cliff.*

Curious, Marie made her way cautiously through the bramble, but not without accumulating some scratches and a torn shirtsleeve.

As she stepped past the bush, the full entrance became visible. It was about five feet high but extended back into darkness.

She stepped inside and discovered a ceiling high enough to stand in comfortably. The floor near the entrance was smooth, yet appeared natural. Without a light, she knew she couldn't explore the cave further, but her desire to do so seemed more compelling than mere curiosity. It called to her somehow, an invitation to enter. She vowed to return when she was better prepared.

---

"Did you like the cave?"

She paused and answered slowly. "The cave is nothing special. It's just a hole in the ground until you are several feet inside. Then it changes—it becomes something else."

"Something else? What is *else*?"

"Like a large room, a place someone has built, but with cavern walls and ceiling. The place feels occupied as if someone is there. And there's an entrance to another chamber in the cavern. The feeling is only a sensation until you cross into the other room." She frowned.

"You've been back to it, after your initial discovery?"

"Yes. I wanted to see it again and explore the second room."

"Then what happened?"

I was trying to be patient and continued to hold her as she shivered once again. She put her arms around my waist and buried her head against my chest.

"I love you," she said. "No matter what happens, I love you."

The way she said it troubled me. It wasn't a reassuring declaration. She said it as if saying goodbye, as if parting was inevitable. I prompted her to continue.

"I returned three days later," she said, "wearing jeans, sturdy boots, and a hardhat. I carried a machete and a flashlight. I thought about bringing a rope as well, but decided if that proved necessary, I'd return with you." She squeezed my hand and we exchanged smiles.

"At first, I thought of the cave as *my* place. That was odd as if I had decided to keep it a secret from you. But we don't keep secrets, do we?"

She looked at me for confirmation and I nodded.

"I hacked a passageway through the berry bush, but not so wide as to make it visible to someone casually passing by. I wanted to keep the cave hidden until I knew what was in it, if anything." Another smile. I could tell Marie was a bit more assured.

"What did you think it might contain?" I asked. "Indian skeletons or the bones of Ice Age animals?"

She laughed and looked up at me. "Maybe loot from a bank or train robbery," she replied. "Maybe the cabin was the hideout of some old-time crooks. The Old West still has some mysteries to solve. You never know."

But then she became still and somber. "I might have found the remains of Uncle Charlie. But no treasure; no signs of people or animals."

"Not even bats or rodents? Most Western caves play host to something."

She paused. "I didn't see anything, not until I noticed the other entrance."

---

MARIE TURNED HER LIGHT ON AND STEPPED INTO THE CAVE. The ceiling was higher than the entrance, about seven feet, and she could walk easily across the smooth floor. It was dry and cool, with no indication of a draft. She stepped further into the room, shining her light to the rear wall, about twenty feet away.

That was when she first noticed the feeling as if someone was in the cave watching her. It didn't feel threatening—it was just there, a sensation that she wasn't alone. She flashed the beam around the walls and discovered a five-foot entrance to another room at her right, near the rear wall.

"Is anyone here?" She asked in a quiet voice, feeling foolish as she did so. She didn't want an answer, but she had to ask.

She was the intruder, so she waited a few seconds before walking toward the entrance to the inner room, the space she would later call the "portal." As she neared the dark opening, the feeling of a presence grew, but now it changed in character. No longer just a vague impression of something coexisting in the space with her, it seemed like a magnet, drawing her toward the inner chamber, filling her with an irresistible desire to enter.

At the same time, she could sense an undercurrent of dread growing, a warning to leave. She stopped two feet from the opening, flashing her light into the darkness, but nothing returned the beam, as if it was an endless void. *Not a very bright light*, she thought.

Despite her fear, the compulsion to discover any mysteries in the darkness was stronger. She stopped on the threshold of the entrance. *I'm not ready for this. I need a weapon of some kind, at least the machete I left at the entrance.*

Deciding to retrieve the blade, she turned and moved toward the entrance. As she did so, the sensations subsided. She picked up the machete, started to return to the inner doorway, but stopped, overcome by a wave of common sense. *I also need a stronger lamp and a camera.* She quickly left the cave, replaced a few branches across the opening, and went home, puzzled and somewhat shaken by her experience.

---

"And yet you returned?" I said.

"Yes, I returned, two days ago. I brought a small digital camera, LED flashlight, and my dad's 45 Ruger. I also did one other thing. I left a note in my apartment about where I had gone and how to find the cave. Just in case."

I must have frowned because she looked at me and gave me a playful punch in the stomach.

"Just in case I fell, sprained my ankle—you know, had trouble getting back."

"Yeah, dark bears in dark caves do things like that," I said, meaning it as a joke.

"I didn't smell a bear or any wild animal. In an enclosed space, there would have been a strong odor, even if the animal wasn't there at the time."

"You're probably right. So, then what?"

◆

Marie entered the inner room, the flashlight in her left hand and the pistol in her right. Once again, she experienced the opposing sensations of her first visit, but when she crossed the threshold into the inner chamber, they stopped. She felt normal, as if she was outside of the cave.

She looked around at the large space.

The light barely reached the far walls to her left and right. The rear was still in darkness and the ceiling appeared to be twenty feet or more above her. But something was present in the center of the room, a raised platform of stone about fifteen feet from the entrance. It appeared to be a natural part of the cave floor, which resembled smooth rock like the outer chamber.

As she approached the platform, she placed the gun in her holster, but kept her right hand near it, ready to draw if necessary. There was a large crystal sphere, about five or six inches in diameter, at the center of the platform, too well placed to be natural. The sphere reflected a shimmering golden color from the light.

The height of the almost circular platform came to mid-chest and the width was about six feet across. The near walls appeared to be dark basalt in natural patterns of a lava flow. The far wall was still shrouded in shadow. The platform with its jeweled centerpiece was the only feature of the room she could see.

She set the flashlight down on the edge of the platform and bent closer to the crystal. Although roughly spherical and appearing to be a natural mineral, the object was incongruous with the setting. As she leaned further forward and her head crossed an invisible extension of the platform edge, Marie became aware of a whispering noise, resembling the sound of water spilling over rocks backed by a vocal chorus, chanting without distinct words.

She pulled back, standing erect, and the noise stopped. She leaned forward again, and the sound resumed, as if it was coming from some distance but echoing through the large chamber. She carefully reached toward the crystal with her left hand. She had to stretch the full length of her arm and lean her body across the platform to reach it. As she did, the volume of the rushing sound increased, filling the chamber. She stopped without touching the rock and once again withdrew.

*Something is triggering the noise, associated with my presence at the platform.* She didn't recognize the type of crystal but realized it was probably unique and potentially important. *I need to tell Rod about this.*

She picked up the flashlight, turned on her heels, and started toward the inner chamber door. A wave of nausea enveloped her immediately and she staggered, almost dropping the light. Gasping, she stopped—the sickness eased but didn't disappear.

She stepped toward the opening again and it returned, only stronger and accompanied by an overwhelming sense of dread, as if leaving the room was the worst possible action she could take. Again, she paused, considering what to do.

*Can I make it to the doorway? Should I move slowly and try to endure or should I make a run for it and throw myself through the portal?*

Believing she would be safe once she was in the outer chamber, she steeled herself, grabbed the light with both hands, and ran at full speed for the inner entrance. The fear intensified as she reached the opening, pounding her with an unbearable mix of horror and revulsion. Her legs wanted to freeze, to paralyze, and prevent her from leaving.

She made it past the threshold only by ignoring her heaving stomach and by sheer desperation. In the outer chamber, she collapsed on the floor and vomited. Only then did she feel physical relief and the absence of mental anxiety.

The outer entrance beckoned. She quickly stood and walked out of the cave, not bothering to brush off her clothes until she was a few feet from the entrance. That was when she discovered she no longer had the pistol.

*It must have come out of the holster when I fell to the floor.* Wanting to go back in and retrieve it, she couldn't force herself to reenter the cave. *I'll get it later after I have time to recover. As long as I don't enter the second room, I should be okay.* As she walked back to her car, she thought, *is this horrible discomfort only mine, or will other people feel it?*

Marie didn't sleep that night. The feelings returned as she tossed and turned, although not as intense. Rod was out of town, but she decided she could enter the outer chamber and retrieve the pistol. The next day, she did so without incident, experiencing only the slight push-pull feelings of the first day. She glanced toward the inner opening, the portal to the jewel, but didn't go near it.

---

After Marie finished her story, I told her I would like to see the geode, or whatever it was, and explore the rest of the inner cavern.

"There might be other things, maybe other rooms beyond where the light fell," I said.

"But the feeling, the sickness—I don't know if I could stand that again—it almost stopped me. I might have been trapped inside of the cave, unable to move."

She looked at me, her nervousness at the prospect of returning to the cave visible in her hands, shaking slightly again. Her eyes were moist as I held and tried to reassure her.

"There will be two of us," I explained. "I'll go in first to see if it has the same effect. You can watch from the outer chamber and get help if I can't make it out." Her look of alarm was immediate. "But I'll make it out. If I have the same feelings, we should know it in the outer chamber, right?"

Although I smiled with confidence, I also knew Marie wasn't prone to hysteria or baseless fears. Something had scared her and worse. That, and the mysterious jewel, only made the quest seem that much more necessary. We decided we would go together on the weekend.

---

Saturday morning dawned bright and clear, not a cloud in the sky. September on the wooded high plains near the base of the Cascades always seemed brisk and more refreshing than at any other time. Marie and I prepared a light lunch, brought rope, and we each had a miner's headlamp so we could keep our hands free. I had a large Bowie knife strapped to my belt and Marie wore the holster and Ruger, "just in case." If possible, I wanted to walk well back into the inner chamber. Marie wasn't sure about this, even if the sickness didn't reappear.

The cave was about a hundred yards from the dirt road. We parked my Jeep in a small clearing and hiked in together. We had left notes at our respective apartments to indicate where we were. I also told Keith, my best friend, about Marie's experience and what we planned to do.

Our unanswered question concerned the mineral on the platform. Should we bring it back? More importantly, could we bring it back?

Marie had never touched it. Her hand was still a few inches short of contact when she decided to retreat. My longer reach should remedy that, but with what result? I brought a lined plastic bag and some bubble wrap in case the mineral was fragile.

We neared the entrance, removed the loose branches, and walked into the outer chamber, stopping a few feet inside.

"Do you feel anything?" I asked.

"Just a little, mostly a pleasant hint of attraction, like a place I am comfortable in." She shuddered, commenting on how different it was on the other side of the threshold. "There it is, the other chamber."

Her light revealed the portal as she pointed. I watched her beam play across the edges of the entrance. Only blackness beckoned on the other side.

"How are you feeling…anything?" She looked at me, searching for some sign that I was sharing her experience.

"Some excitement—anticipation, I guess. But no, I can't say I am feeling anything positive or negative." A pause. "Shall we proceed?"

"I love you, Rod."

She lowered her head and stepped closer so we could touch. Once again, she said it as if she was sending me off to war, quiet and fearful. I squeezed her hand and stepped back.

We walked toward the inner portal. I was two steps in front of Marie and stopped at the threshold to look back at her. She gave me a weak smile.

"Feel okay?" I asked and she nodded, but her anxiety was apparent.

I stepped across the threshold as my light revealed the platform and the golden crystal. Marie stood on the other side of the portal, watching me. I took two more steps toward the platform and felt suddenly as if the platform was inviting me forward to learn its secret. I looked back at Marie, but she stood motionless, hands at her sides as if resigned to whatever fate awaited us. Turning back to the platform, I walked forward with a long decisive stride.

The geode gleamed and shimmered as the headlight beam crossed its surface. The shimmer was particularly mesmerizing and most unusual for a crystal, as if the structure was moving like a liquid. My left hand held the plastic bag, open and ready to receive the treasure.

As I reached forward, a murmur of voices rose. As Marie had described, I couldn't make out distinct words, more like nonsense syllables that increased in volume as my hand touched the crystal. The rock was cold—very cold. I lifted it easily from the platform surface and wrapped the bubble pack material around it. I placed the crystal carefully in the bag, sealing it. The noise increased in volume and pitch.

As I turned, I saw Marie take one step inside the chamber, but she immediately lunged back into the outer chamber. Mindful of her experience, I started quickly for the portal as she watched with an open mouth. I stumbled but kept my feet as an intense paralysis and fear clutched at me. I was sick and could barely see the entrance, but kept moving, understanding that hesitation could mean disaster. Less than five feet from the threshold, I bent over double, the pain in my stomach blinding me to everything else.

Marie ran to me and pulled me toward the entrance, ignoring her own discomfort. We collapsed in the outer chamber in each other's arms, sick and vomiting. Panting to catch my breath, I could feel the stomach cramps easing, but it took me a full minute to stretch out and stand up. Marie remained sitting, her arms wrapped around her knees. She was mumbling something to herself.

"What did you say?" I asked, kneeling and putting my arm around her.

"I said, was it worth it?" She looked up at me and slowly rose to her feet. "Maybe we should have left it in there. Maybe we made a mistake."

"Too late now; I'm not going back. We have it. Let's get it analyzed at the State Museum and find out what this is." I put the plastic bag in my backpack.

"Listen, Rod, I can still hear the noise from the inner room." She cocked her head to one side.

"Yeah, but it's not near as loud out here as it was in there, even though the entrance is open. It's like a doorway to...*what*?"

She was staring at me like I had missed the point of her comment. I had.

"Rod, when I was here alone, the noise stopped as soon as I crossed the threshold. It was silent out here as if nothing had happened. Is it because we have the crystal?"

"I don't know, but let's go. The farther from this cave, the better, at least for today."

We walked back to the car in silence, but both of us could hear a very slight murmur as if we were experiencing a strange form of tinnitus.

---

THE HALLUCINATIONS STARTED THAT EVENING AFTER WE FINished dinner at Marie's apartment. She didn't want to be alone, not even for a few minutes. The murmur was still there, a background noise that had not abated. I called it an "after tone," something similar to an "after image" from staring at a bright light. Marie kept shaking her head—whether to try and clear the noise or to make sense of what had happened, I wasn't sure.

We put on some light music, opened a bottle of wine, and tried to relax. The mineral sat on the kitchen table under a light, but the crystals seemed dull, more like the color of old urine. There was no glitter, no shimmer. At eleven, we climbed into bed, tired but not at ease.

The first dream woke Marie just after midnight. Screaming and holding her head, she threw up on me and started crying. I had dreamed also but not as vividly. The stomach cramps returned, but I wasn't sick. I took Marie into the bathroom, removed our bedclothes, and we took a quick shower. The murmur had now risen to a dull roar and we had to speak in loud, clear voices to be understood.

"This is crazy. What is happening to us?" she said, in between sobs as I dried her off.

"I don't know. Whatever it is, it seems you are more sensitive to it than I am. I can feel it, everything you described, but it isn't as bad as what you're experiencing."

"I dreamed about my uncle," she said. "I could see his face—it was blurry—but his hand…it was reaching toward me, almost touching me as if he was trying to…I don't know…warn me, push me back."

She sobbed and buried her head in my chest as I held her. After sitting for a while, we decided to try again for sleep. The symptoms had lessened and we were both exhausted. Sleep came in fits and starts, interrupted by dreams, but not as dramatic as before.

At breakfast the next morning, Marie told me she wanted to take the crystal back to the cave.

"Marie, after what we went through to get it out? You can't be serious. Let's identify it first, then make a decision." I reached across the table and took her hand. "I know this has been really rough for you, but we have it. Besides, I'm not sure either of us is strong enough to face the inner room again."

"Oh, Rod, I know, I know. It is a nightmare and the nightmare is still with us. It followed us home. How will this end?" Her look was pleading, searching for an answer, for a solution I didn't have. Finally, she said in a husky low voice that I barely recognized, "I love you Rod. I always will, no matter…."

I nodded, squeezed her hand, and told her the effects should eventually lessen and then disappear as if I knew what I was talking about. I told her, if it was important enough, other people could enter the cave and solve the mystery of the place and the psychotic images it generated. I kissed her and left at eleven to bring Keith back to inspect the sphere.

---

BY ELEVEN THIRTY, THE NOISES HAD GROWN LOUDER AGAIN, but without nausea or fear. Marie kept staring at the dull yellow crystal on the table and became increasingly obsessed with taking it back to the cave. She didn't want to spend another night like the last one. At noon, she picked it up, stuck it in the plastic bag, and walked out to her Corolla.

*This might be my only chance to end this nightmare before I go completely crazy.*

She drove quickly to the dirt road, got out, and walked to the cave entrance. She cleared the entrance and entered the outer chamber, recognizing the feeling of attraction and familiar comfort. Turning on her headlamp, she walked to the threshold and stood there, gazing at the empty platform in the light beam.

---

KEITH AND I RETURNED TO MARIE'S HOUSE A FEW MINUTES after noon. I noticed Marie's car was missing. *Probably went out to get something for dinner tonight.* I entered the house and took Keith into the kitchen. The vacant space on the kitchen table told me all I needed to know.

"She's taking it back, damn it. We need to stop her."

We raced outside for the Jeep. I drove quickly to the dirt road and parked next to Marie's car. Jumping out, I ran toward the cave, with Keith close at my heels. When we entered the outer chamber, Marie was standing at the portal, as if in a trance.

"Marie, wait, don't go in," I shouted. We walked quickly up to the threshold. I took the mineral from Marie and showed it briefly to Keith.

Marie grabbed my arm. "No, I need to put it back. *Now!*" The urgency in her voice indicated that it wasn't up for discussion. I nodded to Keith and took the crystal from his hands.

"We'll put it back, together. Keith can wait out here, in case we need his help."

Keith nodded, obviously disappointed about returning the rock.

"We can always get help with this later, from professionals who are better prepared than us." I smiled at Marie and indicated where Keith was to stand and watch.

The background murmur was pleasant as we held the crystal in front of us, the geode sparkling and shimmering as before. I gently placed the rock at the center of the platform as Marie's lamp lit the scene. The return glare from the crystal was almost blinding and the murmur rose to a crescendo—then there was silence.

We looked briefly around the room and turned for the run back to the portal. After two quick steps, we realized that there was no pain, no feeling of dread or horror. We stopped and looked back at the crystal. Was it over? Had we redeemed ourselves by returning it?

Relieved, we turned once more to the doorway—the disappearing doorway. As we watched, the opening quickly shrank. We rushed to where the portal had been and touched the surface. No trace of an opening, as if it had never been.

Dazed by the discovery, it took us a few moments to realize that the chamber was shrinking, the surrounding space becoming progressively smaller. The platform was now only a few feet away and we could see the back wall. It looked like a large plate glass window, from floor to ceiling. Marie's light reflected from its surface.

The platform was now touching our legs. The rock table and the geode were the only things in the room not growing smaller. As the platform pushed against us, we fell onto it, to lie beside the glittering geode. Marie and I looked up to see the ceiling descend and the walls envelop us, enclosing us in the void, the blackness within. Our final words of goodbye merged with the rising chant of others—so many others.

---

KEITH WATCHED IN DISMAY AS THE OPENING TO THE INNER chamber shrank to nothing, becoming part of the featureless wall. He called out but could hear nothing from the other side. He ran quickly out of the cave to seek help. Looking back at the entrance, he was shocked to see that it had disappeared—not a trace, as if the cave had never been there.

Maybe it hadn't. He wasn't sure.

When he approached the road, he saw two parked cars, a Jeep and a Toyota. *Not mine*, he thought. *Must have walked here.* He couldn't remember; things were fuzzy, as if it had happened in a dream that was already fading.

---

"Capture is complete," indicated the first observer behind the glass window.

"It appears we captured two of them," answered the second observer. "We were only after the female."

"No problem. The chorus is diverse and there will be places for more in the future. Restore the chamber."

A slightly different version of "Threshold" by L. Wade Powers first appeared in *Doorways*, the 2017 anthology published by the Northwest Independent Writers Association (NIWA).

# Shroud

*Some boundaries are more difficult to cross than others. There will be times when we don't know we must make a decision and, in many cases, we may not have an option. What will be, will be. Wait, isn't that an old saying, something about fate and inevitability?*

Once again, the blanketing mist lightens and vague shadows emerge from the grayness, forming the boundaries of my existence—the box that enfolds and holds me. From the nebulous cloud to which I wake, from the nothingness that comforts rather than confronts, the mindless geometric reality confirms the indisputable outline of my confinement. Dull white walls are relieved only by a small window, complete with unyielding bars. The opening provides a tantalizing, teasing glimpse of freedom, but one unattainable, beyond reach or hope.

There is no sound, except my breathing and the subliminal awareness of a heart beating. I move slowly, always slowly, through an indistinct medium, as if suspended in water. It is a dream, isn't it?—a reoccurring nightmare of entrapment in a place whose purpose I know not.

Is it a torment of the unconscious? I'm not sure anymore. I have difficulty recalling a different existence, an awakening or a life that I once dimly remembered as being normal, a conscious state of action and decisions, sadness and joy, accomplishments. They all have faded into distant memories that were, or never were.

I remember occasional pain in that time and place, but not now. There is no pain in this misty present; there is no emotion of any kind.

There is nothing but the fog and the walls and…a door.

Yes, there is a door, an outline in the wall, but without a handle, knob, or other feature. My attempts to reach it, push against it, to force myself through it all fail. Always, I am too far away, as if the unseen liquid that holds me and slows me thickens with my effort, preventing my approach.

The window is different. I can step to the sill, grasp the vertical bars, and touch their smooth metallic surface. Most importantly, I can see a world outside. There are no clouds in the bright azure sky—nothing to mar the intense blue above. An intensely bright white landscape of immense sand dunes stretches to a distant horizon. There is no other feature—no trees, buildings, roads, nothing.

Why do I remember those things? Should they, would they, belong here? Dunes and sky only, but delightful to behold from inside the gray box. The sun lights my face. I feel no warmth, but it yields the only joy to which I am entitled.

What did I do? It must have been something terrible to deserve such a confinement of endless duration without distraction. I do not eat or sleep, and I know not if time passes. It must because I can remember attempts to reach the door and other times gazing at the landscape.

But how often and when, I have no means of calculating. It is as if every time I emerge from the amorphous cloud, it is for the first time, but I know it is not. After a time—how much time?—the walls dissolve and the grayness re-asserts itself. I become nothing again.

---

THE CLOUDS RETRACT AND THE WALLS APPEAR. THE DOOR OUTline is unchanged, in its usual place. The window remains where it always is, but this time different. The bars are not outlined by bright light as before. Instead, the light is diminished, the room darker.

I move to the window and look out on a dim landscape, consisting not of endless dunes, but a hillside of grass and tree. There are oaks, majestic towers of hardwood, and spreading branches laden with the beautiful leaves of summer.

How do I know they are oaks? There must have been something…what? I am confused. I know but I don't, as if a veil of ignorance has been dropped on me, blocking comprehension and confounding my attempts to remember, to understand.

It is raining, a gentle shower carried by a breeze that…I can feel. I can feel! I now understand that touching and feeling are not the same. I could touch the bars, but now when my hand makes contact, they are cold. The stone sill is warm. The wind and wetness stroke my face, refreshing me like nothing ever has before.

Or is that only in the box? Have I experienced these sensations before, in another place? I must have because I recognize the delight this produces, a familiar but almost forgotten piece of the past.

I search the vista before me, watching clouds pass overhead, some lighter or darker than others. The wind eases and strengthens and the leaves respond accordingly, performing a dance for my benefit. I am the only witness, the only eyes. Now I hear the wind, deafening in comparison to the inhalations and exhalations that were my previous auditory companions. See, touch, hear. What next? The view dissolves and the gray shroud returns. I fade away once more.

---

WHEN THE ROOM RETURNS—OR WHEN I RETURN TO THE ROOM, I am not sure which—I recall the last time, the window view with the rain, wind, and oak trees. The window, once again, shows sunlight and I fear the dunes may be all I'll see. But when I step to the window, it is the hillside and the spreading oaks and…flowers! Blues, violets, yellows, reds—the hillside is covered with bright blazes of wildflowers. They must be wild because they are free to live, grow, and dance in the sunlight. The grassy field is a green carpet of luxuriant growth. And the aroma of life, of earthy soil and sweet nectar, drifts on the breeze and calls to me like a siren to a sailor. The bars remind me I have no choice but to watch and wait. Grayness.

NEAR THE WINDOW I CAN SEE SMALL MOVING CREATURES FLYING about the brilliant petals, and a slight buzzing sound fills the air. I breathe it in, slowly and deeply, and marvel at the panorama that has materialized during the past few awakenings. I now remember these occurrences, the multiple appearances of sterile walls and harsh desert landscape and now, this.

There is something else. The bars are no longer metallic, cold, and unresisting. They feel like rubber or soft plastic as I press my face against them. They are still bars but less like barriers than ornamentation, a decorative design for a window that looks on paradise.

I turn from the window and stare at the door. It is no longer a line in the wall. There is a slight recess around the border and a small gap on the lower edge. There are no handle or hinges, but a lightly colored circle, without a defining edge, exists in the center.

The door is inviting and I start toward it, my right arm extended. My steps forward are sure and lack the syrupy resistance as before. I will reach it—but I don't. The dissolution comes as before and the room disappears.

SOMETHING WAKES ME. THIS IS THE FIRST TIME I FEEL AS IF I am not alone. I didn't just reappear in the room. Someone or something aroused me from the gray oblivion. The room is very dark and I can barely discern the window. The door on the far wall is invisible but I suspect it is there, waiting as before.

I cross to the window and peer out into the night. There are small points of light above and a half-moon sheds enough light to reveal the hillside and trees, but there is no color. I am reassured by an occasional gust of wind and the sound of rustling leaves. I have lost nothing since the last awakening. My senses are intact, and I know the night. It holds mysteries but no fears. The darkness displays objects and features within it. The night is not impenetrable nor is it suffocating, unlike the grayness, to which I seem destined to forever return—the muzzling sheath of numbness over which I have no control. Why?

I turn toward the door, where I believe it must be. I walk slowly from the window, arms outstretched, to feel for the wall. I cannot see the door but, perhaps, I can reach it, perhaps this time....

---

Lana, it is time. Awake and arise.

It is very bright inside the room and the window has no bars, merely an unobscured rectangle. The opening reveals a majestic scene, resplendent with flowers, deer, rabbits, and many other animals. Several species of birds fly, hover, or sit in the oaks, aspens, and willows. Mountains with snow-covered peaks rise in the background and the sound of surf crashing on rocky cliffs is near but the seashore is out of view.

The sun is warm and inviting as I push my head out from the window, inhaling the fragrant air like a hungry woman seated at a banquet. I turn toward the door, a distinct portal with a bright circle in the center. I move to it without hesitating, wanting to reach and touch it before the gray shroud descends. My hand makes contact with the circle and it yields. The door opens and I step into a bright, blinding light. *I am free.*

---

The sun shines brightly on a large metallic disc in the meadow. The surrounding hills are bright green, dark with distant evergreens and brilliant with pastures typical of a pleasant Oregon countryside in late spring. A portal opens in what was previously a seamless surface. The long awaited release begins—multitudes of gossamer-winged entities exiting, silently floating like bubbles to blend into the quiet coastal landscape. Lana breathes deeply. A new home, a new beginning. She is free.

A slightly different version of this story by the author appears in *Escape*, an anthology published by the Northwest Independent Writers Association (NIWA) in 2020.

Photo Essay III.

# Alien Places

—◆—

They seem to shoot up without warning—exotic beings waiting below the surface, incubating in tropical soil, anticipating the opportunity to come forth, one that would favor their ascendancy into a world that humans believe they control. No more! Domination will be their destiny, displacing all other life forms, tolerating no resistance. They arrive in many guises, include many species in diverse forms, but are united in purpose and coordinated in effort.

Propagation is accomplished and they disperse, reproduce, disperse, and breed again, claiming their place, any place, in the humid landscape. They are silent but ignore them at your peril.

What will stop them? You? Your companions, your armies? You can win an occasional battle, shrink their numbers for a time, but they will return, bigger and more numerous than before.

An alien invasion? Not quite. It is merely a closeup of tropical vegetation along a roadside in Poas, in central Costa Rica. But I don't know; it looks peculiar to me. Maybe we shouldn't go there. Let's not take any chances—you know what I'm saying?

# Expectations

*Life is full of surprises. People don't do what we expect; things don't always turn out the way we envision. It makes it all unpredictable, interesting, and also challenging. One can't but help wonder when things do go as planned.*

The afterlife isn't what I thought it would be. I wasn't expecting Saint Peter at the pearly gates or angels strumming harps. Ambrosia might have been nice, but I don't know what it tastes like and you don't miss something you never had. In some ways, it was a relief. What would I tell the gatekeeper, if there had been one?

Not that I was some evil underworld character who killed, robbed, or abused family and neighbors, but I wasn't particularly strong on redeeming qualities either. I was just the average Joe trying to make it in the living world, then suddenly finding himself somewhere else.

That was the strangest of all. I didn't know I was somewhere else. I mean, everything looked like it always had. I woke up that morning, got dressed, ate breakfast, and headed to work in a car I had been driving for six years. There were other cars on the road and people going about their business, as people usually do.

The first clue that something had changed was at the coffee kiosk. I picked up a latte on the way to the office, a practice I had followed for several years. Lenny waited on me each morning and didn't need to ask me what I wanted. He would see me turn into the driveway and by the time I pulled to the take out window, he was already filling my order. The routine had varied little and changed only if a new gal or guy was temporarily filling in.

A new face greeted me as I stopped the car. Instead of explaining what I wanted or waiting the minute or so for it, she handed me the sixteen-ounce Styrofoam cup of latte before I could turn off the ignition.

"Good morning, Joe. Need anything else?"

I told you I was an average Joe (formally christened Jonathan but everyone called me Joe instead of Jon). I smiled, mumbled something about nothing else needed, and paid her. I figured Lenny must have told her about me and probably described my car (a green Subaru Outback). My usual morning stop was eight fifteen, give or take five minutes, so she must have anticipated my arrival and had it waiting. I made a mental note to mention the speedier service to Lenny and the considerable improvement in the looks of the server.

Sipping my brew, I pulled into the parking lot of the local community college, where I teach as one of their few full-time instructors, and found my usual spot. After locking the car, I started for the two-story brick building that housed most of the faculty offices and secretarial support. Carrying the latte and my briefcase, I opened the door and stepped inside to greet my departmental secretary, Gloria. She had been on the job two years and had been a tremendous help in organizing the materials I needed to publish during the next year or so. Besides, she was one very attractive looking female, single and willing to date a man at least ten years her senior. We hadn't consummated the relationship, but there had been hints, looks and flirty encounters that left little doubt that she was willing and ready. So was I.

"Hey there Glo....!"

I stopped. It wasn't Gloria. She was someone else, equally attractive, but not the familiar young woman I expected.

Her gaze was intense and direct, as if measuring my academic and personal assets for a future job or the prelude to a sales come-on. She smiled and nodded, "Good morning, Jonathan. I have the draft of your magpie paper ready for your review. Would you like me to print it out or send it to you?"

Jonathan? No one called me Jonathan, except Mom and my brother. It was a family secret. True, my employment papers, driver's license, and other official documents declared "Jonathan Hardaway," but none of my colleagues and friends ever used it. To my students, I was Professor Hardaway. To most everyone else, I was "Joe."

"Where is Gloria? Is she ill?"

I was hoping that whatever kept her from the office would be short and easily resolved. I had wanted to ask her out for the weekend and had arranged a couple of reservations to make it a memorable occasion.

"There won't be a Gloria, Jonathan. She is not here. I am here. My name is Sylvia."

She said this matter-of-factly as if it had always been true and I was remiss for not knowing it. She continued to smile in her charming, half-quizzical, half-seductive fashion. My next thought was that this was some elaborate joke, engineered by students, colleagues, or both. She was charming, no doubt about it. First the gal at Lenny's Coffee Stop, and now this "secretary."

"Uh, send it to me, if you will."

With that, I started down the hallway to my office, expecting to encounter someone else in on the scheme, perhaps saving a final surprise for my office. It wasn't my birthday or any other occasion I could remember, but I guess I would find out soon enough.

My office was the fourth door on the right—the second door on the left was open. It belonged to Shirley, an adjunct who taught chemistry, mostly at night. She sometimes worked in the afternoons, but it was rare to see her at this time in the morning. I stopped and rapped on the doorframe. The person behind the desk looked up, flashed a smile, and said, "*Que pasa*, Joe? Doing okay?"

"Okay," I said, becoming less sure of myself with each moment. "Where's Shirley and who are you?"

"I'm Roberto. Shirley won't be here. I hope that's good with you. If not, say so and we can get someone else."

"Someone else?"

"Sure, another person—someone, anyone except Shirley."

"What about Gloria? What about our secretary? Is she gone too? Can I get her back?"

Roberto paused and ever so slightly sighed. "I'm afraid not, Joe. Gloria won't be here either. Neither will Lenny. There are a few things you need to know."

There were, indeed, a few things I needed to know. Roberto had me sit down. I still had my latte, but it was disappearing in nervous gulps. Roberto nodded at the door and asked me if I would like to have another coffee at the College Union. I politely declined and asked him to explain what was going on and why three different people I knew had been replaced by three strangers I didn't know.

"At two-thirty-six this morning, Joe, you had an acute coronary, a heart attack. You were dead within three minutes." Roberto's eyes never left mine, intense but not unfriendly.

"This morning?" I glanced at my watch. "Like, seven hours ago this morning? That doesn't seem very credible."

"Why not, Joe? What's not to believe?"

I took a last sip of the latte and tossed the cup into his trash can. "Well, for starters, I'm not dead. Not even remotely. I feel fine, no chest pain, no head cold, nothing." I stated it with complete conviction, daring him or anyone else to deny the obvious fact of my existence.

Roberto said nothing but continued to look at me, as if waiting for some sign of acceptance of my current status, one that he and I were at complete odds about.

"And how would you know the exact time of a coronary, if there had been one? Do you even know where I live? Do you know who I am? I've never seen you before in my life."

I suddenly relaxed and grinned. "Of course, this is all part of it. Scary, though, coming on like this and using these other people. So, who put you up to this, and who all is in on this?"

I looked down the hallway, expecting my colleagues to emerge from their doorways. I still could not imagine a reason for the ruse or why it had the morbid flavor of an early morning heart attack.

Roberto turned back to his desk and spoke toward the wall above and behind me, "Joe, it will take some getting used to, and I can help you when you need it. Others around here will help too, just ask. We're not going anywhere and neither are you, but it isn't bad—just different. You'll see." He put his head down and remained silent. If it was an elaborate joke, it wasn't going to end here and now.

I shrugged and walked down the hall to my office. Everything was familiar—the messy desk, a pile of books in one corner that I was using for my current courses, a note-filled bulletin board to the right of the door, a large poster of Yosemite National Park on the wall opposite the desk. An easy chair for me and a stiff wooden chair for students and other visitors completed the furniture. A small window looked out over the parking lot.

I was staring at my Subaru when it finally occurred to me. All of the people in the lot, students and staff, were strangers. The thought gnawed at me, and I decided I did need another cup of coffee. The College Union was several buildings away. Surely, I would encounter a familiar face, either on the way there, in the Union, or on the way back. I couldn't remember a time in the last two years when I didn't meet several people I knew in the few minutes it would take to get there and back.

Although several people waved, smiled, or called me by name, I didn't recall seeing any of them before before. Not one face could I name, but I politely nodded and carried on the pretense, despite a sinking feeling in my gut.

*This is wrong, so wrong. It doesn't make sense. The whole campus can't be in on this.*

I bought coffee and quickly returned to my office and shut the door. I didn't need visitors at this moment. Not until I sorted a few things out.

I picked up the desk phone and punched in a familiar number: Lindsey would give me a lifeline. She was my anchor, my port in the storm. Four years older than me, she was an artist whom I dated occasionally. More often, she was a friend and confidante. We had shared a lot of thoughts and had provided each other with support when other relationships had failed.

The number rang once and was interrupted by an automatic message stating that the number was not recognized by the phone company. *Not recognized? I don't remember hearing that before. Out of service, changed, wrong number, sure! But, not recognized?* I had just talked to Lindsey a couple of days ago at the number I had just dialed.

I tried several other numbers external to the college and got the same result. Glancing at the College Directory, I opened it and began to scan up and down the faculty-staff list of office numbers and phones. All different! Every name in the directory, from the president to the custodian, was new, except for one. Mine. Yes, my name, number, and office were there. So was Sylvia's, listed as Biology Department secretary, Sylvia Porter, and Roberto, listed as Roberto Hernandez.

I looked at other papers on my desk. Student names on papers were there but new. I had never taught these students and never received a paper from them. The courses were the same, and the dates were consistent, but all of the people in my life were gone, replaced by others—by strangers.

My feeling of amusement, followed by dismay and disbelief, gave way to dull shock. I couldn't focus. I sat there staring at the park poster, clinging to something familiar as my mind refused to engage in an unacceptable tableau, a chimeric composition of the familiar and the alien. The unassuming acceptance and warm greetings by my new colleagues were not reassuring.

The desk phone rang. I wasn't sure I wanted to answer it. What now? Who else would take up this pretense of just another day at the office? I pushed the speaker phone on button.

"Hello, Joe Hardaway here."

"Joe, this is Sylvia. Can I come to your office for a few minutes? I think we need to talk."

The growing numbness of mind was becoming a chill in my chest and gut. Maybe I really was dead and rigor mortis was next. I looked at the speakerphone, then up at the poster.

"Joe, are you there? Are you okay?"

"Yes, sorry. I'm okay. Give me just a minute. We do need to talk, don't we?"

I pushed the off button and sat back to think. Would Sylvia confirm what Roberto had told me, that I was dead and now existed in some other place? And what was dead? The coffee tasted the same and was just as hot. Women, like Sylvia, stirred the same warm reactions of desire. The entire world seemed normal, full of activity. If this was a stage set for my benefit, it was one hell of a theater. I felt my pulse. It was regular and a bit faster than normal, but considering how the morning had progressed, faster would be expected. A knock on the door, and Sylvia's voice interrupted the reverie.

"Come in, please."

She entered and gave me a matronly smile, something to provide comfort to the lost and weary. She sat in the hard chair, legs crossed, arms in her lap.

"I'm very sorry, Joe. This must have been a rough morning for you. We didn't do a very good job of preparing you for entrance into your new life. Your sudden demise was not expected, so we had to rush preparations. Fortunately, your daily routine was predictable and allowed us to anticipate what you would do."

"Predictable? Yes, I can see that. Must have been boring to review. So, who are you and where am I? Roberto told me I died this morning, and you just said the same. What now?"

She smiled. "A lot of questions, Joe, and it will take some time for you to understand and to adjust. You probably believe in the Christian account of heaven and hell, and you were expecting something more along the line of a utopia or an inferno. Am I right?"

"I wasn't particularly expecting anything. I am…I was, an atheist. Now I am not sure what I am. If I have really passed on to some afterlife, it is a strange one. My life, minus the others I lived with. Only the players have changed. I seem to be still an untenured professor at a small community college, teaching biology courses and preparing an ornithology monograph for publication. On target so far?"

"Right on, Joe. As you said, the names of people you knew before are gone, unless…."

"Unless?"

"Unless they have also passed on. Your mother and father, for example, exist here, appearing about the same as when they died. They will look healthier because they are, but their age and general behavior are preserved forever."

"Forever, as in immortality, eternal life?"

"Yes, kind of. That will be true of Gloria and Shirley, also Lenny at the coffee kiosk. Each of them will join your world when they pass on, but only when they reach the time and age when death overtakes them."

"So why the replacements, the surrogates? Wouldn't it have been simpler to just transfer me to a new life, a new me, without recreating all of the details of my former existence?"

"It doesn't work that way, Joe. You are here and so are we, and your life goes on."

"But it won't go on, will it? If I don't age, will I be an assistant professor forever? What about marriage and children? Is this a "Groundhog Day" cycle where I repeat everything and never grow older? Can I move out of this town, quit my job, and start a new life somewhere else?"

I stopped, realizing that I was talking fast and my voice was rising. I was becoming hysteric.

"Slow down, Joe. You can continue living just like you did before, but you will have different people around you. Each individual is unique, each person exists as one soul, if you will, that is preserved intact from death to this new life. We call it simply the present."

"The present? Meaning that everything I remember is the past, and it is gone?"

"Good. Well put. It is gone, and it will eventually disappear from your memory as if it was a dream. The details will become fuzzier, and finally, any recollection of your life before now will be gone."

"So I won't remember Gloria, my beautiful and efficient secretary? You replace her, Roberto replaces Shirley, and that young girl at the kiosk is in for Lenny. And I won't recall any of my friends or the good times I've had up until this morning."

"I may not be as beautiful as your former secretary, but you will find me as efficient and as knowledgeable to help as she was. It's not all bad, Joe, you just have to get used to a few differences. You probably noticed that most of the people on campus know you. Even your morning latte routine will continue, but with a different person handing you the cup."

"Okay, it seems like I have no choice but to accept all of this as a done deal. But who is in charge? I mean, why does everyone know me? How did you, or someone, know what I would order this morning? Who chose the substitutes for my coworkers and friends?"

"I can't tell you that because I don't know. Neither does Roberto or anyone else I know. We appeared in this world, the present, at the same time you did. Like you, we have a memory of who you were and so we know you, just as if we had been living and working with you all this time. There is no one in charge, except you. You have free will to go and do what you want, where you want, and with whom you want."

She delivered the last few words with a smile that left little doubt about the implications for her and me. The same flirty look, the same inviting expression, and posture that had attracted me to Gloria in the past. I didn't want to forget my former coworker, my presumed date, and romantic interest, but if I did, Sylvia Porter would lessen the loss.

"Do I stay young, regardless of what I do or where I go?"

"No, Jonathan, you won't. And please let me call you by your full name. It sounds very distinguished, and it will help you transition from the past to now. You will age as before, and you will pass on at some time. It could be hours from now, or weeks, or after a decades-long life. You can have a fatal accident or die of any disease that is still prevalent in the present—your present—and you will cease to exist here."

"Will I be reincarnated in another present, like this one?"

"I don't know that either. I don't have a past—I only know that I have an existence at this time, associated with you and your time. I don't know if I exist outside of this context."

"Oh, wow."

The thought suddenly occurred to me that I was unique in this world, and all of the others were projections or actors or something created for my benefit, like a Star Trek holodeck. That they might not have any other rationale for being was difficult to fathom. I looked again at the attractive woman sitting in my office. *Should I pursue a relationship with her? With anyone?*

"I can have children and live a normal life here?"

"As far as I or any of us knows, yes. So can we, even those you will never know or come in direct contact with. Others will appear as you see them, read about them, or become aware of their presence. When that happens, they will be. Will that answer your questions, for now, Jonathan?"

"Just one more, Miss Porter. This is still Friday, is it not?"

"Yes, the day you left is the day you arrived." She stood up and started for the door.

"Would you be free tomorrow evening? I have reservations for dinner and a great show at the local nightclub."

"That's two questions, Professor Hardaway. Come by the front office and ask me before noon. I'll give you an answer then." She turned, walked through, and closed the door. No smile but no frown.

*Just as in the past, navigating the land mines of a personal relationship promises to be a challenge. But challenges have always been welcome, especially ones with great expectations. Give it a go, Jonathan; give it a go.*

# The Love Shop

*Love can be one of the greatest challenges of all. Finding love means identifying and recognizing it. What kind of love? Love of parents for children and vice versa? Love of music, animals, and life? What about romantic love, the need for companionship that is deep and intimate? And lust—does that figure into the formula? This might be where the boundaries dissolve...where our desires are difficult to separate.*

It was inevitable that online social hookups and matchmaking would lose appeal for the masses of lonely men and women desperately seeking companionship, whether for a quick fling in the proverbial hay or a longer-term relationship.

Brothels and prostitutes had been around in one form or another for millennia to satisfy sexual needs, for men and women, and all flavors of desire, but there was often little satisfaction or challenge in the sterile business transaction. You got what you paid for and many people wanted more.

Digital pornography could be convenient and inexpensive, but like virtual dating, it didn't involve enough of a person's sensory capacity to be truly satisfying. After a while, it was repetitious, boringly predictable, and depressive.

As people put down their cell phones, logged off their computers, and returned to real-time shopping in physical stores and markets, they also began to search for a return to traditional and more socially acceptable ways of finding partners. They wanted to not only see and hear romantic and sexual fantasies, but also to smell, taste, and touch them. They needed to do this without giving up the convenience of being the shopper or instigator, being able to realize instant gratification when they found what they desired, and and to have the ability to start and terminate a relationship whenever the urge arrived.

Create a demand for something by willing purchasers and someone will meet the challenge and provide. As usual, many people will respond and the competitive race for dollars, euros, and pounds will proceed rapidly and efficiently.

In the year 2031, the first boutiques for romance arrived in major cities. Love Shop Unlimited became one of the first franchises to provide a one-stop location for the lonely. Everything from cards, candy, and flowers to woo someone the old-fashioned way to exotic lingerie, sex toys, magazines, books, and videos could be purchased, just as in times past. But wait—as the ads used to say, there is more…much more.

There was a contact desk where you could arrange a casual date with a paid friendly escort, the girl or guy next door variety, or purchase time with a skilled sex worker engaged in the age-old profession. Everything from talking over coffee or dinner to the kinkiest demands in a well-provisioned bedroom could be had for a price. But wait, there's more.

Looking for something more lasting, something to build on? Willing to play the courting game, to establish friendships and arrange for lovers the way it used to be? Additional resources could be had from the store's catalog of available, interested individuals.

Like the online catalogs, the in-store lists provided an illustrated database that presented ages, education, occupation, hobbies, preferences, and other information a person might want before deciding to make contact. Prices varied according to physical desirability and social popularity, but there was something for everyone, or so the advertising stated.

And the advertising was pervasive, once the stores were operating. They saturated the airwaves and print media with announcements, contests, and special deals to bring in the hesitant, the curious, and the bold. Customers—or clients, as the shops preferred—trickled in at first, skeptical and reluctant as many social misfits tend to be.

The problem in 2031 CE was that a major portion of the population easily matched the description of the socially maladjusted. Two generations of surrogate connections and virtual satisfaction had left a deep imprint and ugly scar on Western culture. The birth rate was less than sustaining—not necessarily a bad thing, in the short term—but people were increasingly depressed and dysfunctional. They needed to be exposed to and relearn the joys and advantages of physical and emotional pleasure.

---

It was April and the skies were clear and bright. A temperature of sixty-seven degrees Fahrenheit and a slight breeze heralded shirtsleeve weather in Eugene, Oregon. Crowds took advantage of the change from rainy skies and chilling winds—downtown squares were packed as shoppers passed from store to store with bundles of clothes, toys, and Easter artifacts in their bags and carts.

Denny paused in front of the ostentatious store window, filled with teasing hints of what could be found inside. Nothing in the displays sparked outrage or protest from the more conservative individuals hurrying by. It might as well have been Victoria's Secret or a Hallmark gift shop, but the signs were there. A banner over several well-dressed mannequins asked:

> *Are You Lonely? Need Some Help in Having Fun,*
> *Enjoying Life? We Have What You Seek,*
> *Even If You Don't Know What You Are Looking For.*
> *Money-Back Guarantee. You Will Be Satisfied!*

Denny had seen the ads and read many of the commentaries on the new commercial businesses. Labeled "Love Stores," "Romance

Shops" or "Horny Houses" by some uncharitable wags, they had become increasingly prevalent during the past six months. A bachelor and untenured professor of anthropology at the University of Oregon, Denny had not been as successful in the dating department as he had expected.

Six foot one and in fair physical condition, he wasn't male-model or movie-star handsome, but he could stand out in a room of ordinary men. At twenty-six he wasn't particularly shy and could even be considered aggressive after a few drinks—but the few opportunities to establish a meaningful relationship with a woman had not materialized into anything satisfactory.

He finally recognized and admitted to his ineptness at moving beyond the initial contact and trivial chatter phase to present himself as a worthwhile partner.

Even a follow-up date for a dinner or movie seemed to elude him. It wasn't bad breath or body odor. A good male friend at school told him, "You just don't have much to say to anyone outside the classroom, do you?"

It was true. Denny found it difficult to carry on a conversation that didn't involve the technical details of his specialty in paleoprimatology and human origins. Unless he was at an academic conference, most of his casual acquaintances were either overawed or pointedly uninterested in the evolutionary comparisons of molar patterns and limb joints. The result of too many parties was often one or two drinks by himself and a slow walk or drive back to his two-bedroom apartment.

In addition to the large inviting banner in the window, one figure on the right side caught his attention. It was a very lifelike mannequin of a young woman in a gold mesh, one-piece bathing suit. She had long black hair, minimal makeup, and looked like the idealized next-door neighbor he wished he had. She held a small sign in her lap. It read:

*Ask About Monica. You'll Be Glad You Did!*

*Ask what about Monica?* he thought. The figure looked quite different from the others, which were mainly used to model suggestive clothes or represent men and women associated with Love Shop Unlimited. This one had a name and appeared to be very sophisticated. There were no obvious seams at the arms and legs, like on a typical mannequin. The face looked very realistic and the mouth was slightly open, showing a row of upper teeth. Her inviting expression was the hook that pulled Denny through the front door and into the store.

The first thing he noticed was the soft, subdued indirect lighting and music. Not elevator pop but lively light classical—not highbrow and not jarring, just…well, comfortable and relaxing. The store was spacious, with adequate floor distance between well-designed counters, kiosks, and shelving along the walls. Items were beautifully displayed, giving the impression that each object was precious, as if in a museum.

The overall aspect was one of luxury and privilege, but without seeming to appear priceless or unaffordable. Only a few customers were present in the large front room, but he noticed several wide corridors branching off, like spokes from a central hub. Other rooms could be seen at the end of the corridors and other customers came and went from view.

"May I be of assistance, sir?" The voice came from his right and he turned to see a smiling woman of about forty, attractive and well-dressed.

"I, uh…just thought I'd drop in and see what this was all about," he said, but in a voice that was probably too low. He started to repeat his response, but she understood.

"I suspect that this is your first visit, not only to our store but to a love shop?" She said it with a slightly amused tone, one that reflected more than occasional practice. He probably seemed out of place and his hesitant answer only confirmed it.

"Yes, it is. I was curious about what you provided, or…what you do in here." Again, his voice trailed off, not sure what to say. Then he remembered the strange window model. "Your sign said to ask about Monica. What about it, uh…her?"

The woman smiled again, projecting a warmth that belied her role as a sales clerk. "I recommend that you speak with Anadeane. She is one of our android specialists." She motioned for him to follow her down one of the central corridors.

*Android! That's why it looked different from the others.*

He walked beside her as they entered one of the back rooms, an area with three glass offices surrounding a reception desk. The receptionist smiled at them as the sales clerk led him to the office on the right and stopped at the door.

"I'm Mrs. Clarke and I can help you later if you have other questions or needs. But first, I'll have you meet Anadeane Markova and she can tell you all about Monica."

She led the shy shopper inside the office and introduced him to a tall, willowy blonde, appearing to be in her mid-twenties. When she stood, she was almost as tall as he was, but Denny couldn't tell if she was wearing high heels. She shook his hand and invited him to sit in front of her desk as Mrs. Clarke closed the door and left.

"Mister Rathbun, where would you like to start?"

As with the older sales clerk, she was casual, without the false friendliness that seemed to haunt so many people in the sales industry.

"Please call me Denny. Even my students are on a first-name basis with me."

He sat back in his chair, already convinced that his decision to enter the store had not been wasted.

"Teacher? At what school and what do you teach, Denny?"

She also sat back. The desk was mostly clear, with only a notepad and a small book in sight. The office walls sported two romantic paintings and a small crocheted sign that said: "Every day is Valentine's Day." A computer on an adjustable table, left in stand-up mode, was pushed against one wall.

"I'm an assistant professor at UO, in the anthropology department," he offered, painfully aware that other attempts to describe his profession often ended in blank looks and lonely trips home.

"Is it Doctor Rathbun, then?" She said it without undue emphasis. But Eugene was still a college town, despite recent growth pushing it to over half a million. PhDs were not uncommon and he was near the bottom of the academic ladder.

"Yes, but 'Denny'—just 'Denny' will be fine. I was curious about Monica. The sign said to ask, so here I am."

He gave her a hopeful look, one that was sincere because he did want to know how the android was connected to the romance business. He knew that commercially available androids had been on the market for the past fifteen years and models included pet dogs, cats, parrots, and a variety of service modules that mixed drinks, greeted visitors, conducted tours of facilities, and yes, provided doll-like companions.

Some of them were equipped to satisfy sexual needs and many of the recent models could carry on engaging conversations, with the ability to learn advanced skills in social engagement. Most of the better androids were not compatible with his modest pocketbook and, even if he could afford one, the thought of using a mechanical doll for his "girlfriend," no matter how visually appealing, was more depressing than facing a silent apartment.

"Monica is the latest in a series of remarkable developments in humanoid manufacture," Anadeane explained. "She has evolved beyond the android stage and her capacity for artificial intelligence rivals that of many of our fellow inhabitants and coworkers. Perhaps, not yours, professor, but I believe the average person would have difficulty in matching her knowledge, intelligence, or wit."

"Wit? Do you mean she has a sense of humor?"

"Oh yes, intelligence and humor. It is optional and programmable, as with all of her linguistic characteristics. She not only can recite jokes and funny anecdotes, but she can recognize aspects of satire, parody, and even sarcasm. She responds to vocal inflections that can distinguish factual statements from those intended to flatter, persuade, or deceive."

"She can detect if someone is lying? That's amazing."

"If the tone and rhythm of speech are correct for deception. A practiced liar can deceive her, just as one could deceive any human. Her superiority is based primarily on her capacity to store knowledge and master any number of foreign languages. And she can anticipate your interests and needs as she learns elements of your behavior."

"My behavior?"

Denny was amused at the thought of interacting with Monica. It—she—might be more sophisticated than a robot, but it was still a manufactured contraption, controlled by a computer and software designed by humans to please humans. It was an expensive amusement park and he had no delusions about what type of amusement it could and would provide.

"I would like to see it...er, Monica...in operation, if that is possible, but I must in good conscience also tell you that I could never afford to purchase one." *I assume there is more than one; that this item can be individually programmed, and that there must be many Monicas in the world.* "Are there other models with different names? I mean, if someone wanted a short redhead, or an athletic type, would these also be available?"

"We currently have nine models available and, yes, they each have a name. But, of course, you can rename them anything you wish. Not only are different languages available, but different accents and dialects can be programmed, along with the cultural traits you would like to have. I am sure, as an anthropologist, you can appreciate that."

She smiled again.

"Let us go for a short walk into one of our showrooms and you can see an activated Monica. You'll be able to talk to her, inspect her, and realize the potential that she and her humanoid kind can have for the rest of humanity. Monica, or one like her, might be more affordable than you realize."

The showroom was just that. A stage dominated the center and a small section of chairs designed for an audience filled one side. The rest of the room contained furniture including a bed; a kitchen space with a counter, stove, and refrigerator; and a living room space with a rug. A vacuum cleaner stood next to the rug. A windowpane in a frame was perched in a corner with a variety of cleaning tools.

Anadeane pushed a button on a remote control and spoke into a built-in mic. She rattled off a few numbers and letters, an activation code that brought a look-alike Monica sitting in a chair to her feet. Denny and his hostess were the only ones, not counting the humanoid, in the room. Monica turned toward them and walked to where they stood, showing no traces of mechanical stiffness. Denny couldn't help but admire the slight slinkiness and hip movement—enticing indeed.

Anadeane spoke to the android. "Monica, I would like you to meet Dennis, or Denny Rathbun, a professor of anthropology from our university."

"Pleased to meet you, Professor." She extended her hand toward Denny.

After a moment's hesitation, he took her hand. It was warm and the texture of her skin or outer coating was soft. He examined it and saw it had a pore-like quality, almost indistinguishable from real skin. He let go and she dropped her hand, stepped back, smiled, and looked him in the eye.

"What would you like to see me do, Denny?"

Anadeane said nothing, standing to one side as she watched Denny and Monica interact without further prompting. Denny quickly adapted to the situation by treating the android as if she was just another person, someone who was going to demonstrate some simple skills. She did so, messing up the sheets on the bed, then making it. Next, she sprayed the windowpane with soap, applied rinse, then carefully used a rubber squeegee to dry it.

"See, I even do windows," she remarked with a light lilt, almost like a song.

The most remarkable task, however, as Denny followed her to the kitchen counter, was when she removed a carton of eggs from the refrigerator. Grabbing one egg and a small pan, she broke the egg perfectly. Her finger control and ability to manipulate them was better than Denny's. He gave a sharp whistle and looked back at Anadeane.

"What can't she do?" he asked. It was mean to be rhetorical, but Anadeane answered immediately.

"She can't harm anyone physically and she can't be required to harm herself. She has several built-in behavior paradigms that will signal an alarm or seek help if she believes someone is in danger. This can be expanded for models that are used as medical caregivers for the ill or elderly."

She paused for a moment, looking at Denny for additional questions.

"She has no moral inhibitions about anything unless it would harm someone else or herself. There is an accompanying digital manual that provides the details of her capabilities and her few shortcomings."

Denny walked back to where Anadeane was waiting at the door. He wasn't sure how to ask the next question. *What the hell, I won't be back and I can't let this opportunity slide.*

"Is she preprogrammed for sex or does she learn that as she goes?" He felt stupid as soon as he said it, but Anadeane took it in stride, as if it was a common question. *It probably is, considering the wealthy assholes who would spring for an uninhibited sex slave.*

"She knows the basic moves and the situational paradigms, but she is quite capable of learning and expanding on that foundation. Monica can follow and will obey your instructions unless they violate the basic inhibitions."

"Sort of like Asimov's Laws of Robotics, huh?"

"Yes, something like that, but don't depend on her to sacrifice her existence if you do something stupid and out of her control." She punched several keys on her remote and Monica resumed her chair, settling into a relaxed but alert pose. After a few words into the mic, Anadeane slipped the remote into her suit pocket.

"Very enlightening, Anadeane. This has been a real eye-opener. I can see that, in the future, anthropology will need to develop a new subspecialty, one extending past artificial intelligence and modem man. You have given me a lot to think about and some material to present to my students. Would it be permissible sometime to have one of my graduate students spend some time here to research Monica?"

Anadeane ushered him out of the showroom and back along the corridor. When they reached her office, she turned and took his hand. "Yes, I think we can arrange something, as long as it is not destructive or does not involve intimate contact, we are open to the benefits of learning more about our creations and products."

"And you? If I want additional information, can I call on you sometime?"

She shook his hand and took a step back. "Yes, that would be fine. Call ahead and I'll make time." She looked at him for a moment before continuing. "It doesn't necessarily have to be during work hours or here in the store. Let me know what you need. Thank you for coming in, Denny. It has been a pleasure to talk with you." With that, she gave him a final smile, turned, and retreated to her office.

Denny walked down the corridor to the front of the store. Mrs. Clarke caught his eye and he nodded toward her.

"Get your questions answered?" she said from a nearby desk.

"Yes, that and a lot more. Thank you."

He left the store, his thoughts muddled by the recognition of disappearing boundaries and changing relationships between man and machine, creator and creation. The fantasy and science fiction worlds of literature and film never seemed so close, so immediate. Then there was Anadeane. Not at all like most women he had met. He needed to discover more and he had an ideal pretense to engage her further. After all, he was an anthropologist, wasn't he?

It wasn't until after he was sitting on the sofa in his apartment, recovering from a quick dinner and a much-needed stiff drink, that he realized he hadn't explored the other attributes of Love Shop Unlimited. The advertised sensory pleasures, opportunities to hook up—all of that was forgotten because of Monica. Monica and Anadeane, one of wires and plastics, one of flesh, and both desirable in their own way. One involved a simple command. Yes, sir; as you wish, sir.

He had not asked about maintenance, but food and medical care were not requirements. Presumably, some scheduled checkups would be needed. Machines, human or otherwise, were subject to failure and required repair and, possibly, upgrades. All at a cost, of course, and that would be in addition to the purchase price. Were long- or short-term leases possible? What would the terms be for a night? A quickie? His alcohol-numbed thoughts relapsed into a jumbled reverie of two women, a long-haired brunette and a tall blonde. Strangely comforted, he slept well that night.

---

Professor Rathbun related his Love Shop experience with two of his colleagues over a beer at a neighborhood pub the following evening. It was a Friday and a pub crawl was scheduled at least once a month for the three bachelor academics. One was a psychologist and the other a cultural anthropologist.

Both were mesmerized by Denny's account. Both wanted to visit the store themselves, but unlike Denny, had not coughed up the nerve to do so. They shared his experience in a nerdy vicarious manner that kept them safe, with their dignity intact.

"Maybe if the three of us, together, went in on something like Monica, we could afford it," offered Bill Behrens, the psychologist.

He was always proposing communal models of sharing something, be it transportation, housing, or the latest flames. All three still had their cars and houses, and Denny didn't have any latest flames to share. For that matter, neither did Steve Dersham, Denny's colleague. That didn't stop them from scheming and dreaming.

"So, what about this android specialist, Anadeane? Got the hots for her, do you?" Steve had been especially interested in Denny's description of the blonde.

"Remains to be determined, lads."

Denny took another sip of suds, purposely leaving a trail of foam on his upper lip to accompany the mischievous grin he couldn't remove.

"I will call on her again because I need to find out more about the franchise, their products, and I am even more interested in what they might be working on for the future. If I hadn't already been told, I might easily have mistaken Monica for another woman, a real one."

They let it register while they ordered another round. It was time to hit the next tavern on their planned tour, but they silently and unanimously decided to remain in place. The topic of the evening dictated study and serious academic debate—no time to be stumbling down the street just to get a fresh beer somewhere else.

"What's next, Denny? We have a college-wide mixer tomorrow night. Why don't you invite your blonde friend and introduce her around?"

Bill looked at Denny with the intensity of a counselor trying to save his client's marriage. Steve raised his empty mug in a half-sober gesture of agreement.

"We'll tie Steve to a chair and put him in a closet, so the horny bastard doesn't crash your party, okay?"

Denny grinned and patted Steve's hand. He had little to fear from the anthropologist. Bill was more accomplished at meeting and greeting the ladies than either of them, so it would be the older and more experienced psychologist who Denny would need to keep an eye on. His brow creased as a thought popped through the alcoholic mist.

"This is Friday. The store will probably be closed tomorrow. I don't have her address or phone. Shit, I don't even remember her last name and I didn't take a business card. Figures. I am so organized, such a player."

Bill, still the soberest of the three, sat back and stared at Denny.

"Go by the store tomorrow morning, after nine. I bet they'll be open and, even if she's not there, I bet you can get her card. They are salespeople, selling stuff. Saturday is a big day for that. Go do it, man. Invite her to the wingding. Let's see what you're made of."

Denny had no doubts about what he was made of. He gave his patented chicken call on the way to the men's room. His last words to the table as he left were, "Beer, I'm made of beer."

---

Skipping breakfast and sleeping in late after the previous night of imbibing, Denny found himself walking into Love Store Unlimited on Saturday morning. A new sales clerk, with the name tag Glenda, greeted him as he started toward the central corridor.

Before she could give him the official welcome, he turned to her and said, "I need to see Anadeane, your android specialist. Is she in?"

"She will be in this afternoon, sir. Can I take a message for her?"

"Do you have her card? I can call her later, if that's all right."

"Of course." She walked back to a central desk and returned with a bright embossed card. It read: "Anadeane Markova, Love Shop Unlimited, Specialist in Android Persons." Her email, office, and home phone numbers were listed.

*Ambitious…an attractive woman listing her home number on a business card.* He put the slick card in his shirt pocket, thanked the clerk, and walked out. He would investigate the other offerings in the store some other time.

He was hungry and wanted to reflect on what he would say to the blonde. Perhaps nothing. He could simply not call, avoid the embarrassment of a refusal, and tell the guys she wasn't there. And yet, she had indicated she could be available outside of the store and at times other than business hours. Sales hook or a social invitation? She didn't sport a ring; there were no family pictures apparent in the office. What did he have to lose?

He spent much of the afternoon with busywork, forestalling the moment to commit. At three o'clock, he finally composed himself and dialed her work number.

*Funny,* he thought, *I don't usually have this much difficulty approaching a woman, much less following up with someone I've already met. But there is something intimidating about her. Attractive, yes, but there is a challenge in her eyes, a self-confidence that appears extraordinary even for a successful businesswoman. Am I up to this?*

She picked up on the third ring. "Good afternoon. This is Anadeane at Love Shop Unlimited. How may I help you?"

*Her voice is cool and calm but warm and inviting at the same time. How does she do that?*

"Hello, this is Denny, Denny Rathbun. I hope you remember. We spoke yesterday and you gave me a demo of Monica."

"Of course, I do, Denny. She must have impressed you favorably."

"Yes, you did. I mean, yes *she* did, but I was also impressed by your store and your staff, and by you. It's all very futuristic and fantastic. I'm not quite sure what to make of it all."

"Not an unusual reaction, Denny. What can I do for you?"

*Oops, back to business? Here goes nothing.*

"I really would like more information about Monica, your company, and… about you. How did you get into this business? I am especially interested in how one becomes an android specialist—what type of education or training is required."

A brief and quiet laugh preceded her answer. "I am willing to share what I can with you. I am sure some of it will be of interest to your students as well. There are a few proprietary secrets I must withhold; I'm sure you understand."

"Yes, of course. The real reason I called at this particular time, is to ask you if you might be free tonight to meet some of my colleagues at a social mixer, held every spring at the University Faculty Club. I know this is extremely short notice and, if you're not available, I understand and apologize, but I would be delighted if you could come. There will be an informal dinner, appetizers, drinks, and a live band to provide music for listening and dancing, if you are into that."

He trailed off as he recognized that he would soon be babbling like an idiot. There was a moment of silence and he feared he had already passed the idiocy boundary and she had hung up.

"I was going to get together with a few friends from work, but nothing planned, so yes. I would be very interested in meeting your colleagues and seeing you again. We can continue our discussion about Monica and…about other matters."

The vocal friendliness had returned, as if she was a casual date and he was again in control.

"Great, can I pick you up about seven and where would that be?"

"Seven will be fine, but I know where the club is on the campus. Why don't we meet there in front of the main entrance? Should I assume casual dress or something more formal?"

"Uh, casual will be fine. We're a very informal crowd. I'll see you there, then."

"Looking forward to it. Goodbye, Professor Rathbun."

She offered the latter with a hint of flirtation, as if teasing him with his title. Yet, she didn't want him to know where she lived.

*Not yet. Maybe never. Hard to figure out the juxtaposition of business and social relationship. Tonight will be interesting, to say the least.*

---

SATURDAY EVENING WAS BRISK BUT PLEASANT, A TIME FOR walking through parks, feeding ducks, bicycling around town, and for greeting the interesting but enigmatic Anadeane. She was waiting at the main entrance of the club, dressed in black thigh-hugging tights and a simple but short black-and-white patterned dress that also showed her form to best advantage. She wore no jewelry and only a trace of lipstick and eyeliner. She was too stunning to be ignored by the faculty and their guests arriving for the annual party.

Denny quickly strolled up to her before either Steve or Bill could take advantage of an unattended young woman. That neither of his bachelor friends knew her by sight would not stop them from finding a reason to satisfy curiosity, academic or otherwise.

"Been waiting long?" he asked.

"Just arrived. It is very busy, a bigger group of people than I had imagined." She reached out and took his hand as they started up the stairs. "Hope this is okay for tonight." She looked down at her dress, then into his face as they reached the landing and walked through the open outer doors.

"Better than okay. I am close to being overwhelmed."

It was true. As lovely as she looked at the store, her everyday casual attire placed her on a higher pedestal. *Hopefully, not out of reach.* The looks he received from his faculty friends and their respective spouses provided another big bonus. She slipped her arm inside of his as they continued toward the large ballroom, set up with dining tables, side bars, and a stage where a small orchestra was setting up.

They stopped frequently for Denny to introduce her to faculty. When she indicated that she could use something to drink and that a White Russian would be perfect, he all but ran to a nearby bartender and ordered it and a rum and tonic for himself. Big mistake. As the drinks were being mixed, he glanced back over his shoulder for the distant view of his date. She was not alone.

Bill was at her left chatting away, his arms in rhythm as if he was conducting a marching band. Steve was on her right, standing by but close to drooling. They must have seen him enter and were now making up for lost time. Or were they making time? He paid for the drinks and quickly made his way back to the trio.

Handing her the sweet drink, he said, "I see you've met my friends." He put just a bit of ice on the last word, a not-so-subtle nudge to let them know he didn't completely appreciate their sneak attack, although he could hardly blame them. In a room full of young and older adults, many of them attractive females, Anadeane stood out like a neon sign—a magnet for wandering eyes and potential opportunity.

Bill had wasted no time. "Doctor Rathbun tells me you are a specialist in androids, including those that serve primarily social functions." He held a whiskey, straight up, in one hand and continued to gesture dramatically with the other. "Please tell me, what's that like…the kinds of behavior patterns and how they interact with humans." His beaming face made it clear that his interest extended beyond that of an academic psychologist.

Steve nodded from time to time, grasping onto a beer bottle as if it was a lifeline to a passing ship. He was never as aggressive or as self-assured as Bill, so Denny focused his attention on placing himself slightly between Bill and Anadeane, who was listening with polite attention. She took the drink and a small sip before answering.

"Denny has seen Monica perform and can probably answer your questions on her domestic capabilities. She can have other, more intimate functions, as well. They are programmed according to the wishes of her purchaser. We collect a great amount of data on what her owner might want, how he wants her to converse, react to situations, respond to him or her."

"Her?"

It was the first time since joining them that Steve had said a word and it was only one word.

"Oh, yes. You don't think that Monica would only be desired by men, do you?" Another smile at both of his friends before turning slightly to face Denny.

"Actually, Denny and I still have a lot to discuss in that regard and I hope we can find time to do that tonight." A bigger, more relaxed smile bloomed as she, once again, slipped her right arm through his.

He walked her away from the two men on the pretense of finding a table. He didn't want to insult his buddies, but he knew that he wouldn't be able to carry on an interesting, possibly fruitful, dialogue with her if they remained close by. A dinner spot shared with two other couples, preferably ones he didn't know well or at all, would work perfectly. Animal behavior was one of Denny's special biological interests and he knew the rules of the mating game. He was sure Anadeane wasn't naive and would understand his strategy.

The evening wore on with no surprises. They ate, drank some more, took a few turns on the dance floor, fast and slow, and greeted others, including Bill and Steve who had found some temporary companions for dancing. Anadeane had answered many of his general questions about the Love Shop and how she had been recruited and trained. He told her a bit about his background, where he was raised, and his ambitions for an academic career.

Many of the others, especially the older faculty, had already exited. Bill and Steve were still hovering in the background, occasionally throwing glances his, or more correctly, Anadeane's way. He and she found themselves dancing slowly and closely a few minutes before the soiree was to end.

She wore loafers but her height allowed her to remain face to face with him, her mouth very close to his left ear when she softly whispered, "What now, Professor?"

It sent a shock through him, from his lower spine to the top of his neck and he felt his hands perspiring. She clasped them a bit tighter and he could feel her breasts against his chest, her knees brushing his as the last number, a romantic oldie, finished.

The dance floor embrace ended and as they walked back hand-in-hand to their table for her purse, he offered the possibility of a late-night dance place.

"I had your place in mind, Denny, if it is convenient." She looked at him with hopeful eyes, like a little girl asking for a birthday puppy.

"It's a small apartment and it can be noisy on a weekend night. Students live there, but it isn't expensive, and I usually don't have… um, overnight visitors. Would your place be more comfortable and, or, convenient?"

"No, we can't use my place. I don't mind noise. If it is all right with you, let's do our next dance at your apartment. Besides, I'm curious to see how the young single professor lives."

No arguing with that. With a brief look and wave at his friends, Denny escorted her out of the building, into his car, and they made the drive across town to a modest apartment building. He parked around the back and used the rear stairway to his second-floor abode. As predicted, a number of parties were in progress in the complex, including several semi-naked bodies gathered around the pool. They slipped into his apartment and closed the door.

The next morning, Anadeane climbed out of his bed, used the bathroom, and got dressed. Denny woke up to see Anadeane putting her hair up.

"Going so soon? It's Sunday and we might want to get some breakfast. I know of a great place for a late brunch, if you care to come back to bed and linger a while."

He gazed at her longingly, not nearly satiated from a night of heavenly delight. He was in a trance, as if charmed by a siren from a Greek classic. "Besides, I may still have a few questions about Monica and her, well, you know, intimate functions."

She crossed to the bed and took his hand. "Professor Rathbun, I believe we covered the subject thoroughly—exhaustedly, I might add." She smiled like she had the night before, but there was also a trace of something else…a partial return to the business countenance of Friday.

"You not only know about Monica, one of our standard pleasure models, but you have experienced some, but not all, of the repertoire of the self-activated Anadeane model. She has just developed past the beta version, but there is only one functional entity at this time—me. You have had the opportunity to try the best that Love Shop Unlimited has to offer. I hope you enjoyed yourself and you will quietly spread the word. We do believe in the old slogan, it pays to advertise."

She stood up, walked to the bedroom door, turned, and said, "Now I must return to the shop and prepare for Monday. Thank you, Denny."

She left a stunned assistant professor of anthropology bewildered and wondering how he could have been so easily deceived.

# The Miracle Workers

*What is a miracle? Is it decreed by fate alone, or can one or more persons make it happen? Are miracles impossible or simply unexpected? Why do some people seem to be more likely to experience such an event and others not?*

Dawn comes as a grayish-blue haze through curtained windows, alerting them it is time to leave and the growing light isn't to be ignored. Rarely do they linger past five-thirty and never until six. It is an integral part of their disciplined success and they obey it faithfully, until now.

The six of them move as one, each carrying a small bag of treasures sought and found, each quietly surveying the rooms as they pass, not wanting to miss any easy opportunity. Two of them move quickly ahead to the staircase as the others slow. Albert and Rachelle descend from the second floor to the large atrium at the front of the house, observing the circular driveway for surprises.

Surprise! As they watch from the dark interior, two vehicles stop in front of the broad, raised veranda that runs the full frontage of the manor. A chauffeur in a white, starched uniform emerges from the first car, a dark blue limousine. He hesitates a moment, then opens the passenger door for a tall man in a dark suit. Albert nudges Rachelle and nods toward the staircase. They meet the others on the second-floor landing.

"They're back," whispers Rachelle. "Back up the stairs; we can't risk the back door."

Carolyn, the freckled blonde, starts to protest, but Albert cuts her off with a hiss.

"No time for this—just go, find a closet, under a bed, as far up as you can, and be quiet."

They lose count in the maze of hallways and alcoves, but the house has four stories and at least seventeen rooms. Two libraries, three parlors, two offices, and an unknown number of bedrooms are distributed among the first three floors.

Silently climbing the stairway, they hear the front doors unlocking and opening. The others find doors on the third floor, but Rachelle and Albert continue to the fourth story. One large double door greets them at the top of the stairs. It opens on a large, nearly vacant room, covered with a vast expanse of bright blue carpet. Scattered around the periphery, against a glossy white wall, are several chairs. At the far end of the room, a vacant stage with open red curtains looks over the emptiness.

They close the door gently and walk quickly and silently toward the stage, climb the few stairs at one side, and duck behind the curtain. The two listen as other vehicles arrive in the driveway below the window. There are several, as indicated by many doors opening and closing, and a growing murmur as people enter the house.

Pete and Mary sit in a bedroom closet on the third floor. Several large robes provide a screen as they wait patiently for a chance to escape. At seventeen, Pete is the oldest of the group, but not the leader. That honor belongs to sixteen-year-old Albert upstairs, but Mary always feels the most secure with Pete. He understands her when she tells him she is unique. She is also small, a pixie with short dark hair and a dark complexion, derived from her Puerto Rican parents.

Pete has one arm around her shoulder and she leans her head on his chest. Whispering in her ear, he tells her they will be safe and she isn't in danger as long as she is with the group. Mary needs to hear this because she is often afraid, convinced that her small size signals "victim" to others. She is as tough as nails in an old barn and takes shit from no one, but Pete's assurances offer a comfort and she presses herself into him as if it confers invulnerability.

The other two girls, not realizing they had the time to climb higher, opt for a hiding place on the second floor at the far end of the hallway. They open a door and enter to find themselves in a spacious bathroom, with a Jacuzzi tub and double counter but nowhere to effectively hide.

Carolyn and Megan step into an adjoining shower and stand behind the curtain. They can hear people below them talking, some in loud excited voices, others barely audible. It sounds like chairs scraping on a hardwood floor and at least one heavy footstep dominates other sounds of movement.

Carolyn clutches her cloth sack in front of her. She opens it to glimpse at the jewelry inside, part of their night's take.

*Was it worth it? Not if we are caught. We've had a few close calls before, but nothing like this, trapped in a house with so many people.*

She whispers to Megan, pressed against the wall, almost in tears. "We'll be okay. Let me think what I'm going to say if we're discovered. Let's stash the bags somewhere. We don't want to be caught with their stuff. It might be real hard to explain our way out of that."

Megan nods and gives her sack to Carolyn. The blonde has the street smarts and the boldness to take charge and Megan is more than willing to let her. Carolyn steps out of the shower and places the two bags in a linen drawer, tucking them under a pile of towels. She returns to the shower stall and puts her arms around Megan.

---

THE LIVING ROOM COULD HAVE BEEN A PARTY SCENE, FILLED with almost two dozen people, every chair and sofa occupied, with several standing. But what a strange party it would have been. Only a few of them circulate, talking to each other and occasionally to those who sit in somber silence, staring at their feet or some unseen vista on the walls or ceiling. The walking and talking group—three men and three women dressed in conservative suits and dresses—seem to serve as hosts for the others.

Even a casual glance would tell an observer that the others are not the usual casual crowd. Many of them appear severely retarded with droopy eyelids and unfocused pupils, slack jaws, a few of them drooling from the corners of their mouths. Postures make some seem spineless, like reclining jellyfish, with arms loosely dangling at their side. One of the men has wet his pants, but he doesn't seem to notice. All are adults, ranging in age from young to elderly, but the few words most speak are infantile, more of a babble than a structured conversation. One middle-aged woman exhibits spastic arm movements and can't hold her head upright.

One of the active women leaves the room and returns a few minutes later, pushing a large cart with three shelves laden with plates of food and cups of liquid. The well-dressed ones pass out the refreshments carefully, supervising those who need extra help. Large napkins are provided and some are tucked in at the tops of shirts or blouses. They eat and drink. One of the men, taller and older than the others, excuses himself and walks up the stairs to the second floor.

He strolls down the hallway and enters the bathroom. Unzipping his trousers, he is about to relieve himself at the toilet when he hears a faint gasp. Turning toward the shower, he can see a shoe beneath the plastic curtain and the vague outline of a body. He quickly turns, zips up his pants, and crosses to the curtain. He is both curious and a bit outraged at this intrusion, but not afraid.

The body does not appear to be of great size and he can handle most people without much effort. Ignoring the possibility that the intruder might be armed, he yanks the curtain aside and is surprised to find two teen girls facing him, a small brunette cowering in the corner and a thin blonde facing him with a scowl and her fists clenched.

"And just who in the hell are you two?" he says, more amused than angry. It is obvious that they are not a physical threat, but their presence is not welcome at this particular time. He notes that neither of them is bad-looking, although the brunette has traces of mascara on her face and red puffy eyes. Both are wearing work jeans, pullover sweaters, and tennis shoes.

Carolyn gives him a coy smile, her hands now open and her shoulders relaxed. She thrusts one hip suggestively to the side as she shifts her weight to her left foot. The right leg is poised if she needs it, but she decides to play the ingenue first. It often works with older adult men and she looks him directly in the eye.

"We're visitors and we've come to help you." She says it simply, convincingly, as if nothing else could be a possible reason for their presence.

"Interesting. You have decided to visit our bathroom and our shower. Should I let you bathe or would you like to step out of there?"

Carolyn takes Megan's hand and they step out onto the tile floor. The man doesn't advance but stands with his hands on his hips, awaiting a more appropriate answer. Carolyn eyes him as she quickly concocts a story, one that might rescue the entire group.

"There are others here, hidden in the house."

"How many?" he asks, still not moving but staying between the girls and the bathroom door.

"There are six of us," she replies. "I can call them for you and we can help you, whatever you want."

She glances at Megan, who says nothing and stands partly behind her. *I hope she trusts me and doesn't try to make a run for it.*

"All girls or do you have some guys with you?" *I don't want to say boys; that would be an assumption. They are obviously housebreakers and amateur burglars or they wouldn't have been trapped so easily. But they might have adults with them and that could be dangerous, especially to my people downstairs.*

"Two guys. The oldest is seventeen. Nobody is armed if that's your worry." She smiles, turning it on, lowering her eyelashes slightly. "We just want to help."

"Hmm, we'll see. Call the rest of your party out into the hallway. And I want everyone who is with you—no holdouts." He walks to the door and opens it. Carolyn passes him but he stops Megan. "You stay here for now, just in case your girlfriend decides to run for it. I'll be in the hall with her."

Megan looks at Carolyn, eyes as big as shining saucers, "Don't leave me, please Ca…"

Carolyn, standing behind the man's back, puts her fingers to her lips and scowls.

"Don't leave me alone." Megan is about to cry again.

"I'll be right here, in the hallway. I need to call the others down. I'll be back for you in just a jiff. Okay?" Megan nods. Carolyn and the man step through the door and walk toward the middle of the hallway and the staircase.

"Your name is Kathy or Carol?" he asks.

"Cassandra. I'm Cassandra." She looks up at him, hoping he will respond in kind, but he doesn't. Instead, he points to the stairway and holds onto her arm.

"Call them down, from here."

"Hey guys, it's me. Come on out and meet our host. I'm on the second floor. Roger A."

"Roger A? Is that a safety code?"

*Ooh, this guy is no dummy. He picked up on that right away. I just hope when they come they leave their sacks somewhere.*

All is silent for about thirty seconds until a door opens on the third floor. Footsteps sound overhead and two faces appears on the stairs—Pete and Mary.

"Come on down, Steve. You too, Sue. Meet mister… uh, mister…"

He ignores Carolyn but looks at the two as they slowly descend. The boy is of medium height, not very muscular, and doesn't seem to be a threat. The girl is only about five feet tall and though she looks like a young teen, in her baggy clothes she resembles a small child.

"Martha's waiting in the bathroom and will join us in a moment. Are the others coming?"

She is relieved to see they are carrying nothing.

Pete and Mary quickly realize that all of their names are false and they relinquish control of events to Carolyn. The break-and-entry survival game, when successfully played by a group, depends on tight communication and cooperation. Wits have served them before and will do the same now. They reach the hallway as another pair of feet appear on the stairs. Albert and Rachelle, hands empty, step down quickly to join the group. Albert notices Megan is missing and is about to ask when Pete tells him Martha is in the bathroom.

Carolyn smiles. *So far, so good.*

"Go get your friend," says the man as he surveys the group. *All young, no adults. What were they doing? Did they take anything or did we come home before they had a chance?*

Carolyn returns to the bathroom and speaks quietly to Megan before they leave. "Your name is Martha. And I am Cassandra. Pete is Steve and Mary is Sue. Don't forget."

"I don't know, I…too many names—what if I can't remember?" Her hands are in motion and she is starting to shake again, tears not far behind.

"Martha, get a hold of yourself. We need you, so don't screw this up. Follow my lead and keep quiet. Don't say any names, not even mine. Just respond if someone calls you Martha, okay?"

Megan nods and follows Carolyn back into the hall to join the group. The man hasn't said anything to the others and they wait in silence. Albert and Rachelle are alert to Carolyn's ploy and wait to see what develops.

She doesn't hesitate. "I told him…." She looks at the man to see if he wants to volunteer a name, but he doesn't. "I told him we were visitors and we were here to help."

She says it brightly, like an airline attendant welcoming passengers aboard. They nod as if that has been the plan all along, but they say nothing, not knowing what else she may have told him. Megan still looks terrified, but that isn't unusual for her.

The man takes charge. "Let's go downstairs. Stay together and no one leaves unless I dismiss you. Understood?"

They nod, but Carolyn and Albert don't miss the "unless" instead of "when."

The living room group is silent. The seated ones finish their food and drink and only a couple of them look up to watch the teens and man descend the stairs. He motions for them to stand by the landing and quietly tells one of the other men to lock the front door and stay near the atrium.

The man raises his eyebrows as he looks at the kids, but the older man shrugs his shoulders and says, "Perhaps we'll have some evening entertainment, an unscheduled performance or two."

Rachelle tries to whisper something to Albert but a sharp look from one of the women silences her. The man who found and led them to the first floor walks back into the living room and stands before them.

"I am Ward Brookings and I own this house, this place you decided to invade. My associates…," he nods toward the other normal adults standing about the room, "believe you are burglars and have been up to no good during our brief absence. It seems we have several options."

He has their full attention. Other than a burp from one or two of the others in the chairs and some restless movement here and there, the room is silent.

Ward continues, "One, we can simply call the police and turn you over to them. Since most of you are juveniles, you will probably not suffer unduly. Your imprisonment will be short, relieved by your parents…" he looks at each of them, "if you have parents. That would be the simplest solution, wouldn't it? You'd be gone and we can get on to our interrupted business."

Albert takes a chance. "Your second option?"

Ward fixes him with a steady gaze. "Ah, I don't believe we caught your name earlier. I detect a leader if there is one. Well, sir, our second option is to follow up on your young comrade's suggestion." He looks at Carolyn, then turns back to Albert.

"She seems to think that you are going to be of some immediate and great service to us. Remarkable, since you don't know us nor do we know you. I would be curious as to what she or the rest of you have in mind. An agreement of mutual benefit is not out of the question. And, I hate to add, a third option is also a possibility."

Albert doesn't flinch. "And that would be?"

"We abuse each of you in any way we please and see fit. I'm sure we can come up with some amusing games and tasks for you. We can be quite creative when we need to be or when circumstances dictate." There is no smile, nothing to blunt the implied threat.

Rachelle takes over. She is sixteen but appears to be older. Statuesque, a shapely brunette with a tan complexion and the makings of a fashion model, she also exudes a commanding presence.

"We are the Miracle Workers. We serve the community and can serve you as well. It's true we intruded, but we also believe we can be of help. We weren't expecting so many of you, so we hid until we could evaluate the situation."

"Impressive, my dear. Miracle workers, you say? You may need a miracle or two before the night is over. You speak well, but do you speak the truth? I believe you are a gang of common thieves, young ones at that, but thieves nevertheless. It would still be easier to exercise the first option. A simple phone call and problem solved."

He stands in front of them, grim and resolute, hands folded across his chest.

Carolyn speaks next. "I told you we would be willing to do what you want." She looks toward the group of seated strange adults. Some seem harmless but others give her the creeps, like one obese man whose bulk occupies almost half of the sofa. He looks back at her and she turns away.

"Indeed, you did. Cassandra, was it? I see you are fascinated by some of our guests. You will have time to make their acquaintances if we let you stay. For the time being, let us adjourn to the library where you can sit. I want to know more about your miracle business."

He smiles as he waves them toward an open door off the living room. One of the women follows him and the teens into a large room filled with tall shelves containing thousands of impressive-looking books. A large crystal chandelier dominates the high ceiling and a study desk with several comfortable chairs completes the room. There is no other exit door.

"Please be seated. Mrs. Schmidt, would you have John bring us some refreshments for our young guests? I would guess soda pop would be better than coffee, correct?" He looks at the teens and a couple nod their assent.

Carolyn, sitting on the edge of her chair, decides to maintain a token sense of confrontation. "I could go for something stronger. How about some rum in a coke?"

Albert and Pete both give her a disapproving look, as if to say, "not now girl; let's keep our wits and see what these people are up to." Despite the overt manners displayed by Ward, they have no illusions about the precarious position they are in.

"Colas or whatever you have will be fine, Mr. Brookings," says Rachelle. She looks around at her friends and no one disagrees.

Mrs. Schmidt leaves the room and Ward remains in front of them, with his hands behind his back. He begins pacing back and forth in a tight figure eight, head down. "How about we start with your real names?" He looks up, stops, and stares at Pete. "You look like you might be the oldest. Tell me your full name and how old you are."

Pete glances quickly at Albert and Rachelle, seated side by side at his left. "My name is Peter Santiesteban and I'm seventeen." He speaks softly but without hesitation. The others recognize there is no longer a need to continue using phony names.

Mary, sitting at Pete's right, gives her name and age, fifteen. Ward smiles, thinking she doesn't look older than twelve or thirteen. Albert and Rachelle go next. She states her name and age decisively as if announcing her candidacy for a political race.

Ward turns to Megan. She has recovered from her initial fear and sits quietly, hands folded in her lap. Her voice is little-girl soft, but she tells him she is fourteen and apologizes for giving him a false name earlier. Carolyn, still somewhat defiant, looks away when Ward steps in front of her.

"Dear Cassandra, you are an interesting one. No need to give me your name now. I'll spend time with you later."

Mrs. Schmidt returns to the room, followed closely by the chauffeur Albert and Rachelle spotted earlier. He has a tray of glasses and a choice of several bottles of soda. He passes them around the room as Rachelle takes note.

*Great, there are seven adults, in addition to the creeps.* She glances at the first-floor window. It has small square panes contained within a gridwork of sturdy metal bars. *Bet anything that is locked. We are indeed trapped.*

One of the other women, trim and in her late twenties, enters the room and talks quietly with Mrs. Schmidt by the door. Ward walks over to them, listens for a minute, then turns back to the kids.

"John will remain with you while I confer with my colleagues. Finish your drinks and I will return in a few minutes."

John stands by the door but doesn't seem interested in them. They risk a few words and huddle together around Pete and Albert. Carolyn faces John in case he decides to come closer. Pete bends his head down.

"Stay cool, everyone. We'll get through this. It's weird, but I don't think we'll have any trouble as long as we cooperate. We call ourselves the Miracle Workers, but that's our street name. I don't know what we're going to do if they expect us to cure one of the charges, or patients, or whatever."

Looking up at Carolyn, he says, "And don't get sassy with them. We all stay together and we all leave together, but don't make trouble. Got it?"

She nods but says nothing, keeping her eyes on the chauffeur. They break apart and return to their seats when the door opens. Mrs. Schmidt points at Megan and Mary.

"Upstairs, you two. We need to talk. Actually, *you* need to talk."

Her manner leaves no room for dispute. Megan and Martha follow Mrs. Schmidt up the stairs to a second-floor room. She opens the door and the girls go inside and sit on the bed.

"I'll be back in a moment; that's a promise." Her tone is not encouraging.

A few minutes later, Mrs. Schmidt enters the room with Ted. He was one of the seated ones who Megan had first noticed. Hard to miss at almost three hundred pounds, much of it gathered around his waist. His baby face and small beady eyes remind her of an oversized rodent. She recoils automatically but Mary sits defiantly on the bed, her arms folded. She must show courage when Megan is the target, but she is mistaken. Ted walks over to her as Mrs. Schmidt stands by the door.

"Ted is fond of dolls, Megan. He thinks Mary is a living doll, petite and pretty. He likes to undress and put clothes back on dolls, don't you, Teddy?"

Ted grins and sits beside Mary, who slides a few feet away.

"Don't be shy, Mary, Ted won't actually hurt you. He is a gentle giant and only wants to touch, to play. Now that we know your real name, it is time to find out a few other things. For instance, where did you hide the jewelry and cash you took before we arrived? Tell me and maybe we will have Ted play with something else."

Megan starts to tear up, but Mary gives her a hard stare. "I'll be fine. Don't tell them anything. This fat slug won't dare mess with me."

Mrs. Schmidt flashes an evil grin. "Sure about that, are you, honey? He will be very good to you, the very epitome of gentleness. But, as I said, he does love pretty little girls. And, unfortunately, those big hands are not all that skilled with buttons, so I hope he doesn't ruin your lovely clothes."

Megan is crying openly. Ted grins and leans toward Mary, hands extended to lift her bulky sweater. Mrs. Schmidt turns to Megan.

"You don't want to see Ted touch your friend, do you? You're not that much bigger than she is and I'm sure he would like to play with your clothes after he finishes with his first toy."

Mary is struggling on the bed as Ted pushes her sweater over her head. He has both her hands wrapped in one huge fist and one knee pins her legs to the covers. The other hand undoes the top button of her blouse.

Megan screams, "Leave her alone. I'll tell you. We hid our sacks in your towel drawer, in the bathroom where we were hiding." Ted fumbles with the second button.

"The bathroom? Which floor were you on?"

"The second one; that's where Mr. Brookings found us, Carolyn and me. Please make him stop." Frustrated with the stubborn button, Gentle Ted rips it off her blouse and continues to the third one. A lacy slip covering Mary's small breasts is exposed.

"So, it isn't Cassandra after all. Carolyn, the wise-mouthed one. Ward was right on all counts. You are a bunch of bratty little thieves. What about the others? Where did they hide their—pardon me—*our* stuff?"

"I don't know; I don't know. You'll have to ask them, please…"

Megan is trying to reach toward Mary, as if making contact would be of any help. The fourth and last button above her belt pops open and a slow chuckle comes from Ted. He slowly reaches out and touches the outline of Mary's navel, visible under her slip. Mary is swearing now but not crying.

Mrs. Schmidt stands up and puts a hand on the big man's shoulder. "Enough for now, Ted dear. Maybe later you can play some more, but let's go see if Megan has been truthful. I do hope so." Ted pulls back, obviously disappointed at the interruption. They leave the room and the girls hear a solid click at the door, followed by footsteps headed toward the bathroom.

Mary stands up and fastens all but the broken button. She is angry, but Megan is still frightened. "Mary, what are we going to do? He'll come back and he'll do whatever he wants. I just know he will and I don't want his hands on me and…"

"Megan, you'll be okay. That was just to frighten us into talking. I doubt if that overstuffed ham could do anything."

"He could hurt us. He could crush us after he strips us."

Mary puts her arms around Megan, even though she is five inches shorter. "They'll find the bags and they'll ask the others. They won't hurt us. You did the right thing, telling them. I think they knew we had swiped their jewelry and money after that woman came into the library. The others are probably being questioned right now."

Mary was correct. Three of the other four are undergoing individual interrogations in different rooms, each by one of the adults. The fourth, Carolyn, is in the library, still guarded by John. The sun is up and many of the strange adults have been taken to rooms throughout the house. Some are put in beds, a few remain awake in chairs on balconies outside bedrooms. Ted is with Mrs. Schmidt. Ward returns to the library and asks John to help one of the women prepare breakfast.

"For them as well?" John indicates Carolyn and Ward nods yes.

After John leaves the room, Ward walks to where Carolyn sits and pulls up a chair and faces her. They are about four feet apart and Ward studies her for a moment before speaking.

"We've recovered some of your ill-gotten gains, Carolyn, including what you and Megan stowed away. We'll have the rest very shortly. Your group has been reasonable and cooperative—that is, everyone but you. You seem determined to resist our generous offer to forgive and forget. And for what? What do you gain by playing the angry rebel?"

Carolyn's eyes drill into his, accusing. "Forgive? Forget? Sorry, I hadn't heard that was part of the deal, if there was a deal. And what about the scream I heard? I'm sure that was Megan. What were you doing to her?"

"Nothing to her. She was reacting to Mary, sweet little Mary, who was being introduced to Ted, the big guy. I'm sure you know which one I'm talking about. Oh, don't look like that. He didn't hurt her. They are both fine. It was just a quick way to loosen her tongue. Lena, Mrs. Schmidt, has a genius for coaxing the truth from reluctant lips. But I'm not here to talk about that, am I?"

He looks at her and she sits back, folding her arms across her chest.

"What do you want? Why am I alone here?"

"You're not alone. I'm here with you. I am curious—incredulous, in fact—about the story you concocted about miracle workers and how you could help us. Your tall friend, the pretty one, said the same thing. Did you think you were providing invaluable assistance by removing our valuables?"

Carolyn says nothing. She sits still, not wanting to contribute further to the conversation or to invoke his anger. The first waves of fear arise as she becomes aware that, without her group, she is vulnerable—not a tough, practiced housebreaker, just a young girl whose only chance lies in keeping and using her wits.

"In a few minutes, we will have breakfast. The doors are locked and we will remain vigilant in case any of you has the urge to go shopping, here or anywhere." He gives a short, dry laugh. "Meanwhile, we will decide what services you will provide to compensate us for the inconveniences your uninvited arrival has caused. Be assured that the ideas of some of my companions are harsher and more demanding than my own."

He rises, starts for the door, then turns back to the girl. "By the way, Megan told us your name, but she didn't mention your age."

"I'm fifteen, almost sixteen. I suppose you and your group have some ideas about Rachelle and me?"

Ward starts for the door but turns before leaving. "There are always ideas, Carolyn, some good and some not so good. As I indicated, some of us might have some particular—let's say, unusual—plans for you, but no decisions have been made. Your continued cooperation could be a factor in what kind of decision."

He closes the door, leaving Carolyn to think about what she might have to do to earn her release. *And what about Megan and Mary? The boys and Rachelle can take care of themselves, but the other two are just kids.* That made her smile. *What the hell do you think you are, Miss Fifteen-Going-on-Sixteen?*

None of the abnormal ones are at breakfast. That's what the kids now called them, but only when talking amongst themselves. Their captors—the normal ones they refer to as creeps—eat in another room and allow the kids to converse while still keeping an eye on them. Only John moves back and forth in the dining room, silently refilling glasses of juice and cups of coffee. Pancakes and sausages help ease the tensions, but it has been a long night and Megan is fading fast.

Mrs. Schmidt walks into the dining room. "We are a bit short on bedrooms and," she pauses, "we weren't expecting guests lacking reservations." She smiles at her little joke as if she was running a B&B. "We have two rooms and each has two beds. They are on the third floor and the windows are locked. For the protection of our clients, you know. Divide them up as you want. Get some rest and we'll see you this afternoon."

Rachelle and Albert take one bed and Pete and Mary another, in separate rooms. That leaves Megan and Carolyn with their own beds. Megan decides to stay with Pete and Mary. Carolyn isn't sure she likes the arrangement, but she believes that none of the gang have ever gone further than fooling around, necking and some petting, but nothing intimate. However, she is not thrilled about being a witness to Rachelle cuddling with Al, innocent or not.

As they remove their outer clothes and climb under the covers, Carolyn broods. *Mr. Brookings isn't that bad looking. Maybe he wouldn't be so terrible. Just to snuggle with, of course.* It is her last thought until the afternoon shadows darken the windows.

---

THE MIRACLE WORKERS ARE AWAKE BY THREE AND ALLOWED to gather in Pete and Mary's room. All have benefited from food and sleep and they are ready to assess their options.

"Do we have any?" Pete's first question is directed primarily at Albert, but he knows that Rachelle and Carolyn will have their say.

"Let's be Miracle Workers. Not just midnight house crawlers, par excellence, but let's give these creeps some real miracles." Rachelle seems almost enthusiastic as if this was a job they were applying for and hoping to get.

"I don't want to spoil your pending audition, 'Chelle, but I'm not sure what miracles you have in mind. And which group here do you mean by 'creeps?'" Pete shakes his head as if not hearing her correctly.

Megan clears her throat and everyone waits. "The only miracle I want is to see the fat frog have a heart attack and croak." She throws her arms limply to the side, rolls her eyes up, and lets her tongue hang out to one side.

Mary smiles and looks down at her missing button. "What are you complaining about? I had his pasty face just inches from mine and his hands all over my belly. But, yes, I would vote for Meg's miracle."

Pete looks at her. "Belly, huh? You're lucky the dimwit didn't know what else to play with."

"Let's get back on message, gang. We don't have much time and this may be one of the few chances to coordinate anything."

Albert looks at each of them. Carolyn is the only one who hasn't spoken.

"While you were all busy confessing to the crime, Ward confronted me in the library. He didn't threaten anything specific, but he implied that some of his buddies—men or women. I'm not sure—might have some evil schemes in mind. He hinted that Rachelle and I might be desirable."

She stares at Rachelle as if they might soon be on the auction block.

"Exactly what did he say?" asks Albert, leaning forward to put his arms around Rachelle.

"Nothing much, just that our cooperation might play into it. Just don't know what he means by cooperation."

"I think we should play it step-by-step, offer the creeps help with the abnormal herd, help with meals, clean rooms, maybe even wait on them or talk to them. No one tries to escape unless we can all go, agreed?"

They nod. Albert is again the leader, the thinker, the go-to point person they would take their cues from.

"At some point, we will no longer be 'guests' but captives—kidnapped kids. Then we can go to the authorities. Even if we are punished for breaking and entering, the creeps will be in far more serious trouble. We might be able to bargain from strength."

Rachelle clears her throat. "What if they decide on something more sinister than letting us be helping hands? Suppose Carolyn is right and they have designs to use us as sex slaves?" She looks at Pete and Albert. "And you guys aren't out of the woods, either. How would you like Ted playing dress-up with you?"

They don't have long to reflect on the sobering images of what might happen. A knock on the door and Ward enters the room to tell them it is time for another meeting. They follow him down the stairs. Additional chairs have been placed in the library and all of the normal adults are there except for John. The kids take the empty chairs, distributed among the adults so that no more than two teens sit together. Ward stands in the center of the circular gathering.

"I'm sure you are wondering why we have all been called together."

This brings a few chuckles from some of the adults. The kids are silent, glancing at faces to determine who might be friendly and who might not.

"After considerable discussion among us, we decided to let you earn your freedom. Although we are holding you against your will, at least for the short-term, you will agree to remain with us until you have served the terms of the sentence we believe is appropriate."

Ward steps slowly around in a circle, facing each of the teens as he talks, making eye contact, lingering a little longer on Carolyn than the others.

"Each of you will be assigned to one of us. Six of us, six of you. Not counting John, of course, who is assigned to us as well. Some of you will help take care of our other guests. Some of them require a good deal of supervision. Some are unable to feed themselves, bathe themselves, or even relieve themselves without making a mess.

"Megan and Mary, you will work with Lena (he indicates Mrs. Schmidt) and Molly (he nods toward the athletic woman who had come to the library that morning). You will do what they direct, without question, without insolence, without expressing displeasure. You will serve."

He turns to Albert and Pete.

"Boys, you are strong and can help with some of the more physically demanding chores. Lifting patients, moving furniture and cleaning, that sort of thing. You'll work with Enrique and Freida."

Enrique is a light-skinned Latino. He grins at Pete. "*Como estás?*" he murmurs to Pete. Freida is middle-aged and quiet, a bit overweight, and remains silent.

Ward continues his assignments, facing Rachelle. "You will be with Colonel Wilson. It seems he has taken a fancy to you."

Her look of alarm brings a grin from Ward. Jeff, an older man dressed in slacks and a Hawaiian shirt, acknowledges Rachelle with a grin and wave of his hand. He has dark, short hair, graying at the temples. He carries himself, standing or sitting, like a career ex-military man, which he is.

"Jeff will respect you, Rachelle, but he won't tolerate disobedience, no sir. He plays it by the book and so will you. He is an exception to the first-name basis the rest of us enjoy. You will call him Colonel Wilson." He turns to face Carolyn.

*So I'm last again. Singled out once more and, guess what? I get the boss, the wonderful Mr. Brookings.* She sighs and sits back, legs extended out from her chair.

"Don't be so gloomy, Carolyn. I thought about pairing you with our gentle giant, Ted. I'm sure Mary told you how much she enjoyed his attentions." He glances back at Mary. "Frieda will get you some thread if you want to fix your blouse."

Carolyn retracts her feet and leans forward, not sure she wants to hear what he has in mind for her. But she asks anyway.

"I assume I will be with you. What will I be doing, Mister Brookings?"

"Why, whatever I tell you to do. Maybe nothing. Maybe you will get to sit around the pool and tan while your friends work their butts off. Maybe you will be asked to dance for us after dinner. I'm sure, if asked nicely, you can put on a nice show for us, one that both the men and women will enjoy. You, my dear, will actually have some unsupervised freedom. Along with it comes the temptation to escape, to leave your friends to their fate, and save your own precious ass. If you do, know that they will suffer the penalties and they will be harsh ones."

He turns to Freida. "Make sure we have enough thread."

The others look at Carolyn, not sure whether to be envious or frightened for her. She looks back at them, trying to reassure them she won't betray their trust; she won't run.

"I'll be here," she says.

It's enough. Albert gives her a smile and a discreet thumbs-up, their signal that the message is understood. They are tight. They are the Miracle Workers.

---

THE TEENS WORK WITH THEIR COUNTERPARTS FOR TWO HOURS, most of it with the abnormals. Carolyn sits outside in a lawn chair. She wears a borrowed sunsuit, halter, and tight shorts that expose some front cleavage and long legs. Ward brings her a rum and coke.

"I believe you asked for one this morning."

"What am I doing?" she asks him.

"Isn't it obvious? You are a portrait, a pinup to be admired. Granted, you are not as fetching as the lovely Miss Rachelle, but you deserve to be the object—let me emphasize object—of my attention. As I read at this table, I want to be able to look up and see you in front of me, legs and arms, thin neck, an enticing mid-section, all of the usual attributes of the female persuasion, even though they could stand a few more years of development. Your very youth appeals to my lustful perversion. Now, do you understand?"

"I think so. You just want to look at me. That's all. No touching or kissing or anything else? I don't have to get naked or anything?"

She still doesn't trust him, but so far he has been only a voyeur, not quite a gentleman, but one inclined to watch rather than act.

Her concern remains for the others, especially the two younger girls. *Will their assignments be honored? Will it be merely chores and helping hands?*

Ward picks up his book. "I make no promises. I will look at you, but if I decide that you should remove your top, then you will do it. I won't ask twice."

He begins reading, not waiting for a response. A dinner bell sounds at five-thirty and he motions Carolyn to follow him inside. "Change into something more appropriate. You and the others will find clothes in one of your closets that should fit."

They gather in Albert's room and change. Albert complains about the man who wets his pants. "Almost every hour," he says, "and it stinks. I didn't think pee could smell that bad."

Rachelle tells them about bathing the old woman who couldn't hold her head up. "I had to watch her every minute or she would fall over and drown."

"Probably wouldn't do our work record any good," says Pete. "We've got a rep to maintain, guys."

"How about you Carolyn? What's it like being Ward's lawn model?"

Mary doesn't sound bitter, but she isn't going to give the freckled blonde a free ride, either. Megan starts to protest, but Carolyn puts a hand on her arm and shakes her head no.

Carolyn is wearing some long slacks but is standing next to the closet in her bra. After her afternoon, any residual shyness about undressing in front of the guys has vanished.

"He hasn't touched me. He stares at me every so often and I can't tell what he's thinking, but so far, nothing."

Pete looks at her as she dons a simple pullover blouse. "What if he does? Suppose he decides to take you to his room. What do you do then?"

Carolyn thinks for a few seconds. "Like Albert said, take it step by step. Maybe I'll tell him I have a venereal disease."

This brings a laugh from Rachelle and Albert and they leave the room to walk down to dinner.

Because they slept late that day, the kids are awake at eleven, after the house is almost quiet. They can hear one of the abnormals, a middle-aged woman, crying in the room next to them. One of the normal adults makes a tour of each floor twice an hour. They hear their door move as the lock is checked. Albert, Rachelle, and Carolyn talk softly, huddled together on her bed, next to the wall by the window.

"Carolyn, since you have more outside time than any of us, can you scout around and get a sense of how the house is situated and what the rear of the property is like? We only saw the front and one side when we entered and I'm not sure what way will be best if we do make a run."

Carolyn looks at Albert. "Run? Do you really want to risk an escape? What if we just work here for a while? The food isn't bad, they haven't been abusive, and we don't have parents or anyone else that will miss us until they return from Europe. We're on our own and we can get out of this if we don't panic."

Rachelle interrupts. "Carolyn, maybe Ward has spared you, probably because he knows you are seriously underage, but Jeff has his eyes and his hands on me. Several times today he put his arms around my waist, once on my butt. We were passing in the hall or on the stairs when no one else was near. I'm sure it will only be a matter of time, perhaps today, when he tries to kiss me or make a serious attempt to see what he can do."

Albert lowers his head, confirming that he has the same concerns for her.

"Colonel asshole thinks he is Mr. Rambo and that 'Chelle is his squeeze. I don't know if he does that with Ward's knowledge or whether that even makes any difference. We need to be thinking getaway whenever a real opportunity arises. Be ready. In the meantime, see what you can find out. Use your charm, girl. I know you must have some somewhere."

The next morning, after breakfast, Ward brings Carolyn a package. "Put this on when you come to the pool."

She walks slowly to her room and watches the others getting dressed for work. Most of the clothes are in a closet in Albert's room. Specific items of apparel are mandated for meals, work, and evening relaxation. There seems to be adequate attire for everyone as if someone had made a special shopping trip to keep them dressed for each occasion.

"Not getting into your shorts thing?" asks Megan. She and Mary are wearing nylon jumpsuits. They will be cleaning bathrooms and kitchen floors.

Carolyn holds up the small package from Ward. "I was told to wear this," she says and opens it. Inside a petite flat box, she finds and removes a very small bikini. The bottom is almost a thong and the top barely covers her breasts.

"Wow, two strings and a Band-Aid," exclaims Rachelle. "Don't let Colonel Jeff see you in that. I don't need him any hornier than he already is."

"I'm not going to make anyone horny with my body. This is Ward's idea of my role as his pinup. I'm not sure how far he is going with it, but…" She holds the bikini in front of her face. "It's my very first two-piece. Just hope I can hold it up."

She doesn't smile, not wanting the others to see that she is pleased with the prospect of competing with Rachelle for a man's attention.

Rachelle isn't fooled. She has shared that game with others, but never before with the fifteen-year-old. "Be careful, girl. We are all playing with dynamite. Let's not get blown away."

---

WARD IS SITTING IN A LAWN CHAIR BY THE POOL, WEARING SWIM trunks and reading a newspaper. Carolyn walks onto the deck, a towel wrapped discreetly around her. He drops his paper and sits up. "There she is. Let's have a look."

She slowly drops her towel, using a bit more tease than she had intended. She stands in front of him then turns slowly, anticipating his next instructions. When she faces him again, he has picked up the paper and is once again reading, as if she hadn't appeared almost naked.

"I had hoped for a swimsuit that I might swim in. This isn't very practical for that."

He doesn't stop reading but answers. "If you want to go in, go topless."

She settles into a lawn chair, puts on some dark glasses she found near the pool entrance, and applies sun lotion that came with the glasses. *They think of everything, don't they?* Her thoughts drift back to Rachelle's predicament. *Jeff, although older, is athletic and fit. If I was older...*

The morning wears on and Ward dives into the pool, splashing some water onto Carolyn. She is almost asleep, in the zone and a few nods from dreamland, when the cold drops snap her awake and she sits up suddenly. The flimsy bra slips off her shoulders and one breast is exposed. She grabs the towel but Ward is treading water, staring directly at her. She pushes the bra up and stands. "I think you did that deliberately." She is at the edge with her hands on her hips.

"There is very little I do that is accidental. So here is another decision for you. You can take the top off and join me in the water or you can leave it on and bake for another hour."

"Suppose I join you but leave the top on?"

"If you come in the water with it on, you know what will happen. Your choice, Carolyn."

"I'd like to take a walk on the lawn. I like the grass between my toes. Maybe I'll swim later, just before lunch."

He rolls over and sinks beneath the surface as she walks away from the pool. There is a large hedge that encloses the back yard. Trees and flower beds are scattered about the spacious grounds, but it is the hedge she wants to inspect. Bending down, she can see a sturdy wire fence behind the tightly packed trunks.

"Looking for a way out are you?"

It is the colonel, standing two feet behind her. She hadn't heard his approach and she steps back, almost in contact with the prickly foliage. She places her hands over her breasts as he stares. He is wearing sandals and a Speedo style swimsuit. He has a chest full of graying hair and looks like a model for mature macho males.

"No, just walking around, feeling the grass. I can't run away, remember?" She steps to one side, preparing to pass and return to the pool.

He extends an arm and grabs her elbow, pulling her a step closer. "No need to worry, sweetheart. I never intrude on another man's property. And you don't have all of the equipment you need to make it worth the effort. Someday, maybe, but not today." He releases her arm and she steps back.

"I'm not anyone's property and I never will be. Good day, Colonel."

As she walks away, she hears him laugh. He follows her to the pool and jumps in. Jeff and Ward splash around while Carolyn watches. She catches a few words about "Lolita" and "plaything" and decides it is time to leave.

She shouts to Ward at the far edge of the pool. "I'd like to dress for lunch, if that's okay." He nods in the affirmative.

"How about one quick peek before you go, sweetheart." The colonel is all grin and draped over the near edge.

"Let her go, you horny bastard. You've already got the sexiest one of the bunch," yells Ward.

Carolyn grabs her towel and makes quick tracks for the house. She regrets the interruption to the hedge inspection, but that route does not look promising. Her suit is still threatening to fall off but she holds it in place until reaching the room and changing into casual pants and blouse.

That night, after lights are out, Rachelle pleads her case. "The colonel isn't going to back off." She looks at Carolyn. "I know you didn't mean to, honey, but that son-of-a-bitch was all grabs and feelies today. It was all I could do to keep him from assaulting me, witnesses or not. He told me that your little bikini set him off and he will get me one like it, or smaller."

She turns toward her boyfriend. "Al, what the hell am I going to do?"

He puts his arm around her and his face close to her ear. "Let me talk to Ward. He seems decent enough and maybe he can rein in his pal."

---

THE NIGHT IS A RESTLESS ONE FOR ALL OF THE MIRACLE Workers. Mrs. Schmidt delights in playing pranks on the younger girls, making them repeat some chores and constantly offering derisive comments about their efforts. Pete and Albert work hard, but do not have the problems confronting the older girls. They are also aware that no date or limit has been set for their release. Mary tosses and turns next to Pete and finally shakes him awake.

"What is it Mary? It can't be morning yet."

"It's not, but I need to talk to you, to tell you what I'm thinking."

Megan wakes up and joins them. Pete sits up and shakes his head to clear the fuzziness. Mary waits patiently until both of her roommates are still.

"Pete, you have always believed I'm unique, right?" Pete lifts a finger to affirm. "You don't know I have a few special talents, ones I didn't see a need to reveal. Not until now."

Megan starts to ask a question, but Pete touches her arm and puts a finger to his lips. Mary continues.

"My brother bought me a chemistry set for my ninth birthday. Why, I don't know. Probably because he thought he'd be the one to play with it. But after doing a few of the kit's cookbook experiments, I became interested in something else." They look at her but say nothing. "Poison! I became fascinated with poisons of all kinds, natural ones from plants and mushrooms and toxic chemicals, like rat and bug poisons. And you know what? They have some of these things down in the pantry."

She punctuates the last statement with an evil smile of satisfaction. Peter and Megan look at each other. Neither knows how to respond to this bit of news.

"What do you have in mind, Mary? Are you planning on poisoning all of them, including the abnormals?"

"No, that might be hard to do. They might not all eat it or enough of it, and we only help out in the kitchen. It might be difficult to sneak enough of it into the food."

"Wouldn't it change the taste?" asks Megan. "The first ones to eat it would know."

"Not if I disguised a bit of it in a drink, especially an alcoholic drink. And I'm only thinking about one of them—the colonel. They have one particular poison that doesn't have much of a taste, it's fast-acting, and I can give it to Carolyn or Rachelle to slip in his cocktail, perhaps when he's at the pool."

"Might work, but what then?" says Pete. "They're not gonna let us off one of 'em and then cheerfully invite us to walk out the door. They might even decide to kill one or all of us to get even."

"Hey, I know what I'm doing here—it'll look like he had a heart attack. One minute he's making goo-goo eyes at 'Chelle and the next he's grabbing his chest. Maybe they'll find him floating face down in the pool."

Megan isn't convinced. "It might work and I'm glad you're not thinking about poisoning everyone because a few of them don't seem so bad. Although I wouldn't mind if Mrs. Schmidt and Fat Ted had a taste." She gives them a quick, nervous smile.

"Good, Megan. You can be a distraction while I pocket what I need."

Pete hugs Mary, then Megan. "Okay, girls, work a miracle. Just be careful that no one sees you get the stuff or slip it to him. He's a cagey one and I wouldn't be surprised if he's alert for something like that."

---

THE NEXT MORNING, PETE, MARY, AND MEGAN CONFER WITH the others on what they planned. They have not yet decided what they would do after the event but hope that the ensuing confusion might offer them their chance to exit. As they leave the breakfast table to change into working clothes, Jeff drops a small package in front of Rachelle. He gives her a big smile and tells her it is her uniform for the day.

"Possibly for the evening, as well," he adds and walks away.

In the changing room, Rachelle holds up a string thong knit bikini. "Even smaller than yours," she indicates to Carolyn, donning her poolside outfit.

"At least you have the equipment to keep in in place," she retorts, bringing a few laughs from the boys.

Mary is not amused. "I don't know for sure when I will have a chance to grab my ingredient, so you'll have to be careful what you say and do if you and he are alone." She and Megan finish dressing and leave the room.

Rachelle and Carolyn cover their swimsuits with terry cloth bathrobes. Carolyn puts an arm on her shoulder. "We'll stay together, somehow keep them from separating us. If we can stay by the pool, it will give Mary or Megan a chance to slip us the powder."

"Where are we going to put it? We don't have enough clothes on to hide anything."

"I'll bring my bag, for lotion, sunglasses, whatever. We might have to "entertain" them to stay together, so don't be surprised, okay?"

Albert walks over to the two girls. "Carolyn—fifteen, going on thirty. None of us would be surprised at anything you do." He sees her frown. "That's a compliment, okay?"

Jeff and Ward decide to have a pool party luncheon just for the four of them. Rachelle does indeed look ravishing in her teeny weeny knit, drawing comments from Ward about trading women. Jeff laughs and tells him there is no need to trade, that they can each have both. Carolyn and Rachelle put on lotion and do their best to ignore the men in the pool. Jeff starts some workout laps and Ward does a few dives before grabbing a towel and pulling up a chair next to Carolyn.

"Never mind the colonel. You'll do just fine, just fine," he says to the blonde. He lays back and closes his eyes. Carolyn looks over at Rachelle but her eyes are also closed.

The morning goes without incident. Jeff swims steadily for most of an hour and sleeps after leaving the water. Ward starts for the house to make arrangements for their "picnic," as he calls it.

Jeff wakes long enough to shout after him, "I'll be wanting a double Manhattan when it comes." Ward grins and waves and is gone. Jeff looks at both of the girls, sitting up and trying to decide if a quick dip would be advisable.

"I hope neither of you is shy about seeing others having sex. This afternoon, the four of us can enjoy some aquatic exercises."

His invitation and leer are met with stony silence. They decide to forego the water, at least until Ward returns.

Lunchtime comes, along with drinks for all four. The girls have rum and cokes with slices of lemon. Ward has a vodka martini and Jeff a double Manhattan. Best of all, the food tray is served by Megan and the drink tray by Mary. She hands the drink to Jeff and tells him she will make it again if it is not to his satisfaction. While he sips, she winks over his head at Rachelle.

*"She's done it! Not only that, but asshole Colonel asked for a Manhattan, a sugary drink heavy on flavor. He won't taste anything unusual in that.* Rachelle suppresses a smile as the younger girls return to the house.

"Not bad. If she made it, rather than John or Lena, she might be useful after all. Might even have to have a second."

Jeff sits back and feeds on peeled prawns, his left hand around the iced drink. Ward eats a sandwich and the girls calmly dine on a tuna melt salad.

"I told the ladies here that we might be up for a swim *au naturel* this afternoon. What do you think, Ward?"

Ward shrugs, looks once at Carolyn, but remains silent.

The food is gone, the drinks empty. Carolyn has to admit that the rum has given her some much-needed courage. Rachelle keeps watching, without trying to be obvious, for any signs of distress in Jeff. He is jubilant, feeling the alcohol, and anxious to get on with the show. Only Ward seems to be totally at ease, enjoying the sun and an occasional look at the two of them.

The colonel stands up, stretches his arms overhead, then drops to the tile and does ten quick pushups. Getting back on his feet, he swings his arms back and forth across his chest, taking in several large gulps of air and exhaling nosily.

"Okay, I'm ready." He looks at the girls and drops his trunks. "Hope you are ready, too. Let's hit the water, troops."

Carolyn looks away, although not before getting an eyeful. Rachelle stands up, resigned to whatever fate awaits them.

Ward sits up to watch but seems less enthusiastic about Jeff's proposal.

Jeff motions for Rachelle to undo her top. When she doesn't, he starts toward her. "I can help you with that honey, no problem at all."

To Carolyn's amazement, Rachelle gives him a warm smile and says, "If you'll get in the pool, I'll be right behind you." She reaches behind her and the top comes off in one motion.

"Yes, ma'am." He grins and dives head-first into the water, swims out a couple of strokes, and turns to face the brunette standing on the edge. He raises one hand out of the water to encourage her, then a strange look crosses his face.

"Uhh…what the fuck!" He grabs at his chest and his head sinks almost below the surface. His next and last few words are gurgles and bubbles. He is flailing as if trying to swim back to the side.

Ward is out of his chair in an instant, diving and reaching the man struggling to stay above water. By the time Ward has pulled him to the side, Jeff is barely breathing. Rachelle and Carolyn, feigning distress, help Ward lift him out of the pool.

"Get help," Ward tells Carolyn and she runs to the house, her loose bra flapping, small breasts flopping. Ward attempts to administer artificial respiration as Rachelle puts a towel under his head. "Damn it," Ward exclaims, "just like the son of a bitch to get overstimulated. Between the laps, his silly pushups, and arousal over you," he glances at her, "he probably forgot about his heart condition."

*Heart condition—the big bad colonel had a heart condition? Who knew? First a perfect drink, then a bad heart. It's a miracle!* Rachelle sits beside Ward and the prostrate colonel, feeling helpless and powerful at the same time. *I guess he won't need that second drink*. She quietly retrieves her bikini bra and puts it on, followed by her bathrobe.

John, Enrique, and Molly come running out of the house. Molly kneels and takes over, pumping on his chest, alternating with breathing into his mouth. She feels his pulse and intensifies her efforts.

"We're losing him. Freida called for an ambulance. They had better get here fast."

Ward takes Rachelle by the hand and leads her up to the house. They hear the wailing of an approaching siren as they walk through the kitchen and into the library. Rachelle hands Carolyn her bathrobe and they sit down to await the arrival of their friends.

A few minutes later, the six of them are together. John and Ward stand by the door and they can hear the ambulance departing.

"I'm afraid the news for Colonel Wilson is rather grim. I suspect he will not be returning to us, our little group. The news for you," he indicates all of them as he looks into each face, "is better. Although we had planned to have you stay and help us a while longer, it seems that fate has decreed a different outcome.

"For some of you, the past couple of days may not have been as pleasant as you might have wished, but perhaps a lesson was learned. If you are going to conduct a career in burglary, pay more attention to the place and people you intend as victims. I will abide by my pledge to say nothing of your little escapade and you will say nothing, not to anyone, of what you have seen here. Agreed?"

A few mumbled "yes, sirs" and nods come from the group, except from Carolyn. He smiles when she sits forward in her chair. *I will miss her. Too bad we hadn't met under different circumstances, and when I was thirty or more years younger.*

"Yes, Cassandra?" The use of her phony name brings a smile.

"Mr. Brookings, would you do me…us…a favor? It has been strange being your 'houseguests' and all, even though the food was great, but I think we are all puzzled by your other guests. There are so many and they seem, well…"

"Out of place here? As if either they, or we, don't belong?" He smiles like a teacher responding to a student, a pupil he favors for her curiosity and audacity.

"Yes, sir. It's none of our business, I'm sure, but who are they? Why are they here with you?"

"I will only tell you that they represent a significant source of income for our group, a combination of state-supported care, backed by some healthy inheritance futures. We have invested and we expect large dividends. Now, if you will return to your rooms, change back into the clothes you arrived in, and leave everything else, including the household jewelry, John will drive you to a nearby shopping center. That will conclude our business."

He starts to leave, but Carolyn stands.

"Mr. Brookings?" He turns back to her. "May I keep the swimming suit? It's my first bikini and I thought…"

"Yes, Cassandra. Do keep it and try not to think too ill of me in the days to come. You will become a beautiful and a formidable woman, trust me."

---

AT THE SHOPPING CENTER, THEY WATCH JOHN DRIVE AWAY IN the blue limo. Mary stands a little way from the rest, not sure about what she had done earlier that day. Pete walks over and puts his arm around her and she cries into his shoulder. Albert looks at Carolyn.

"Souvenir, huh? I hope you'll wear it for the rest of us." He turns to Rachelle. "Didn't want yours? Maybe *I'll* have to get one for you."

Megan looks at her cohorts and proudly exclaims, "We *are* the Miracle Workers, are we not?"

Carolyn puts her hands on her hips. "Yes, we are, for many reasons. But maybe, just maybe, we should consider taking up another occupation, like joining a circus, becoming a punk rock band, or, looking at Mary, becoming pharmacists."

## *Acknowledgments*

It is always a pleasure to express how much gratitude I have for those who read, critique, and encourage my efforts to write. Leo Dubray, John and Eva Lund, and William Cook continue to be my faithful beta readers, each offering different perspectives and invaluable commentary. My wife, Alla Vichurina Powers, is my companion in literature and in all other matters—we confront the boundaries together. Last but not least, I acknowledge the expertise and patience of my publisher, Patricia Marshall at Luminare Press, and her great staff who've worked on my books: Kim Harper-Kennedy, Claire Flint Last, Jamie Passaro, Nina Leis, and Melissa Thomas. You help make the dream take shape.

## *About the Author*

L. WADE POWERS has published in the fields of medical technology, ecology, marine biology, and animal behavior under the name Lawrence W. Powers. He also published a critical examination of *The Winter of Our Discontent* for *Steinbeck Review* and several articles on natural history and cultural history for Oregon Encyclopedia Online.

He has served as a contributing editor for the *Journal of the Shaw Historical Library* for several years and as the creative nonfiction editor for the *Timberline Review*.

Larry wrote the narrative film script for *Fields of Splendor*, a 2005 documentary film by Anders Tomlinson.

As L. Wade Powers, he has published two novels, *The Home* (2017) and *The Party House* (2019), and a collection of short stories, *Falling in Love and Other Misadventures* (2019). The current and revised edition of his first novel, *The Home*, was published in November 2019.

He is currently at work on a historical novel about Francis Drake in the Pacific Northwest. This is his second collection of short stories. A retired professor of natural sciences, Larry lives in Eastern Oregon with his wife Alla, with the permission of their cat.

www.ingramcontent.com/pod-product-compliance
Lightning Source LLC
LaVergne TN
LVHW041630060526
838200LV00040B/1513